Redemption

CURSE OF FATE

BOOK FOUR

SAMANTHA BARRETT

Stone Cold Steve "Austin"

11 years of loving you wasn't long enough.
You were the best dog and my first baby.
Xxxx

CHAPTER 1

Dominic

Fuck my life!

Seriously. My life sucks hairy balls right now. I don't want to fucking be here, and I sure as fuck don't want to take over for my dad. I never wanted this life. I never had any desire to lead or be tied to anything. I just want to be free and live my life on my own terms.

I hate living in this fucking concrete jungle; the air is thick and tangy, there is never any silence, and the tall buildings block your view of the sky. It was like living in hell. I miss my home and my friends, and I miss my freedom. Above all else I miss her. I long for her, even though I have no right to want her or even miss her. Sophia Stone was the biggest pain in my ass growing up...then one day she stopped being my best friend's bratty sister and became so much more.

My phone vibrating in my pocket pulls me from my thoughts. I pull it out and groan when I saw the caller I.D but still answer the damn call.

"Five minutes, that's all I fucking asked for!"

"Watch your bloody language, Dominic; you're not too old for me to kick your ass." I smirk; I would love to see him try.

"What do you want, Pops?"

"Get back here now son, we have guests." I stiffen at the tone of my dad's voice. I know something's wrong. I turn and open a portal that will lead me straight to my dad's house. I emerge in the woods that surround our property in New York. Some of my father's pack, mostly the women, are accepting of my dual abilities to shift and to do magic, but of course most of the other bastards are happy to see me burn at the stake for being an abomination.

As soon as I clear the tree line, one of the pack assholes start with their insults.

"You're not natural, you shouldn't even be alive–"I cut the dick off before he can finish.

"Yes, yes, I know. You have said this like a hundred fucking times. Think of a new insult and then come back to me, 'kay? I have a fucken ton of shit that has to be done, so fuck off and—."

"DOMINIC! Language." I flinch at the sound of my father's booming voice. That fucker always seems to appear whenever I'm on a roll with my swearing. It's like he has a GPS tracker on me or something. I turn to see my father standing on the back porch with his forearms resting on the railings. Ian Silver is one big son of a bitch, over six feet tall with the body of a linebacker. Dad and I have the same silver-blond hair, but dad has green eyes; lucky for me I inherited my mother's violet-colored eyes. Before I can sink into the downward spiral of thinking about my mother, dickface speaks.

"Alpha, I know he is your son, but he isn't natural." I smirk when I see my father stand to his full height, he makes his way down the porch stairs toward us. The dumbass gulps loudly when Dad stops a foot away and glares down at him.

"You think *my* son is not natural, Louis?" Louis looks

between me and Dad, clearly at a loss for words, so I throw him a bone.

"You should tell him about wanting to burn me at the stake. Oh, no—what about how you and the others wanting to drug me and then tie cinderblocks to my ankles and throw me in the lake. That one is my favorite. It gives me mobster vibes, you know?" Louis pales and shrinks back a step. My father is vibrating with rage.

"Is that true, Louis?" Louis looks to me for help—fuck that. I smile and wave then give him an encouraging nod. He shoots me a look of outrage and the laughter just bubbles out of me. Dad turns and scowls at me, so I mimic zipping my lips and throwing away the key.

"You dare threaten my son?" Dad shouts, his booming voice garnering the attention of other pack members. It doesn't bother me; I love the attention—thrive on it, even. What can I say, I'm a conceited prick.

"I-it's not like that Alpha," Louis stammers out.

"Then what is it like? He is to be your alpha, and you dare disrespect him like that?" I feel the tiniest trickle of empathy for Louis; my dad is a scary fucker when you get on the wrong side of him. Louis reeks of fear, and I'm surprised he hasn't pissed himself yet.

We have gathered quite the audience now. I nod and wave at the gathering pack members, who glare back at me. It doesn't bother me what the fuck they think I am comfortable with who I am and what I am. I struggled for years with being the first half-breed or hybrid—whatever the fuck you want to call it. Meeting Ryan, another hybrid, changed that for me; I saw how afraid she was of herself, and my heart hurt for her. Ryan was a force to be reckoned with, and now that she has accepted what she is, she is powerful beyond measure. "We would feel better about your son's leadership if he mated with a full shifter." My blood turns to ice; I begin to feel my pulse thrumming in my ears. No, I will do anything but that. I turn pleading eyes to my father, but he isn't looking at me—he's looking at the shifters that are gathered around. More than half the pack is here now. Heads are bobbing in agreement, each of their nods feels like another nail in my coffin. Haven't I given up enough already? My father turns his gaze back to a shaking Louis.

"I will take that into consideration, and we will address it at the next pack meeting." My dad doesn't wait for a reply; he turns and heads back to the house with me hot on his heels. This conversation is far from fucking over!

Watching Lucian learn new things has become my favorite pastime. He knows how to ride a bike now, last week when we went to the Yukon to visit Ryan's grandparents. It was heart-warming to see the love Marcus and Bethany Knox has toward Lucian.

Currently Lucian is rolling down a steep hill with Ryan, like a pair of human burritos. Once at the bottom, they both stagger to their feet, stumbling into each other and laughing like hyenas. I smile at the pair. Ryan, half fae and half witch—only one of her kind—balances Lucian in a way I will never understand. Lucian is also the first of his kind, but I'm the only one who knows that.

Footstep's approach from behind, and I don't need to look to know it's my brother. He never leaves Ryan's side for more than an hour. It's endearing to see the change in him; he is finally relaxed and doesn't take things so seriously since he found his *hugacko*. Ryan balances Nico and he grounds her. They are the perfect fit for each other—fate got their pairing right. I wish I could say the same for myself.

Nico sits down beside me and stretches his long legs out in front of himself, resting back on his elbows. My brother is rocking the casual look these days—jeans and a fitted shirt. He even wears Chucks now. I smile and shake my head. He changed his style because he knows his wife likes that look on him.

"How long have they been doing that?" I look at my brother and smirk. He rolls his vibrant violet eyes. His jet-black hair has stayed long on top and shorter at the sides, but the five o'clock shadow is also new and at the request of his wife.

"Guess."

He scoffs. "Shall we bet on it?" I smile widely. Nico and I have been betting each other since we were young. It's just our thing, I guess.

"Okay, what are the stakes, brother?" A devilish glint enters his eyes, his pearly white teeth on full display.

"I win, you have to answer one question honestly; if you win, I'll give you whatever you want." It's my turn to smile, and he groans. He knows what I want. I offer my hand to him, and he places his much larger one in mine, and we shake on it.

"Okay, on the count of three, we say it together."

Nico nods his understanding, and I have to hold back my glee. There's no way he knows how long they have been doing this. We had to sneak away to ditch the training; Ryan hates training without her cousins and Tyler, so she's always looking to skip out whenever the opportunity arises.

I begin to count, and on three we both say, "Ten forty-five a.m.!"

I gasp and the look on his face tells me everything I need to know: the fucker cheated. I narrow my eyes at him, and he just shrugs his shoulders and leans back on his elbows.

"Don't pout Soph, it's not cute." I grit my teeth and turn my gaze back to Ryan and Lucian.

"You cheated!" I snap, and Nico tuts at me like I'm some annoying kid.

"You never stipulated the rules, little sister."

"How hell did you know?"

"A magician never reveals his secrets." Nico chuckles at his own stupid comment.

"Let's get this over with. What the bloody hell do you want to ask?" Nico sits up straight, all traces of humor gone from his face. The look makes me want to squirm. We sit here staring at each other for a tense moment before Nico asks the one question, I wish he hadn't.

"Why didn't you tell me you're my best friend's mate?" I pull my gaze from his and look back to Lucian and Ryan. They're still running up and down the hill. It amazes me how they're not vomiting from dizziness; I'll never know. "Stop stalling Soph; Dom told me. I just want to know why you and he thought it was a good idea to hide it from everyone...from *me*?" I snap my gaze to my brother so fast I hear my neck crack. God, he is so thick.

"Why in the name of God would I tell you about me and Dom?" Nico returns my glare.

"Because I am your fucking brother Sophia!" I clench my hands into fists. How fucking dare he!

"I never fucking told you because Dominic rejected me! You were too busy being king to notice anything was happening between us!" Nico recoils at my words then jumps to his feet. Not wanting him to have the dominant ground, I stand as well. We're an inch apart, him glaring down at me and me glaring up at him.

"I was never too busy for you Sophia! I would have made the time for you. Instead, you shut me out!"

"I didn't have a fucking choice!"

"Hey, what the hell is going on?" Both Nico and I turn to

see Ryan and Lucian standing nearby, they both wear looks of concern. I move back a step and so does Nico. I hate fighting with my brother, but there's still so much he doesn't know; so much I can't yet say.

"Why do you look so pissed off big guy?"

Nico deflates at the look of concern on his wife's face. Ryan may be tiny and fragile looking, but the girl can sure as shit hold her own. The tiny brunette with strange eyes, my brother's soul mate, is a powerhouse who saved our homeland. Like so many of us, her green eyes with the yellow ring are a hint to her dual nature of witch and fae. Nico quickly closes the distance between him and Ryan, engulfing her in a hug and capturing her lips in a searing kiss, Lucian and I try to look everywhere else but at them.

After a minute, Lucian finally has enough of his best friend sucking face and clears his throat. Lucian looks older than his years; his beautiful violet eyes with a gray ring around his pupils is a dead giveaway for his heritage as well. He has his father's hair: silver-blonde with streaks of black through it. Lucian has the cheekbones of a model and a perfectly straight nose to match. He has *his* height and build as well. The similarities between them hurts me to see. I shake myself out of my thoughts and focus on the three people in front of me discussing the disagreement between me and my brother.

"Little one, I only asked a question. I swear!" I scoff at my brothers' protestations of innocence; he is such a suck-ass when it comes to getting back into Ryan's good graces. Nico turns his head to scowl at me, and I smirk.

"Soph, what did he say to upset you?" Nico groans at his wife's question, she gives him a look that has him snapping his mouth shut and crossing his arms over his chest. Lucian chuckles at him; everyone knows: Nico may be the king, but

Ryan is the one who holds all the power. Ryan spears me with her intense gaze, and I decide to help my brother out and not make a big deal out of this.

"He just wants to know about my love life and I refused to share." Ryan gasps then spins around to slap her husband on the chest. He looks down at her, in shock and throws his arms in the air.

"The fuck did I do?"

"You were being a nosy ass Nico! You know Soph doesn't like to talk about that shit. Now say sorry." I try to mask my laughter with a cough, Nico glares daggers at me.

"I'm not saying sorry, because I'm not. She is my sister, and I have a right to know!" Lucian, Ryan and I all pin death glares at him. Everyone hates it when he demands shit from us, and acts like he has the right just because he's king.

"I swear to fucking all that is holy Nico, if you do not say you're sorry, the Slip'n'slide is shut for a week!" Nico reels back like Ryan hit him. However, his look of shock quickly turns into a look of seduction, and I cringe. I could have gone my whole life without seeing that look on my brother's face.

"You wouldn't dare withhold sex from me love, you enjoy it too much." Ryan closes the slither of space between them and runs her pointer finger down his chest and stops just above his jeans. She stretches up on tiptoes to kiss him. Nico leans down to grant her easier access, but at the last second, before their lips connect, she pulls back and scoffs.

"Try me big guy." Lucian busts out laughing at Nico's expense; I try to cover my laughter but can't. Nico huffs and mutters curses under his breath before turning his gaze to me. He is so far beyond pissed off.

"Fine. Sophia, I'm sorry."

"No, that was a shit apology Nico, do it again." Nico's face turns red as he glares down at Ryan, who simply shrugs at the intensity of his glare.

"I'm sorry Soph, I won't do it again," he growls, then turns to his wife, picks her up and throws her over his shoulder caveman style. Ryan shrieks in surprise, and Nico slaps her ass, as they head back toward the castle.

CHAPTER 3

Dominic

I storm into the house, hot on my dad's heels. I gave up my freedom because of some stupid fucking vow that will send my wolf crazy, but I will not marry in order to keep these fuckers in line. Dad storms past the kitchen and sitting room, making his way down the hallway toward his study. I slam the door shut behind me, Dad already standing behind his desk, gripping his leather chair from behind. If he doesn't release his grip soon, he will leave a permanent imprint on his favorite chair. It would serve him right. I drop down into one of the chairs in front of my dad's desk and cross my arms over my chest.

"I won't do it." Dad sighs and then pulls his chair back and sinks into the worn leather seat. It was my grandfather's chair, and someday it will be my chair. I don't want the fucking chair. I don't want to be alpha. I just want to be free and live my own life.

"I know you don't want to son. But Louis may have a point; an engagement might be the best way to get the pack on our side." I growl low in my throat. My wolf hates being told what to do. I don't take orders from others, not even my father.

"Unless you want my wolf to come out and play, you better take that bass the fuck out of your growl Dominic!"

I throw my hands into the air. "So, you can say *fuck,* but I can't?" Dad narrows his eyes at me.

"You are the child, not me." I glare at the old shit. He hates it when I cuss. God only knows why when he has the mouth of a fucking sailor as well.

"Yeah, good logic Dad. I'm a grown ass man–."

"Who still behaves like a child." I sink back into my chair and push my bottom lip out in a pout. He chuckles at my childishness; we sit there lost in our own thoughts for a long while.

"Shit!" Dad jumps to his feet in a rush, and I do the same, looking around the room for the threat, but I see nothing. Dad makes his way toward the study door and yanks it open. He steps out but stops and turns back to me. "Come on, I forgot about our guest."

We exit through the front door, and no sooner has my foot hit the front porch, I see a blur jump at me. I catch her instinctively and wrap my arms around her, pulling her close. She still smells the same—wildflowers and sweetness. I pull back and cup her face between my hands, smiling down at her. She has the biggest smile on her face, and I can see her eyes tearing up.

"I know I'm beautiful love, but you don't have to cry over my beauty." She pulls back and swats me on my arm. I chuckle and look in the direction she came flying from and see none other than my best friend, Nico.

I make my way over to him and hug the burly prick. Fuck, I've missed him. We pull apart and smile at each other. He looks so happy. Ryan makes her way over to us and slides her arms around his waist. They look good together, and they deserve to; they've been through hell to be together. I'm man enough to admit I want what they have. I knew what it was because I had it, but I ruined it.

My dad breaks up the moment by greeting Nico and Ryan and ushering us all inside. I lead my friends to the sitting room, and Dad excuses himself with the pretense of making us all something to eat for lunch. He's full of shit; we have people to do that. I sit in the single recliner, Ryan and Nico sit opposite me on the couch. Nico doesn't like the space between them, so he pulls Ryan down the couch and tucks her into his side. She sighs but doesn't protest. She's getting used to his possessive ways.

"My dad's disappearing act is a dead giveaway." Ryan drops her gaze to her lap, and Nico keeps his gaze glued to me. Neither of us willing to back down from the staring competition, the longer he holds eye contact, the more my wolf pushes against my restraint. I growl low in my throat as a warning, and the violet-eyed bastard smirks and then turns his gaze to look out the window. "So, who's gonna spill the beans? Why are you both really here?"

Nico exchanges a look with Ryan, and she finally lifts her eyes to meet my stare. I can see different emotions swirling in her strange eyes; she's not the only one with strange eyes these days. I quickly pull myself from my thoughts and focus on the conversation at hand.

"We're worried about you Dom. You barely answer our calls or texts, and Jackson said you're ignoring him too. What's going on? We want to help you."

It's my turn to look away; the uncertainty and sadness in her eyes has my chest feeling tight. I want to turn to my brothers, especially Nico, but how do I tell my best friend that I can't bear to look at him, because he reminds me of his sister? I open my mouth to answer but stop when my dad enters the room. He doesn't know about Sophia being my mate, and I don't know how he will react if he finds out that I have mated outside our race. Dad doesn't want me to end up like him—marrying my mom turned the pack against him, and it took him years to get them back in line. If I was him, I would have killed every single fucking one of the bastards after what they did. They all hate me because I'm a half breed and they don't want to follow a mutt.

"Dominic." My father's somber tone pulls me from my thoughts. I look up and meet his gaze, his brows furrow and worry lines creasing his forehead. I jump to my feet and cross the room to stand in front of him, I feel Nico and Ryan approach, standing behind me. "Son, the council met behind my back."

The look on my father's face has me on edge. He is the motherfucking *alpha*, nothing scares Ian Silver.

"Mr. Silver, what happened?" Nico asks. Dad places his massive hand on my shoulder and looks me in the eyes, remorse filling his gaze.

"Dom, they voted. They knew if I was there, I would have voted against it because you're my son."

"What did they do?" I feel bile rise up my throat, and I know in the pit of my gut what those fuckers have done. I just have to hear the words from my dad's mouth to confirm it.

"Their vote was unanimous, you are to marry Sienna and take her as your chosen mate." I stumble back. *I knew it.* Hearing him confirm it though, is a whole different feeling. "You will marry her by the end of the year."

CHAPTER 4

Sophia

It has been nearly four weeks since Nico and Ryan went to visit Dom. I knew when they got back to Farrarie that something bad happened. Nico has been avoiding me for days, the only information they tell me is Dom received some terrible news, shifted, and took off. Nico has been checking in with Mr. Silver daily to see if Dominic has returned. I'm worried sick about him. Dom has always been a free spirit, but he has never taken off for this long without checking in with someone. I have been pestering my brother for weeks to try and pull the truth from him, but he's like a fucking vault. He won't say shit.

Last night at dinner I declared I was returning to Wonder Lake to seek Jackson's help in locating Dom. I have also been in contact with Kai, who said he will meet me at Jackson's compound. Nico lost his shit, saying he wouldn't allow it and forbidding me from going. He was so angry his magic came out to play. Before we could get into a magical sparring match, Lucian subdued Nico with his magic and pinned him to his seat. Needless to say, Ryan had to come to the rescue to stop my brother and Lucian from going at it.

"Are you sure about this?" I turn to Lucian, who stands beside me. We were standing in front of the portal that will lead us to Jackson's compound. Was I sure? Hell yeah! Was I scared? Fuck yes. I wasn't scared for myself; I was scared for Lucian.

"Yeah, he needs us." I don't know why Lucian feels the need to accompany me on this journey. Last night at dinner, all he said was he owes Dom. I have no idea what the hell that meant.

"Stop it." Lucian and I both turn around at the sound of someone bickering.

"You can't go!"

"Don't fucking tell me what to do!"

"I'll bloody well chain you to my fucking bed if I have to."

"You don't have the fucking balls, Nicky boy!" I smile; my sister-in-law is a fierce lioness. She won't let my brother control her or what she does; Nico hates it, but let's face it, Ryan can kick all our asses with a flick of her wrist. She is the strongest supernatural in the world—well, one of them, but no one knows another one exists. Ryan burst into the clearing with my brother stumbling in after her. Nico is red-faced and giving her his best death glare.

"I can feel you burning holes into the back of my head!" she snaps.

"I wouldn't be fucking glaring at you if you would just listen for once in your damn life!" Ryan halts and spins around so fast that my brother nearly bowls her over. Lucian moves forward to stand behind Ryan. It is his job as her neutralizer, but Lucian prefers to be called her shield.

"So help me God, Nico." She presses her pointer finger against my brother's chest, poking him. "If you don't pull your head out of your ass and come with us, I'll not speak to you for a month." Nico narrows his eyes at his firecracker of a wife; I hide my smile behind my hand.

"You wouldn't last, little one." He smirks down at her. We

all know Ryan can't go a day without speaking to my brother; she try's, don't get me wrong, but she's just not as stubborn as him.

"Oh my darling husband, you're right." Nico pushes her hand down and smiles at her as he opens his arms for her to cuddle him. Ryan takes a step back and confusion colors my brothers face.

"I might lose the silent game, but I am going to Alaska, so I may just win this time. I will be with Lucian, Soph, Aurora, Jackson, Mya, my cousins, and oh, that's right, *Kai* to—."

Nico growls and closes the distance between them, covering her mouth with his hand. Lucian takes a step forward, ready to intervene if he must; I quickly reach out and grab his hand, pulling him back beside me. Nico is vibrating with anger, he knows Ryan doesn't harbor any feelings toward Kai, but it still made him pissy when he thinks about the two of them together.

"Unless you want me to beat the shit out of one of my best friends, you will never use that as a ploy to get your way again." Ryan pushes his hand from her mouth, winds her arms around his neck and reaches up on tiptoes to kiss him. Lucian and I turn away with matching eye rolls. No one needs to see their public PDA; it's nauseating.

We exit the portal at the back of Jackson's property, where the chapel used to stand. We don't waste any time hoofing it to the back door and continue onto Jackson's office. I never bothered to knock, just open the door and walk right in like I own the place.

Jackson jumps to his feet, ready to have a go until he sees it's us. The look of irritation evaporates, and a huge smile graces his handsome face. Jackson is the type of guy who can pull off a suit and tie but also look so natural in jeans, a plain tee and a flannel shirt over the top. He is the most laid back, out of all my brother's friends. It doesn't hurt that he is drop-dead gorgeous either. His chocolate brown eyes can see into your soul. Jax has natural highlights, the lucky bastard—light brown with streaks of golden blond through it. He makes his way over to us and embraces each of us before directing us to the couches to sit, so we can all catch up.

"God, it is so good to see you guys." I smile, I feel the same. I loved being here when I first came back; there were always people milling about and you were never alone. Back in my realm, I am always alone, except for when I'm with Lucian and Ryan or my brother. Solitude is not my friend; the darkness would creep in and try to pull me back under. I quickly shake myself out of my thoughts. I refuse to let anyone see that I'm struggling. It's easier for me to focus on everyone else's problems instead of my own, hence why I am here now trying to help locate Dominic.

"It's good to see you too, brother. Sorry it's taken a while to get back here, but after everything that happened—." Jax raises his hand, cutting Nico off.

"Believe me, brother, I understand. It has been hell trying to get everything back in order and fixing shit around here. The packs are divided—."

"What? Why?" I cut in. Jax turns soft eyes to me, and all I can see is pity shining in them, why is he looking at me like that?

"Because the alpha of the New York pack is electing that his mixed breed son take over for him." I cock my head to the side, confused. "A lot of the packs are pissed that a full-blooded wolf from a high-ranking family is marrying a mixed breed—."

"Enough, Jackson!" My brother cuts in, and I turn my gaze from Jax to look at my brother, and then to Ryan, who is looking at her Chucks like she's never seen them before. My stomach sinks. Lucian places a comforting hand on my shoulder, offering me his support, and I feel a rush of guilt. It isn't his job to comfort me; it's my job to do that for him.

"So, Dom is getting married? That's why he ran, isn't it?" Jax looks from me to Nico and then back again. Jax curses under his breath and pins my brother with a look of fury.

"You didn't tell Soph, did you?" Nico at least has the decency to look sheepish.

"I didn't want to upset her," Nico replies defensively, and Jax growls.

"So, now I'm the asshole for telling her?" Jax hates hurting anyone's feelings; it is one of his most endearing qualities. I'm angry at my brother for keeping this news from me, but most of all I am hurt that Ryan never told me. She is more than Nico's wife—she is my friend.

"You never learn, do you?" I turn and see Lucian glaring at Nico. "You never learned from the shit you pulled with Smurf, and now you're doing it to your own sister." Nico tenses at Lucian's words, redness creeping onto his face. I have a strange feeling in my chest at Lucian's need to defend me.

"Stay out of this, boy." Lucian chuckles and shakes his head.

"Oh *Tink*, when will you pull your head out of your ass and realize that these women have no desire for a man to fight their battles or shield them? They want a man who will stand *beside* them, not behind or in front of them. You may think you were protecting your sister, but in reality, all you did was hurt her." Nico flinches at Lucian's words, his gaze darting to me. The look he sees in my eyes has him deflating and hanging his head. Ryan clasps his hand and threads her fingers through his. She takes a deep breath and sits up straight, looking directly at me.

"I'm sorry, Soph. It wasn't just Nico—I told him not to tell you." I reel back at my friend's betrayal.

"Why the hell would you do that?" She looks from Nico to Jax then she looks to Lucian, and her gaze lingers on him for a moment before turning back to me.

"Because I knew, finding out Dom is marrying someone else would break your heart." I gasp in shock at her admission. Dominic said he only told Nico about me being his mate, not the others. "Don't look so shocked, Soph. Anyone with eyes can tell you and Dom have something going on, the chemistry between you two is off the charts. If that's not enough, the night of my wedding, Dom swore to destroy Farrarie if it meant saving you!"

I don't get a chance to respond the office door opens and in walks Aurora. I am so thankful for her interruption, I don't know how I would have answered Ryan. I thought I hid my feelings for Dom, but I guess I was wrong.

"I had a vision." The tension in the room enhances. Jax is across the room and standing in front of his mate within seconds. They make a stunning couple. Aurora is pure silk and reminds me of a goddess. Her long blonde hair looks like it is almost white, and her huge baby blue eyes shows nothing but kindness and love. Aurora is good people, and I am grateful for her help, after I escaped Randall fucking Cane. I shudder at the thought of him, but I see Lucian watching me out of the corner of my eye and quickly slip my mask back in place.

"What did you see, love?" Jax speaks to her like she is made of glass; you can see in his posture that even without mating with her and claiming her fully, he is falling in love with the seer. Aurora still refuses to mate with him, until the threat on his life is eliminated. If you ask me, I think she is full of shit and is just using that as an excuse.

"We have to find Dom now!"

"Why?" Lucian asks the seer, and a look of dread crosses her face. She turns those blue eyes to me, and I gasp at the look of horror in them.

"Because we need his help to save you, Soph. Randall Cane is coming—for you."

CHAPTER 5
Dominic

I don't know how long it's been since I shifted; this is the longest I have ever stayed in my wolf form. My wolf doesn't deal with human emotions. He is simple: all he cares about is hunting, running, pissing on everything, and his...*Mate*. The thought of her has my chest constricting. I can never be with Soph. I will not risk her ending up the way my mom did. I won't survive losing Sophia. I shake myself out of my thoughts and continue running up the mountain. I was smart enough to change back to my human self after running out of pack lands and opened a portal to Montana, where I met some local wolves. They were really nice and allowed me to stay in their territory. Jackson had never mentioned a pack in Montana, so when I see Jax next I will have to ask him about them.

A sharp pain in my chest has me stumbling, but my wolf manages to get our paws back under us before we roll down the mountainside. I stop running once we are at the top, panting hard. What the hell is that pain, and where the hell did it come from?

The pain hits me in the chest again and has my wolf whimpering.

"What is that?" I ask my wolf. It's pretty cool being a shifter, it means you can communicate with your wolf telepathically.

"Mate," he grits out.

"What's wrong with Sophia?"

"Scared, hurt."

"Where is she?" I snap.

"Alpha pack."

My wolf doesn't fight me or wrestle for control this time; he knows me being on two legs will get us to Soph faster. I feel my bones break and muscles tear, then rejoin themselves. It doesn't hurt to shift anymore; when I was a pup, it used to hurt so badly that I would pass out from the pain. I'm on my hands and knees panting, and as I push to stand and prepare to open a portal, I realize I'm in my fucking birthday suit. Oh well, good thing I'm not insecure.

"Portaly openinga matee laska!" I feel the air shift around me as the portal starts to open. I know my dad's pack hates my mixed heritage, but I love it. I have the best of both worlds: part fae and part shifter. I love having magic inside me, and I am fucking good at it. Once the portal is formed, I step through without hesitation.

In typical me fashion, I open a portal into Jackson's office, thinking that will be a more subtle entrance. The gasps, groans and giggles I hear upon my arrival tells me I'm wrong. Fuck it. I place my hands on my hips and smile wide.

"Hello fuckers, did you miss me?"

"Put some fucking clothes on!" I smirk at the annoyance in Nico's voice as he hurls a throw blanket at me, which I tie around my waist like a towel. I scan the room and see a blushing Ryan as Nico pushes her behind him, and Jax has his hand covering Aurora's eyes like she's a child. I wink at him, and he narrows his eyes and bares his teeth. Lucian is a few feet away, and the smile drops from my face as I catch sight of the woman next to him, who has plagued my dreams for the past eighteen years. There she stands, as beautiful as ever, her long, black, curly hair tumbling down her back and resting just above her luscious ass. She looks gorgeous in skin-tight black jeans, shit kicker boots, a tight white crop top that shows off her abs, and her signature flannel shirt wrapped around her waist. Just looking at her has my cock hardening.

Down boy! Now is not the time. I can't hide you in this flimsy blanket.

"Where the fuck have you been, Dom?" Jax barks. I growl, my wolf hates being questioned. I don't give a flying fuck if Jackson is *the* alpha of all wolf packs; he can kiss my ass. Jax's eyes turn from his normal brown color to the yellow of his wolf; he doesn't like me growling at him. Aurora slaps his hand away and moves to block my view of Jackson. He reaches for her again, but she bats his hand away.

"What Jackson means to say is we have all been worried about you." I deflate at the look of concern in Aurora's eyes.

"I haven't been gone that long, sweetheart." Her brows furrow and she looks to the others in confusion. Ryan steps out from behind Nico, much to his consternation.

"Dom, you've been gone for a month." *What the fuck? It can't have been that long!* I look to Nico and then Jax, both of them nodding their confirmation.

"I...I didn't know I was gone that long. I just needed to get away." I tried, I swear I did, but my eyes on their own accord drift to Sophia. The look she gives me tells me all I need to know. She knows about the marriage to Selina. Just then a thought crosses my mind. I snap my gaze back to Jackson and growl.

"You fucking knew!"

"Knew what?" Him playing dumb doesn't fool me for a second, and I feel my magic surge to the surface. I know my hands will be glowing yellow.

"You knew the council was voting; you're *on the fucking council* Jackson!" Jax glares at me and takes a few steps forward, nearly closing distance between us.

"I was fucking left in the dark like your father. I would never do that to you, Dominic. They knew I would vote against it, so they met without me and your father via Zoom. They want you married quickly to try to ease the distrust among the packs."

I stumble back and plonk down into one of the single chairs, leaning my head back and closing my eyes, I feel like shit for accusing one of my best friends for betraying me. I take a few deep breaths and then open my eyes and look to Jax. Everyone has taken a seat.

"I'm sorry brother, this whole situation is fucking with my head." Jax smiles sadly. Everyone knows I don't want this; they just don't know the real reason why. I let them all think it's because I want to be free and have no responsibilities, but the truth is way, *way* deeper than that.

"How are you holding up?" I turn and smile at Ryan. That's a loaded question.

"I honestly don't know how to answer that, love."

"We want to help you." I appreciate Ryan's offer, and I know four people in this room mean it when they say they want to help. I don't know if the other two are here out of coercion or because they actually care. My eyes stray to Lucian and Sophia again. Both of them have their eyes on their laps and refuse to meet my stare. Ryan follows my gaze, her shoulders hunch. I don't know if Nico told her about the night of the shifter burial, but I have a sinking feeling she knows more than she is letting on.

"I appreciate that, I really do, but I have to deal with some things first. Jax, can I have some clothes. And then can I need you all to give me and Sophia a minute."

Sophia and Lucian both look up at me. I see a look of hesitation and worry in her eyes, but Lucian has a look of mistrust in his.

"Number one, we can do, number two, you can get fucked." Nico grits out. We both jump to our feet, standing nearly chest to chest.

"Don't interfere, Nicky boy," I hiss.

"Go fuck yourself, Dominic, she has been through enough." I growl low in my throat.

"I fucking know! You need to back the fuck off now, Nico."

"Kiss my ass, Silver. Ever since she came back, all you have done is avoid her and fight with her." That pisses me the fuck off.

"And all you've done is bury your face between Ryan's legs and kiss her ass instead of worrying about your own fucking sister."

Oops. As soon as the words left my mouth, I instantly regret them. Nico cocks his arm back, and I am not going to do anything to stop it, I deserve it after what I just said. His fist doesn't connect though, I peek one eye open and see his hand suspended mid-air, yellow magic swirling around it. Only one other person has the same color magic as me. I turn to see Sophia's arm outstretched and her eyes narrowed at her brother.

"I don't need you to fight my battles Nico. I am not a child. Stop treating me like one." She turns her angry gaze from her brother to me, and I gulp I see Jackson's shoulders shaking with silent laughter; the bastard heard me gulp. "And you, what on fucking earth makes you think I want to hear anything you have to say?" It is now or never.

"Because I'm sorry. I'm so sorry for everything, little dove." Sophia gasps and drops her arm. She may act tough, but deep down I know she is still the same little girl that wears her heart on her sleeve.

CHAPTER 6
Sophia

Guilt is nagging at me. He isn't the only one who should be saying sorry. Yes, what he did broke my heart, but what I have done is so much worse. When he finds out the truth, will he ever forgive me? I'm being selfish by keeping this news from him. I keep telling myself I'll tell him the truth when the time is right, but that's a cop-out. There will never be a right time.

"Am I missing something here?" Jax asks. I don't break eye contact with Dom. I can't seem to pull my gaze away from him.

"If you can't feel the raw sexual tension in the air and read their body language, Alpha, then there is no help for you." I can hear the humor in Aurora's voice.

"Oh...*oh*, I get it now–." Jax is cut off mid-sentence, and the spell I was under breaks as the office door flies open and hits the wall. Everyone turns to face the intruder and gasps ring out around the room. Kai walks in carrying an unconscious Mya in his arms. They're both covered in soot and have cuts and dried blood all over their skin. What the fuck is going on?

"You all need to hurry the fuck up! He followed us here, and he has at least five hundred with him." Nico is the first to snap out of his shock.

"Who's here, Kai?"

"Randall Cane and his army," is Kai's somber reply. The room erupts into chaos. Aurora and Ryan guide Kai over to the couch to lay Mya down, Jax is linking with his healer and calling for his wolves to return to the compound to prepare for battle, *again*. Nico opens a portal and tries to pull Ryan through with him.

"I can't go!" She snaps, shaking off his grip.

"Why the fuck not? We have to retrieve our army."

"Nico, I have to go to my cousins and ask them to help us. We need the witches and warlocks." I can see how torn my brother is; he wants to keep his wife with him, but he knows what she says is true. My brother turns to look at Dom and asks.

"Can you open a portal to the Knox coven for her?" Dom is already shaking his head before Nico finishes.

"I can't. I'm opening one for Kai, so he can bring his men through."

"Fuck!" Nico yells, and Dom places a comforting hand on his shoulder and then looks to me.

"But So-So can open one, can't you, little dove?" I gape at him. I have no idea how he knows that. Nico flicks his eyes to me.

"Since fucking when can you access your fae side?" I start shaking my head.

"We don't have time for this shit, Soph. Open a portal to my cousins, please. Dom, get Kai's men here. Jax, you go ready your pack. Aurora will stay with Mya until the healer gets here. Nico, you go get our army. Lucian, you come with me to the Knox coven." The chaos in the room stops as everyone turns to the tiny woman who is barking orders at us. Ryan is a fucking badass!

"I may have a semi right now after that display, love." Nico lunges at Dom and slaps him on the back of his head. In true Dom fashion, he just grins at my brother.

"Come on, let's move!" We all take our orders as Ryan instructed. I open a portal to the coven for her, and she gives Kai a quick hug before clasping Lucian's hand and walking through without so much as a backward glance. My brother looks shell-shocked that his wife didn't even say goodbye. I chuckle at the perplex look on his face. She never fails to flummox him. He shakes his head and quickly opens a portal of his own to our realm so he can prepare our army.

Is it weird that I'm not scared? Let me rephrase that—I'm not scared for myself, but I'm scared for the others. I know Randall isn't here for Ryan—not this time at least. He's coming for *me*. He always told me I will never be able to escape him; that he will always come for me. The thought of having to go back there and be at the mercy of that disgusting pig, sends shivers down my spine. *Now* I'm scared for myself. If he does capture me, I know he will make me pay for escaping; that's the real reason he wants Kai dead. He doesn't want to kill him because he is his blood heir—he wants him dead for letting his most prized *treasure* go. I would rather die than ever be at the mercy of that man ever again.

The healer entering the office pulls me from my thoughts. Dr. Jeremy makes his way over to the couch to assess Mya's injuries while Kai fills him in and tells him he and Mya were attacked by rogue witches and fae. Murmur's ring out around the room. We assumed Randall only had vampires with him. This isn't good news.

"So, he has vamps, fae, witches...what about shifters?" Trepidation is clear in Jackson's voice. If Randall has shifters on his side, Jax will take this personally. He prides himself on keeping *all* shifters in line. Melakai's somber look tells me all I need to know. His gray-blue eyes hold so much regret. He doesn't want to be the one to tell Jax. Melakai Cane may be a hulk of a man, but he has a heart of gold. With his blond hair and beautiful eyes, the woman that ends up with him is going to be lucky as hell.

"Yeah, brother, he has shifters with him too. I don't know how he managed to amass such an army."

Jax doesn't get a chance to answer, when Ryan comes back through the portal with Lucian and her cousins, Alex and Chase Knox, kings of the Knox coven. I wait a moment longer to see if anyone else is coming through with them before closing off the portal. Kai looks to Dom and nods his head before entering the portal Dom opens for him to return to the mansion to gather his army. Nico still hasn't returned yet with reinforcements.

"I never thought I would be glad to see you two knuckle-heads." Alex and Chase both grin at Dom. Alex and Chase greet everyone around the room but when their eyes land on an unconscious Mya, they both scramble over to the couch she lies on. Alex drops to his knees by her head, careful to stay out of the doctor's way.

"What the hell happened?" Alex snaps. Alex is the more relaxed brother; Chase is the hothead. Alex's blue eyes shone with anger, and his jet-black hair is a tousled mess. Chase places a hand on his brother's shoulder, trying to offer his comfort, but Alex shrugs his hand off. Chase's sky-blue eyes fill with sadness, and he drops his head, causing his sandy blond hair to fall over his forehead. Something has happened between these two, and they never fought. I can see the divide between them so clearly, and I can see both their hearts are in pain. I have the useless gift —more like curse— of being able to see others love lives; some-times I am able to see people's emotions, like right now. I can see how hurt their hearts are, but I can't see the reason why.

"She was attacked by magic users on their way here," Aurora answers.

"Where the fuck was Melakai? He was supposed to protect her." Jax and Dom both growl, and Ryan moves to stand by her cousins, glaring at both Dom and Jax.

"He did protect her! He brought her here, didn't he?" Alex opens his mouth to reply but is cut off as Nico, Maverick, Larick, and Cyrus come barreling through a portal. Ryan ran to my brother and throws herself at him, and he catches her without hesitation. A moment later, Kai returns with two vamps either side of him, and he announces that the vamps are on their way to Jackson's. Dom offers to open a portal out the back so the vamps can get here quicker, and Kai sends one of the men that came with him back to let the others know. Nico sent Maverick and Larick out back to open a portal for the fae to enter through.

"Why is Randall here? It's not like he can close the portal anymore." Chase voices the question everyone is thinking.

"He should have taken the opportunity to run when he had it."

"He ran for seven months, Dom. He was always going to come back." Kai is so resolute in his response.

"Kai, you know him better than anyone; why do you think he's here, and why has he not attacked us yet while we wait for our troops to arrive?" Kai's gaze slides from my brother to me; he is thinking the same thing I am.

"Why are you looking at my sister like that?" Nico knows what that look means; he just wants to hear Kai say it out loud.

"There is only one reason I can think of why Randall would risk his life. He isn't here for Ryan. He's come for his *treasure*."

CHAPTER 7

Dominic

I can't think straight after Kai's declaration. Randall *motherfucking* Cane is here for Sophia... My girl. She's not my girl though—I rejected her and broke her fucking heart. Soph was taken because of me. It's my fault Randall took her. I will never forgive myself for that.

"Here put these on." Jackson throws a stack of clothes at me, which I am grateful for. Fuck knows where he got them from, since I didn't see anyone enter or leave the room. Granted, my gaze has been glued to Sophia since Kai's mic drop. I mean, I wasn't ashamed of my body, but I didn't exactly want my sword popping out in the middle of a battle.

"He won't fucking touch her," Nico grits out then turns his gaze to his sister, he softens at her frightened look. Sophia is one of the toughest women I know. She puts on a brave face and hates people fussing over her. At the end of the day, she is still the same girl that used to make Nico and I check for monsters under her bed every night.

"Soph, I want you to do as I ask and go back to Farrarie." Sophia's already shaking her head.

"I will not run from him, brother; he has controlled my life for long enough."

"Dammit, Sophia, just fucking listen for once and let me protect you!" Soph narrows her eyes at Nico, steels her spine, and holds her head high.

"That cunt took everything from me, Nico!" she yells, and I can hear the devastation in her voice. It breaks my heart hearing it. "I will not allow him to do that to me again. I will kill him for what he did to me!"

"What did he do, Soph? You won't even tell me!" Sophia recoils at her brother's question, and her reaction has my mind reeling and thinking about all the worst scenarios.

"Nico, don't." Those two words from Kai hold so much weight. Kai was there the whole time with Sophia; he's the one that finally set her free after being held by Randall for seventeen years.

"Shut up, Melakai! She isn't yours to protect," Nico roars, and Kai doesn't flinch or shy away. Instead, he moves to stand beside Sophia. I can't help the growl that slips out at his close proximity to her.

Kill, my wolf orders.

No, Kai is my brother. He's protecting our mate.

I thought I had the ignoring the mate bond under control. After all, I have been doing it for years. But since Soph came back, it's getting harder and harder to ignore it, and the need to claim her is consuming my thoughts. Hiding out in New York has been a blessing, being so far away from her and not having to hear about her or see her helped dull the urge to claim her. Sophia's frosty glare pulls me from my inner thoughts. I smile sheepishly at her, and she makes a gagging sound then focuses back on her brother.

"She isn't yours either, Nico." Kai's gaze slides my way

before quickly going back to Nico. Does he know? "She is stronger than you think. She can hold her own."

"No, she fucking can't!" Sophia flinches.

"For fuck's sake, *Tink*, you never fucking learn. You tried this shit with my cousin and look where that got you! Don't do it to your own sister, man, trust me. It's not worth the fallout, fighting with your sibling." Chase speaks like he's been through a similar situation, and judging by the tension between the Knox brothers, I will say they are going through that very thing right now.

"Before you carry on and continue to fight among yourselves, I had a vision." Everyone turns to Aurora. Jackson has his arm around her waist, supporting her. She must have just had it, and we were all too preoccupied to notice.

"Randall is only here to show his force and prove that he can reach us. He won't attack us now; he knows we have reinforcements. He simply just wants to *talk*."

The room erupts in chaos once more. Everyone is shouting at Aurora and demanding answers until Jackson's ferocious growl has everyone stunned silent.

"Next time you all think you can yell and demand shit of my mate, I'll tear your fucking throat out. She isn't some fucking carnival attraction. Treat her with some fucking respect!"

Everyone mumbles out an apology and expresses their gratitude for all Aurora has done for us. Without her, we would have been fucked and blindsided by Stevie Knox and Randall Cane last time. Dr. Jeremy stands and makes his way over to Jax and whispers in his ear before leaving the room. Jax releases a long sigh before turning his gaze to the Knox brothers.

"Doc has done everything he can. He thinks Mya was hit with a spell, not an energy ball. He will be back to retrieve her and take her to his clinic on the south side of the compound to hook her up to an IV and keep her for observation." Alex and

Chase exchange a look between themselves before giving Jackson a curt nod.

"I'm glad Mya is going to be okay, but what the hell do we do now?" Ryan asks no one in particular.

"Now we wait for Dom to change and then we meet Randall," is Aurora's cryptic as fuck reply. I drop the blanket around my waist and smile to myself when I hear gasps and giggles followed by growls and grunts. I pull on the jeans first then the socks and tennis shoes., The shirt Jax gave me is tight and stretches across my chest, but it will have to do for now.

"All right, fuckers, I'm changed and ready to do this shit."

"Try take this seriously, Dominic," Sophia snaps, and I turn to see her glaring at me.

"I am, Sophia, what do you want me to do? Sit in the corner and cry about it? Not my style, babe." She narrows her eyes at the word *babe*, and I roll my eyes in response.

"You're such a fucking child! Grow the fuck up, Dominic." There is only so much shit I can take before I snap. I wipe my face clean of emotion and square my shoulders before meeting her icy gaze.

"I may be a fucking child, little dove, but at least I have never lied to you." Sophia looks stunned, and her eyes dart to Lucian, who has been quiet this whole time. *I fucking knew it! She's hiding something about the kid.*

"You don't know what the hell you're talking about!" I growl at her dismissive tone.

"You fucking know more than you say! I wouldn't have been able to enter his fucking mind in the field if he's not somehow linked to me, Sophia!"

CHAPTER 8

My eyes dart to Lucian again, and he's looking between me and Dom. Lucian had pulled away from me since the showdown at Lake William. He may not know the truth, but he suspects, just like Dom does. Neither of them will actually guess correctly, as neither of them know the truth. My time of hiding it is running out. I have to woman up. I've hidden it this long in order to explain to them, I have to tell them how it happened and why they didn't know.

"Sort this shit later, we need to prepare and gather the armies that are coming through the portal and cut Randall off before he hits pack lands." At least Kai is thinking straight. Everyone else in the room is looking at me, Dom, and Lucian. Both Lucian and Dom have narrowed violet eyes on me, Dom's blazing with fury, and Lucian's eyes shining with questions. I sigh then drop my gaze to the floor.

"He is coming to the field where Ryan met Stevie." I saw my sister-in-law flinch out the corner of my eye at the reminder that she nearly killed her sister that day.

We all shuffle out of Jackson's office after Dr. Jeremy came to collect Mya. We make our way to the back of the property, near where the old chapel once stood. Hundreds of fae, vamps, shifters, and coven members litter the yard. Nico, Jax, Kai, and the Knox boys all went to inform their people of the situation. The guys agree that it will be wise to send a small party of men ahead to check the field and make sure Randall isn't setting a trap.

Nico is arguing with Ryan to sit this fight out; as you can imagine, that isn't going down well with the tiny hybrid.

"So help me God, Nico, I will cut your fucking balls off and make you eat them if you tell me to stay behind one more fucking time!" Nico moans and stomps away like a spoilt child. Ryan, Chase, Alex, Lucian, and Aurora all chuckle at my brother's retreating frame. Hell, even I'm giggling. My laughter stops abruptly the moment I see Kai approaching me. I know he worries about me, but he needn't worry. I'm not that same defenseless girl anymore.

"Are you sure you're ready for this, So-So?" Am I sure? Hell yes! Am I ready? Well, the jury is still out on that one. I don't want Kai to worry, so I lie.

"Yeah, I'm ready for this." Kai nods his head. He looks around to see if anyone is paying us any attention before he whispers.

"Is the boy who I think he is, Soph?" I swallow loud enough for all the fucking supernatural's around us to hear. Kai knows everything that I went through.

"The look in your eyes tells me everything I need to know, Soph. Don't wait too long. You know this will all blow up if you keep him waiting." I nod my understanding and hug Kai, and he rests his chin on top of my head. Kai has been my comfort for so many years. I love Kai like I love Nico. A throat clearing has us pulling apart. I turn to see Dom standing next to us with a face like a slapped ass. Uh, no—he doesn't get to be pissed that I was hugging Kai.

"Wipe that fucking look off your face, Dominic!"

"Why, Sophia?" he hisses.

"Because you rejected me, asshole!" I whisper-shout. "You don't have the right to glare or comment on *anything* I fucking do." Dom doesn't listen, as usual. He closes the space between us, and I refuse to move back a step. I will not let him intimidate me.

Our chests were nearly touching, and I have to crane my neck back so I can see his face. He wraps his arm around my lower back and pulls me flush against him, pulling a gasp from me. The heat radiating off him is seeping into my body. Being this close to Dominic Silver is doing things to my body that I don't want to admit out loud. Kai tries to step forward to pry Dom off me, and Dom growls low in his throat, his eyes changing from violet to the gray of his wolf. Dom's upper lip pulls back in a snarl, and his arm around me tightens.

"Let her go," Kai grits out. Dom is still growling; he doesn't like how close Kai is standing to us. Well, how close he's standing to *me*.

"Back the fuck up now, Kai!" We have gathered the attention of the supes surrounding us, and it is making me uncomfortable. I'm getting pissed at Dom's blatant display of dominance. He doesn't own me; I am not a possession to be owned. I try to wiggle out of his grasp, which only causes him to grip me with both arms, his gray eyes peering down at me. He has an evil smirk on his face.

"If you keep wriggling like that, babe, I'm gonna go from

semi to fucking hard in a split second." I gasp at Dom's crudeness, though I don't know why; he has never been one to filter the shit that flows out of his mouth.

"Go fuck yourself, Dominic!" I mentally slap myself; I sound way too breathy and turned on for my own liking.

"I would much rather be fucking you, little dove; it would help release some of the pent-up anger I have toward you."

I can see anger swirling in her eyes, but there's something else there too–desire. My wolf is riding me hard, and I'm hanging on to the control by a hair. He wants to shift so he can claim his mate. Being this close to Sophia is torture. I have no fucking idea what possessed me to grab her but seeing her in Kai's arms made something inside me snap. I'm too distracted by looking at Sophia to even hear the others approaching.

"I am going to say this once!" Nico booms. "The next time you even so much as think about fucking my sister, I will take a meat tenderizer to your fucking dick, Dom."

Laughter burst out of me. Oh, Nicky boy, if only you knew. "Step the fuck away from her now, Dom, you're losing control."

The insinuation that I would hurt my own mate if I lost control has me vibrating with rage.

"Are we missing something here?"

"Seriously, Alex, you haven't clued in yet?"

"No, Chase, I fucking haven't!" I can hear the annoyance in Alex's voice, and I can't afford for Chase to voice his answer in case he's right. There are too many shifters here, and word will get back to my dad. I reluctantly release Sophia and step back.

My wolf is pissed at the loss of contact with her. Sophia stands there, eyes wide, so many questions swirling in the depths of those beautiful violet eyes. I am going to fucking hell. I turn and shoulder my way past both Nico and Kai. I can't deal with this shit right now.

I rejoin the others after the search party comes back declaring that there are no traps to be found, and no scent to detect. Which means Randall isn't here yet.

"He was right behind us; he should have been here by now!" Kai is shaking, his fists clenched at his side.

"Something's not right. We all know Randall is one for the theatrics, so he must be planning something."

"It fucking hurts me to say this, but I think Chase might be right."

"Awwww, Tink, hearing that just made my day." Nico's features change to pure joy, and he smiles widely at Chase.

"I hoped it might, *Sabrina*." Chase blanches, and our whole group breaks out into fits of laughter. Everyone knows Nico hates being called *Tink*, Chase started calling him Tinkerbell just to piss him off, and now Nico just one-upped the warlock. Chase turns accusing eyes to Ryan, and she holds up her hands in surrender.

"Come on Chase, he's my husband! I have to help him out."

"You're a traitor, squirt. We're blood and you betrayed me to help the fairy." Chase is pouting like a child.

"Oh, I'll always win, *Brina,* it didn't take me long to convince her to help me. All I had to do was withhold sex for–."

"I get it! You won that round. I don't fucking need to hear more. Please, for the love of all that is fucking holy, stop." Ryan is a bright shade of red and glaring at the side of her husband's head, Chase looks like he's about to be sick, and Nico looks like a smug prick until he turns to see his wife's expression.

"Babe, come on. Don't be mad, please."

"You're such a dick, Nico." He pulls her to him and bends down to kiss her, and the moment his lips touch hers, the anger melts from her body. Jealousy rears its ugly head at seeing my friends so in love and happy. I want that with Sophia, but I could never risk her life. Being with me would be a death sentence, and I care about her enough to never put her in harm's way.

"I love banter just as much as the next person, but we have to focus. Why the hell is Randall not coming at us right now?" Alex looks to each of us as he speaks. The warlock is right; Randall loves to make a show. Something about this encounter is off.

"He's not coming here to fight." All eyes turn to Sophia, but I can't read the expression on her face. She's tense and trying so hard to make sure her emotions aren't seen.

"Why do you say that?"

"I know Randall better than most Aurora; he is a coward. He would have used the element of surprise to ensure he won. He's here to bring news, I guarantee it." Sophia's words hold merit, and by the looks on everyone's faces, they agree with her as well. Before we can discuss this any further, Aurora drops to her knees, shaking. Her face tilts toward the sky; her eyes now white—she is having a vision. Lucian steps forward to help her, but Sophia holds him back.

"You can't touch her while she's having a vision, it could

harm her." Lucian's eyes are wide; words fail him, so he just nods his understanding. Minute's tick by as we stand around, helplessly watching Aurora shake and shiver. We all form a tight circle around the seer, blocking everyone's view of her. She isn't some sideshow act. After what seems like forever, she stops shaking and her eyes start to return to her normal pale blue color. She flops forward on her hands and knees, panting, her long blonde hair acting as a curtain, Jax drops to his knees beside her and gently cups her face between his hands. Fear and concern shine in my brother's brown eyes; he hates not being able to help her through her visions.

"Are you okay, Rora?" She opens and closes her mouth so many times, but the words won't come out. Jackson pulls her to him and holds her in his arms, stroking her back, whispering words of love in her ear. After a moment, she pulls back and looks up at all of us. When her gaze lands on Sophia, her expression took on a look of sadness.

"I know." A beat of silence passes before Soph is clutching her chest and darting her eyes around the circle. They land on me then quickly darts to Lucian before returning to Aurora. Sophia is shaking.

"He's come for him, hasn't he?" Aurora's kind eyes fill with tears, and she nods her head again.

"Can someone tell me what the fuck is going on?" I snap I hate not knowing the full facts; it drives me fucking nuts. Aurora and Sophia snap their gazes to me, and both women now have tears in their eyes. Aurora opens her mouth to answer but is cut off by one of Nico's soldiers.

"Your Majesty, he's here!"

CHAPTER 10

Sophia

I thought I had more time. I thought I could figure out a way to tell them. I follow the others, chilled to my bones. Not from the weather, but from the feeling of dread inside me. My whole world is about to come crashing down in minutes, and there is nothing I can do about it. I should have told them seven months ago when I figured it out, but I was selfish and just wanted to live in this bubble with them. As time went on, it got harder and harder to tell them the truth. A hand grips mine pulling me from my thoughts, and then I feel another hand grip me. I look side to side to see Kai and Ryan holding my hands. Kai gives me a nod of encouragement, and the look in his gray-blue eyes tells me he'll be by my side through all of this.

"I have no idea what is going on, but I just want you to know that I'm—we're—here for you." I smile at my sister-in-law and thank her. She might not feel the same way shortly.

We emerge from the woods to the same place Ryan's power transferred, and it's an eerie feeling being back here. So much changed that day for me: seeing Dom's ability to enter Lucian's mind confirmed it for me. That's when I knew the truth, and I would kill Randall for what he has taken from me. Nico stops moving, and the rest of us follow suit. Kai gives my hand a reassuring squeeze and then bends to place a small kiss on my head before leaving to stand up the front with Nico, Jax, and Dom. I can't see around them, but I assume we stopped because Randall and his men must be there.

"Either you're stupid and want to die, or you're here because you want to see my beautiful face one more time before you die." I roll my eyes at Dom; he can be such a child.

"The sight of you makes me sick, boy!" His voice sends shivers down my spine, and I go from cold to freezing.

"Cut to the fucking chase, Randall. Why are you here? You must know that you will never get out of here alive?" Kai's deep baritone has me standing ramrod straight, so much authority in his tone.

"That's no way to speak to your father, son." I see Kai flinch at the word. "Give this up and come join me, my boy." Dom breaks formation and takes a menacing step forward, his growls clear as a bell, even from here. His wolf is riding close to the surface.

"He won't be going anywhere with you! You will die here today." Dom sounds more beast than man. If he's not careful, he will shift soon. Dom is a force on two legs, but on four he is volatile, and he would attack anything he sees as a threat.

"You need me, boy!"

"We don't need you for shit!" Nico snaps and Randall's laughter has the four men in front of us tensing. We came out here with ten representatives of each race: Alex and Chase lead their coven. Kai leads the vamps, Jax the shifters, and Nico the fae. Aurora, Ryan, Lucian, and I stand in the middle of our small army. The guys told us the only way we could join them at this meeting was to stay in the middle of the army.

"Oh, you foolish pillock! Give me what I want, and I will give you the answer to save the boy." The four guys look between each other; the girls, Lucian, and I all exchange looks of confusion. Randall laughs again, clearly loving the fact he is one step ahead of us.

Nico changes into a fighting stance and moves his hands to form an energy ball, except nothing happens. He tries again...and still nothing happens. Dom sees what Nico is trying to do, and he tries to make a ball of his own, to no avail. I try to call on my magic and feel nothing. Fear ripples through me. I look to Alex and Chase; I see anger on their handsome faces. Without our magic, we are all useless. Jax turns to look at his pack, panic clear on his face. His mental link is gone. There's only one conclusion, Randall is in possession of a moonstone.

"Aurora, what the hell did you see?" I turn my gaze to see Ryan looking to Aurora; Ryan knows whatever Aurora saw in her vision has something to do with this situation. Aurora must have a good reason for not warning us about this. Aurora turns to look at me.

"When Stevie blasted Lucian at Lake William, remnants of her magic remain inside him. Randall has a cure for it." My eyes dart from her to Lucian. I can see it in his eyes. He's pawing at his chest like he could scratch the darkness out of himself.

"What do we do, Aurora—how do we save him?" Ryan's getting hysterical. Lucian means as much to her as she does to him. They are cut from the same cloth, these two. Aurora turns sad, guilt-ridden eyes toward me.

"He wants you in exchange for the cure to heal him." I stumble back a step.

"She is not going back to him! I can blast the darkness from inside him." Panic is evident in Ryan's voice, but the look in Aurora's eyes tells me all I need to know. I move to Lucian and look in his eyes; so much sadness, fear, and unanswered questions swirl in those beautiful violet eyes. I reach up and cup his cheek, and he nuzzles into my palm. Tear's trail down my cheeks.

"Who am I to you, Sophia?" he whispers, and I smile sadly.

"You're everything to me, Lucian." I reach up and place a kiss on his cheek, then pull him into a hug and quickly move away.

CHAPTER 11

"You're fucking mad, Cane. We're not giving you shit!" Jax roars. Randall is out of his fucking mind. He doesn't have anything that we want. Randall's gaze moves from me to the other side of Kai. I peer around the bloody giant to see what has captured Randall's attention and gasp.

"Ahh, my treasure." Sophia doesn't flinch or shy away; she keeps moving so she stands beside Kai. Nico makes a move to go to her but stops when Ryan pushes between the two of us and clasps his hand, shaking her head. Aurora moves to Jax's side, and Lucian pushes to stand between me and Kai. Randall turns his gaze from Sophia to me and Lucian, a cunning smile lighting his face up like fireworks.

"Give me the cure first," Sophia demands. What the fuck? She knows what Randall is talking about—how?

Randall shakes his head and points to Lucian as he answers. "Is he really worth it *treasure*." Sophia moves to stand in front of Lucian, blocking him from Randall.

"Yes!" Is her only answer. Randall's blue eyes narrow, and he runs a hand through his cropped blond hair. He's a short, plump bastard, and truth be told, he's a gutless piece of shit when he doesn't have guards around him. Seeing his ugly burnt face brings a smile to my own.

"Then come to me and I will give the boy the cure. You were always meant to be mine, *treasure*. I miss you every night." Sophia flinches. I growl low in my throat at the insinuation, Ryan and Jax are holding Nico back. With my connection to my wolf severed, I have no access to my magic either, so I'm out here blind.

"You go anywhere near my sister, and I will fucking kill you!"

"Oh, and how will you do that? You have no magic here, boy. I allowed you all to enter here feeling like you had the upper hand. I made sure the moonstones were out of distance to lull you into a false sense of security." Randall turns his gaze to Ryan.

"Hello, feather, it's been a while." Nico snaps, pulling against Jax, Chase, and Alex, who rush forward to help hold him back. Nico will lose; we all will. We have no power here. We have to find out how the fuck he got the moonstones that David said were now gone.

"Enough!" Everyone stops moving, and all eyes turn to Kai. He steps forward so he and Soph are shoulder to shoulder.

"I'll take her place. Give the boy the cure, and I'll come with you. I won't fight you, I'll never try to escape, and I'll pledge my loyalty to you."

"Melakai, no! I can't let you do that." Kai turns to Sophia, nothing but love shining in his eyes for my mate.

"Tell them. Be happy and live, So-So."

"Fuck you, Melakai, not this shit again. No one is going anywhere. The kid is fine; he doesn't need shit," I announce.

"Oh, but you might feel differently when that darkness starts to manifest and claims his life like it took Stevie Knox's, especially when you find out who he is." Something isn't adding up.

"We know Lucian is the *trifecta,* or whatever that means," Ryan hisses.

"Oh, Feather, you are so dense. If you really knew why he is called the *trifecta* then you would want to make sure he doesn't get overtaken by this darkness. He may even be stronger than you, Ryan."

Everyone turns to stare at Lucian, who stands there, stunned. His eyes are vacant, like he's lost in his own thoughts. Randall knows more about Lucian than any of us. He seems to think I care a whole lot about the kid, but really, I don't give two shits about Lucian. He intrigues me, but that's about it.

"What is a *trifecta?*" Chase asks Randall. Randall looks to his men and laughs, and his followers follow suit like they have just been told the funniest joke.

"Where's the fun in me telling you that? I am over this little game, *treasure.* If you will?" Randall has his arm out, and Sophia looks from him to me and then to Lucian.

"Don't even fucking think about it, Soph! I will not lose you again!" Nico shouts, and I can hear the fear in his voice. Sophia doesn't move her gaze from mine or even acknowledge her brother. I move toward her, leaving a small sliver of space between our bodies. I lift my hand and cup her cheek, tears rolling freely down her beautiful face.

"If you go with him to save that boy, Sophia, I will never forgive you." She recoils at my words and bats my hand away, fire leaping in her eyes. Sophia hates being given ultimatums.

"I will do whatever I have to do in order to save his life!" she hisses, and I glare down at her.

"Why the fuck would you risk going back to him for that kid?" I yell.

"Because he's my fucking son!" I reel back like she had

slapped me, and my knees nearly give out. I might have fallen to the ground if it wasn't for Kai supporting me. I look from her to Lucian. Sophia is staring at Lucian with so much guilt and sadness. Lucian looks thunderstruck.

"Y-you're my mom?" Sophia doesn't get a chance to answer before Randall's laughter breaks through the tense moment. Sophia won't move her gaze from Lucian, and I can't tear my gaze from her.

How the fuck can Sophia have a son?

"*Treasure*, time to come home now, my dear." No one moves. No one speaks. Everyone stands there looking between mother and son.

"I am so sorry I didn't tell you sooner, I was going to. Then time went on and–."

"So you chose to lie to me? You knew the whole time I was searching for my parents and yet you still said nothing! I have wondered who my mother is since I was old enough to know I didn't have one. Do you even know my birthday? Who my father is?"

"August 7th, and yes, I know who your father is."

"How old am I?" For the first time, Sophia's gaze snaps to me and then back to Lucian.

"You turned...seventeen just over a month ago." My knees buckle and I am dead weight in Kai's arms.

No, no, no. This can't be! It can't be true.

"SOPHIA!" Randall roars, Soph flinches and reluctantly pulls her gaze from Lucian to turn and face Randall. "I am not a patient man, now get over here or the boy dies!"

Sophia takes one step toward Randall and then I snap. I break out of Kai's hold and tackle her to the ground. She lets out a shriek, but I don't give a fuck. I jump to my feet and haul her up by her arm and shove her behind me, then turn my eyes to Randall.

"I will fucking kill you before you ever lay another fucking finger on her!" I see fear enter Randall's eyes before he quickly masks it. I can't believe this bastard came close to breaking my neck at Lake William. I will never let him have the upper hand again. It warms me inside to see half his face is burnt from Ryan's energy ball. His face looks like melted cheese.

"So be it, boy." Randall turns and signals to his men, and the first row start to move forward. Within seconds they have purple energy balls in their hands–they're fae.

"Stand the fuck down!" Nico screams at them, but they don't listen. Fuck, we're about to be slaughtered. We may have Ryan on our side, but she is useless at the moment with the moonstones in play. I look to Kai, Jax, and Nico and see the fear on their faces. I'm no coward, but right now we don't have another choice!

"Everyone fucking run now!" I yell.

CHAPTER 12

Sophia

We all do as Dom says and run; we don't have any choice. Energy balls whiz past us, and I can hear snarls and growls coming from behind. Randall has released his band of misfits on us, and we're being hunted by wolves, vamps, fae, and rogue witches and warlocks. One of Nico's men that's running beside me is taken out by a wolf, and I see another man up ahead taken down by an energy ball. I don't know how, but the woods catch on fire, and there is so much smoke everywhere that I can't see my friends. I feel like I'm choking...the smoke is so thick and suffocating. I feel myself weakening, and I'm coughing so much that it'll be near impossible to be silent and hide. I can hear swords clinking nearby, and screams break out on the other side of me. I stop running and turn in a circle. I'm lost. I don't know where the hell I am. I can't see anything to indicate that I'm going the right way to the compound.

"Sophia!"

"Nico, where are you?" My brother doesn't reply, and I'm so scared. If Randall or one of his men catch me, I'm as good as dead. I will die before I ever let that vile cunt touch me again. I had planned to hand myself over for the cure for my son, and when the first chance arose, I would have ended my life. I will never go back to that life again; I can't. I hear branches snapping behind me and whirl around seeing a figure emerging from the smoke. I drop into my fighting stance. I may not have my magic, but I sure as fuck have skills in hand-to-hand combat—Nico and Dom made sure of that. I try to stop my coughing but am unsuccessful, and I have given away my position.

"Sophia?" I take off toward the figure and launch myself at it. Strong arms wrap around me. After a moment we pull apart and two hands cup my cheeks. "Are you okay? Are you hurt anywhere?"

"No, Nico, I'm fine." I start coughing again. My brother picks me up and takes off running. I'm praying that he knows which way to go. I'm so disoriented and dizzy that I feel like I might pass out.

"Stay with me, little sister, we're nearly there." I try to keep my eyes open, I swear—I really do. Darkness claims me, and as I slip away, I pray my brother will get us to safety.

I come to coughing, my chest is aching like someone has taken a hammer to it. My eyes sting and I can't get the scent of smoke out of my nose. I try to open my eyes three times, but the sting is too painful. I rub my eyes and then try again. It's still sore but not as bad, though my vision is blurry. I feel something on the top of my hand and use my other hand to feel what it is. It's an IV! Where the fuck am I?

"She's awake!" I know that voice.

"Jackson?" I feel the bed dip from someone's weight.

"Yeah, Soph, it's me. How are you feeling?" I don't get a chance to answer before I hear footsteps pounding the floor and so many voices mix together.

"Are you okay?"

"Are you hurt?"

"Do you need anything?" All these questions and the fact that I can't see properly is so overwhelming.

"Shut the fuck up!" He's here.

"Dominic?" I whisper.

"I'm right here, little dove." I feel a hand run through my hair and instantly know it's Dom; his touch always sends tingles throughout my body.

"Soph, I'm gonna get Dr. Jeremy now so he can check you out." I nod my head and murmur my thanks to Jax.

"Did everyone make it out okay?" I ask No one answers for a minute.

"We lost eleven men and at least a dozen others are injured. It might have been a lot worse if Mya and the elders hadn't shown up."

"How did they know?"

"She woke up and had a vision Soph, then went to the remaining fae that were at the compound and sent them to get the elder council. Mya, the elders, and the rest of the men came and saved our asses." My sister-in-law sounds pissed that we all needed saving.

"Where's Randall?" I have to know.

"The weasel got away, and he nearly killed Kai." I recoil at the news.

"Where is Kai? Is he okay?"

"Shhh, little dove, he's fine. The stake missed his heart, and he's with his men now." Dom starts massaging my neck. God that feels so good.

"Hello, Sophia, I'm glad to see you're awake. Is anything hurting?"

"Hi, doc. Just my eyes and chest. I can't see properly." Doc gives me some painkillers and some eye drops and tells me to take it easy for the next few days. He says he will be back in an hour or so to discharge me. I am so thankful to have my eyesight back. I can see now that, Dom, Jax, Nico, Ryan, Chase, and Aurora are in here with me. I'm in the infirmary at Jackson's compound, and I can see so many injured people in here. Their injuries were on me; this is all my fault.

"Don't do that Soph." I snap my gaze to my brother's. I can see he is so angry...at me. "This isn't your fault."

"Your words say one thing...but your expression says another, brother. Just spit it out already, Nico." My brother narrows his eyes at me, but Nico doesn't scare me. But what does shock me is the sound of growling coming from beside me, I turn my gaze to see Dom looking directly at my brother. Is he warning my brother to be nice to me? Is he trying to protect me?

"Aww now that shit is gonna be epic. Now you're gonna know what it feels like Tink." Jax laughs at Chase, which just encourages the young warlock. To break the tension between my brother and my...*Dom*, I ask my most pressing question.

"Where is Lucian?" Ryan's sad eyes turn to me, and I swallow loudly.

"He just needs some time Soph, he–." I cut her off. I don't want her pity.

"Is he okay, though—he didn't get hurt?"

"No, as soon as we all took off, he and Kai found me then we made our way out." I nod my head. That is all I needed to know.

"You owe us all an explanation, Sophia."

"She doesn't owe you shit, Nicky boy, now lay the fuck off her!"

Nico glares at Dom.

"She may be your mate, but she's, my sister!" Gasp's ring out from our group of friends, and Dom's hand drops from my neck. Four pairs of eyes turn toward me. I can't do this. I rip the IV out of my hand and batted away my brother and Dom. I fling my legs over the side of the bed and stand on wobbly legs. Jax helps to steady me. I thank him and then make my way toward the exit. I can hear the others following close behind me.

I storm down the hallway, heading for Jackson's office. I need a fucking stiff drink!

As soon as I'm in his office, I make my way straight over to the liquor cart and rip the cap off the vodka bottle, bring it to my lips, and start to guzzle. A moment later the bottle is ripped from my hand. I glare up at Dominic, my anger spilling over.

"You do not get to fucking act like you care now! You rejected me, Dominic. I loved you, and you pushed me away. You can get fucked and stay the fuck out of my life!"

"I did it to protect you, Sophia! You don't think it kills me to be near you and not fucking claim you? It drives me fucking insane—daily! I hide in New York to be as far away from you as possible, so I don't put you in danger!" It's a reflex, I swear, my hand comes up on its own accord and slaps Dom across the face. Gasp's ring out once again around the office, an angry red hand-print clearly visible on Dom's cheek, I quickly mask my emotions so he can't see the shock on my face.

"He had that coming, if you ask me."

"Shut up, Nico, no one asked you!" Ryan snaps. Dom returns his eyes to me...and I gulp, they are no longer violet, they are the gray eyes of his wolf. Whoops.

"Does that make you feel better, *mate*?"

Dom spits the word mate at me like it burns his tongue. I refuse to cower or show him that I'm hurting. I will not be seen as weak or fragile ever again. I square my shoulders and maintain eye contact.

"I am not your *mate*. I, Sophia Stone, reject you, Dominic Silver."

"I am not your *mate*. I, Sophia Stone, reject you, Dominic Silver."

I recoil at her words, utterly shocked. Her eyes hold so much anger...what the fuck could she be mad about? She hid a kid from all of us—from me! She has no fucking right to be mad. Not to mention she just hit me! As rage simmers inside me, my wolf pushes to the front again. Fuck this!

I step forward and close the gap between us, I grip the back of her neck and apply enough pressure, so she has to lean back and look up at me. I see Nico move toward us and quickly bring my magic out to form a dome around Sophia and me. He starts banging on the dome and trying to break through with his magic, but he won't be able to breach this shield. I focus my attention back on my deceitful mate and narrow my eyes at her.

"You and I aren't done until I say we are." Her upper lip pulls back into a snarl.

"You do not control me, Dominic!" I smile at her; she has no fucking idea what I am capable of.

"Try me, Sophia, you so much as look at another man with fuck-me eyes and I will kill him. You so much as hint to being attracted to another man, I'll fucking kill him." She struggles against my hold, and I release my grip on her and allow her to step back. She's panting, and I can see in her eyes she's conflicted. She wants to hate me but can't; she won't admit it, but she's just as fucking turned on as I am right now. I can scent her arousal, and it's driving my wolf mad.

"You do not get to make these demands! You turned your back on me! You didn't want me, you hid what I am to you for fucking *years*, Dominic... why?"

I can hear the hurt lacing every single one of her words. I see the tears in her eyes and she's furiously blinking; she doesn't want me to see her break.

"Cat's out of the bag now, babe. Everyone is going to know who you are to me soon enough. You have no idea the goddamn danger you are in now that everyone knows you're my mate. I rejected you to try and protect you–."

"Break this fucking dome down now, Ryan!" I snap my gaze to Nico to see he is still trying to break in. His magic isn't strong enough to break through this dome, so he has to ask his wife to do it for him.

"No, Nico, and fuck you. Speak to me like that again and see how long that pretty face of yours lasts." I love Ryan, and I love how she puts Nico in his place. That bastard needs to eat humble pie more often.

"Drop this shield now, Dom, I want to leave." My anger flees my body at the look on her face. She looks so sad and hurt. I don't want to upset her, but she has to know the danger she's in, now.

"Soph–." I'm cut off by the office door slamming open and Lucian entering with the rest of the crew. Great. Everyone is here now to see the show.

"Drop the Dome now!"

"No, Sophia, not until you listen to–." A force hits my shield and it shatters I stumble back a step to glare at Ryan, but her gaze is fixed on someone else. I follow her line of sight to Lucian, who has his arm extended. It was *him* who shattered my shield, the little shit. "You little asshole!" I yell.

"Shut up Dominic. Lucian, I can explain everything if you will just give me a chance, please." Lucian's face is void of all emotion; he looks completely uninterested.

"Then explain, *Mother*." Soph recoils at his harsh tone. I move to stand beside Soph. I may be pissed at her, but that doesn't mean anyone else can speak to her like that.

"You don't get to take your anger out on her, boy."

"Fuck you, Dominic, this is between me and the woman who gave birth to me then abandoned me! You fucking left me there, Sophia. Do you have any idea what that was like? I longed for you. I fucking mourned for the mother and father I was told died, and then here you are. You filled me with your fucking lies. You helped me search the files for my parents when the whole fucking time you were right beside me!" I look at Soph to see tears trailing down her cheeks, her bottom lip trembling. She opens her mouth, but words won't come out. I see Ryan move to make her way toward Soph and I. She wraps an arm around Soph's shoulders and then turns to look at Lucian.

"Luce, I know you're mad, buddy, you have every right to be. Why don't you and Soph go somewhere and talk, just the two of you. It might–."

"How can you defend her, Smurf? You know better than anyone what I went through." Ryan flinches at the harshness in Lucian's tone, and I got to admit I kind of feel for the kid.

"You may be hurt and pissed right now but you do not get to talk to them like that!" Nico snarls and Lucian turns angry eyes to him.

"Did you know about this, *Uncle*?" Nico shudders at the word *uncle*.

"Let's just stick to Nico or King, huh?" No one laughs at Nico's dry as shit joke. He sighs then meets the kid's gaze again.

"No, Lucian, I didn't know. If I had known, you would never have been in there. I would have traded myself for your freedom. We may not have known we were family until now, but I swear to you, on my honor, that I would have come for you and ensured your freedom." Well, well...who knew Nico, King Heartless, actually has a soft spot?

"Why didn't you wage a war for her, then?" Lucian says, motioning to Sophia. Nico hangs his head in shame, and I growl low in my throat. The kid is starting to get on my nerves now; he has no idea what we went through to try to get Soph back.

"We didn't know where she was at the start. We tried to bargain and trade with Randall when we found out where she was. Randall refused to trade her for Nico; he said he would kill her before he ever gave her back." Lucian turns and pins Kai with a death glare. If looks could kill, Kai would be six feet under.

"You were at Randall's, weren't you?"

"Lucian, please, he–." Kai cut Sophia off and answers Lucian.

"Yes. Now ask me what you really want to know."

"You knew who I was to her, didn't you?" Kai darts his eyes to a tear-stricken Sophia then back to Lucian.

"No, I thought you died, just like she believed. I helped Sophia deliver you, but before we could formulate a plan to get you out, a guard nearby heard Sophia's screams and alerted Randall that she was in labor. Randall had Sophia and I subdued while he took you away, and an hour later he returned with a lifeless baby and said–."

"Now there is nothing stopping us from being together. You are all mine now, *treasure*," Sophia finishes for Kai. Lucian stumbles over to the single chair, and Sophia quickly follows and drops to her knees in front of him.

CHAPTER 14

I clasp both his hands in mine. He needs to know the truth. Lucian raises watery eyes to mine, and my heart breaks at the look of betrayal in his eyes.

"I thought you were dead. I would never have left you behind if I had of known Lucian. I thought my life was over when he returned with a body of an infant. It broke me. I gave up any hope I had and I...just gave up."

"You knew my sister had a fucking baby, and yet you said nothing? You're supposed to be my friend—my brother—and yet you betrayed me, again!" Nico is pissed, his hands glowing purple. He reels his arm back, ready to launch a ball at Kai, but stops when I jump to my feet and stand in front of the man who saved me.

"Don't, Nico."

"Move, Soph, I will deal with you later!"

"You do anything to hurt her or harm her, Nicky boy, and I will fucking come for you!" My brother turns his angry eyes to Dom.

"Don't you dare get involved! You didn't want her, and now all of a sudden you change your mind because you have some kind of mommy fetish!" Oh my God, Nico went way too fucking far. Dom's eyes change in an instant to the gray of his wolf. In a split second, Dom goes from standing on two legs to four. His huge black wolf now stands there growling and snarling. Then Jackson starts to growl. Oh, shit. Dom just shifted with Jax in the room, and to make matters worse, Aurora is in here with us and is unclaimed by her mate.

"Ryan put a shield around Jackson now!" I scream. Ryan jolts out of her shock and quickly put a shield around Jax just in time. He changes to his wolf form; his gray black wolf now stands caged in a blue prison. My attention is snatched back to Dom as he prowls toward my brother. I have to make a split-second decision. I race in front of my brother and block Dom's path to Nico.

"I know you're angry, and you have every right to be after what my dick of a brother said. Please don't do this, Dom, you will regret it."

"Say you're fucking sorry right now Nico, or so help me God, I will go back to the coven with my cousins until you can pull your fucking head out of your ass." I smile, Ryan is one bad bitch.

"He started it! He had it coming. He hurt my sister!"

"And you're fucking hurting her by hurting *him*, Nico. Anyone with fucking eyes and a brain can see there is history between them.... Oh my God Sophia, is he—?" I spin around to see a look of shock on Ryan's face. "*Trifecta.* I get it now." I see the moment it clicks into place. Her hand comes up and covers her mouth, tears gathering in her strange green eyes.

"Wait, squirt, why did you say trifecta?" I don't take my eyes off Ryan or even acknowledge Alex spoke.

"Ryan–." I stop speaking when I see her shaking her head.

"You need to explain now; I will not hide this from either of them. I suspected the day in the clearing, but thought I was out of my mind. Now I know I was right by the look on your face. Tell them now!" I steel my spine before answering her.

"One, you don't get to tell me what to do. Two, this does not concern you."

"Like fuck it doesn't! He's my best friend, Sophia. He has a right to fucking know." I scowl at my sister-in-law.

"What don't I know, Smurf?" I dart my eyes to Lucian and then back to Ryan, begging her with my eyes to let me explain. She gives a terse nod, and I release the breath I didn't know I was holding.

"Everyone needs to calm the fuck down, take a bloody seat, and I'll explain." I turn back to the black snarling wolf. "Shift back, Dominic, now." I maintain eye contact with Dom and moments later the sound of bones breaking fills the room. I keep my eyes on his face as he stands, not wanting to look at his dick. He is mouthwatering with clothes on, but without, he is any woman's wet dream.

"You ever and I mean *ever* talk about my mother in any way again, Nicholas, I will kill you where you stand." There is so much venom in Dom's tone, and I can see from the look in his eyes that he means every word he just said. I don't turn to see my brother's reaction, but I can hear the remorse in his voice as he speaks.

"I'm so sorry, Dom. What I said was uncalled for. I had no right to speak about your mother."

Dom grabs another throw blanket from the back of the couch and wraps it around himself. Ryan releases Jax from his prison once he is back on two legs, and he darts behind his desk and grabs a spare set of clothes. I claim one of the single seats while Lucian occupies the other. Ryan, Aurora, Mya, Chase, Alex, and Nico claim the other couches while Dom, Jax, and Kai stand. I can feel all their eyes on me, waiting. I take a few deep breaths before raising my eyes to look at my son.

CHAPTER 15

Dominic

Her shoulders hunch, her eyes full of sorrow. The atmosphere in the room is tense and uneasy. I don't know half the shit Soph went through until now, and the thought of Randall ever touching her makes me sick to my stomach. On top of all that, she thought she lost a baby and then found out he's alive, and he was kept as a prisoner in the same house as her. I'm still fucking pissed at Kai for not saying anything, but I will deal with that fucker later.

"Okay, like I said, I thought the baby—you—had died. I had no fucking idea that you were living in the same mansion as I was."

"How did you end up there?" *Fuck,* Sophia's eyes dart to me then back to the kid. Everyone is about to learn what a piece of shit I am. What they don't know is that I did it to protect her.

"I fled my our—realm after I was rejected by my *hugacko*—." Chaos erupts. Questions are being shouted at her, and I can see she's about to tip over the edge. I do the only thing I can think of. I let my magic out and it causes a fireworks display in Jackson's office. All eyes turn to me and glare.

I shrug my shoulders and pull my magic back and say.

"Maybe if you all shut the hell up and let her finish, I wouldn't have done that."

"Who the hell is your piece of shit *hugacko*, Sophia?" Sophia's eyes move from her brother to me, but I won't let her face this alone. I move so I am standing behind Sophia's chair and rest my hands on the back of it, looking Nico in the eye.

"I am her piece of shit *hugacko*." Silence meets my confession, the girls are staring, hands covering their mouths, and the guys look murderous.

"Well, that is a plot twist I *never* saw coming!" I turn and smirk at Chase. I like that warlock; he has a good sense of humor. My moment of distraction cost me though, when I turn back to face the front, a fist hits me square in the fucking nose. I stumble back a step and cup my nose. When I pull my hand back, blood coats my palm. I turn and glare at the fucker.

"Why the fuck did you punch me, you cunthole?"

"Because you rejected my fucking sister, dick!" I throw my hands up in the air.

"I fucking told you that at the shifter burial," I yell. Nico moves around the chair to stand directly in front of me, and no one else in the room moves. We are eye to eye, both of us angry as hell at the other. Nico uses his pointer finger to poke me in the chest as he speaks.

"You told me you rejected her as *your* mate, not *her* hugacko." I spin away from him and begin pacing. I fucked up so bad. I have to smooth things over. I have to find a way to fix this. I run my hands through my hair and start tugging on it from the roots.

"Dominic, what are you not telling us?" I stop pacing and turn to face Kai. I am still angry as hell at him for not telling us about Soph having a kid.

"I rejected her to keep her safe." Saying it out loud feels good.

"Truth." Fucking Jackson and his inbuilt lie detector—it's a handy gift to have though in times like this.

"Keep me safe from what, Dom?" She asks the question so quietly, almost like she's afraid of my answer. I make my way over to her and kneel down in front of her. Nico moves to stand behind her chair, and I let loose a growl.

"I will never fucking hurt her!" I snap and Nico scoffs.

"Yeah fucking right! You already *have.*" I flinch. He isn't wrong. Sophia won't meet my eyes, so I grip her chin in my hand and lift her gaze until it meets mine. I have *never* told anyone this before, but it's time to tell my mate the truth. She needs to know why I rejected her.

"I rejected you that day in the woods Soph, not because I didn't want to be with you, but because I had to." She tries to speak, but I cut her off by placing my index finger against her luscious full lips. "If I had of claimed you as my mate, I would have had to take over being alpha for my father." Her eyes narrow in anger.

"You selfish bastard–."

"Fuck me! Let me finish, Soph." She reluctantly nods her head. "If we became the alpha pair, you will become a target. I already am a target because I'm a half breed. I can take their shit, but I can't take it if you become a target and meet the same fate as...my mother." Sophia recoils at my words, and I drop backward and plop down on my ass. I have never told anyone this before. I swore I wouldn't talk about this again. That's why I never wanted to become alpha; I hate that pack. I can't understand why the fuck my father still stays there after what they did.

Chatter starts to pick up, but I'm too lost in my own thoughts. I'm pulled out of my thoughts when Sophia drops onto my lap and straddles my thighs. I look up at her in shock. Sad eyes stare down at me, and she cups my face between her hands, Nico starts to move toward us like he's going to pry Sophia off me, so I did what I had to do, and with a flick of my wrist I send him sailing back against the wall. Out of the corner of my eye, I see him jump to his feet quickly. But to my surprise, blue vines wrap around him and he stands there like a statue. He turns to glare at his wife. It isn't hard to guess whose powers rendered the king of the fae immobile.

"I am not your mother, Dom, and you are not your father." Sophia doesn't understand; I can't risk her.

"I can't take that chance, Soph; you mean too much to me to ever put you in harm's way."

"You don't get to make that decision for me, Dom—it's my choice."

"You don't know what you're saying! They killed my mother because she was a fae. What the fuck do you think they will do to you, huh? They already hate me and want me dead; imagine if two mixed breeds end up leading that pack?" I can't take it anymore. I try to move her off my lap, but she won't budge, so I stand and she clings to me like a monkey. She locks her legs around my waist and wraps her arms around my neck. I can feel the heat between her thighs and groan this is fucking torture. She wiggles to get comfortable, and all her wiggling does is rub my fucking dick the right way. I grip her ass with both hands and hold her steady.

"Stop wiggling, little dove! I don't want to have a boner in front of your brother and kid." At the mention of Lucian, Sophia's expression changes. She's wiggling for a whole different reason now; she wants me to let her down. I reluctantly place her on her feet and move aside.

CHAPTER 16

Sophia

I can feel myself blushing. What a fucking hussy. I pretty much jumped Dom in a room full of people. Dom moves to stand beside me, and I see a look of horror on Lucian's face. Oh my God, he must hate me.

"I may have just learned that you're my mom, but please don't ever do that again. I feel like I want to bleach my eyes." The whole room erupts in laughter—me included. Lucian unknowingly removed the tension in the room with his words. Ryan releases Nico from her hold, and he stomps over to the couch and plonks down next to her, pouting like a fucking child.

"Aww *Tink*, don't sulk, it's not a cute look on you." Nico's only reply to Chase is to flip him the bird, which causes everyone to laugh again.

"Who's my father?" The laughter stops immediately at Lucian's question. All eyes are on me, and the only one that knows, turns to me with a sad smile. He knows shit is about to go down. I drop into to single seat and cradle my head between my hands. Admitting this is going to change everything

"Little dove, it's okay, I promise not to kill the bastard that knocked you up."

"Fuck that, Dom, I promise to beat the living shit out of the prick for knocking my sister up!"

"Nico, shut up, Dom, stop being a dick. So-So, if you aren't ready, it's okay." I appreciate Jackson's kindness, but I will never be ready to admit this. I need to woman up.

"Your father had no idea I was pregnant with you. I just want you to know that right now. Your father is amazing." I hear Dom growl and Nico snicker but ignore them. I have to get this out before I lose my nerve. "I fled Farrarie after Dom rejected me. I spent a few weeks in this realm and that was when I found out I was pregnant. I tried to return home so I could inform your father, but I was captured by Randall and taken prisoner."

"Who. Is. My. Father?" Lucian grits out. He knows I'm stalling, and his patience is at an end with me.

"Calm the fuck down and give her some time."

"Fuck you, Dominic! This is between me and–."

"Dominic!" I shout.

"Yeah, little dove?" I look to Dom then turn back to Lucian. The room is silent, everyone waiting with bated breath for my answer.

"Your father is Dominic Silver, heir to the New York Pack."

Silence. No one says a word. You could hear a pin drop; it's that quiet. Lucian sits there, eyes vacant and mouth hanging open in shock. I turn my gaze back to Dom, who stands beside me, staring at his son in shock. I look around the room and see everyone except Kai has a look of astonishment on their faces. Kai looks stoic but ready to battle if Dom snaps.

Lucian jumps to his feet and glares down at me. I meet his gaze. I deserve his anger; I should have come clean months ago and told him and Dom the truth, but I was scared. I was afraid Dom might reject his son like he rejected me.

"Thank you for being honest and telling me." His hollow

words cut me deep. Lucian turns on his heel and hightails it out of the room. I stand to follow him, but Ryan cuts me off.

"I'll go after him. I think it would be better if it was me. You should stay here and deal with this," she says, motioning toward Dom. Ryan trots out of the room, Chase and Alex hot on her heels. Mya and Aurora stand and excuse themselves with some lame story of forgetting they have somewhere to be. Nico, Jax, Kai, Dom, and me are left. Nico is still staring ahead in shock, and Dom doesn't move a muscle. Jax is looking from me to Nico then to Dom. Kai moves a few steps toward me and places his hand on my shoulder, offering his silent support.

"How?" Nico's one-word breaks the silence in the room, and he turns his angry eyes to me. He doesn't get to be pissed off at me.

"How do you–."

"I don't want to fucking hear it from you, Sophia! I want to hear it from my so-called *best friend*. I want to know how the fuck he could have gone behind my back and fucked *my* sister and never said a fucking word about it!" I shrink back into my seat. I have never ever heard Nico so angry. Kai squeezes my shoulder, letting me know he's here with me.

"Calm down, Nico, what's done is done."

"Stay the fuck out of it, Jax. How would you feel if you were in my shoes?" Jax flinches, that was all the answer Nico needed before he was on his feet and standing in front of Dom. Nico is vibrating with rage, and Dom has yet to move or say a word. "You are nothing to me. What you have done to my sister is unforgiveable." Nico turns angry eyes to me and points his finger at me. "You will return to the fae realm and remain there until I say so."

I jump to my feet and look my brother in the eyes. He doesn't get a say in my life! I am a grown-ass woman and don't need him wiping my ass anymore.

"One, fuck you...Two, kiss my ass and three, as long as my son–." Dom whirls around to me, and I stumble back a step and bump into Kai. The look in Dom's eyes is a look I have never seen before. He's so angry and hurt, but the way he's looking at me is like he doesn't even know who I am.

"Your son?" Dom's laughter echoes throughout the room, but there's no humor in it. "Are you sure he is mine?"

For the second time today, I slap Dom across the face. It's like he was expecting it, his eyes are now the gray of his wolf. I thought Nico would move to intervene, but he stands there staring at us.

"Fuck you, Dominic, you do not get to stand there and say that to me."

"Why the fuck not, Sophia? Every fucking thing out of your mouth is a fucking lie! It's been nearly a fucking year since he arrived here, and you have said nothing! I asked you who the kid was to me; I knew he was linked to me somehow when I helped him funnel Ryan's power. You could have told me then!"

I snap, I can't take it. "Why the fuck would I tell you, Dom, huh? So, you can reject him like you rejected his mother?" Dom recoils at my words.

"In case you didn't hear me before, I made that decision to save your fucking life! Don't turn this around on me, Sophia, you hid my fucking son from me." I can hear the heartache in his voice, and tears leak from my eyes. "You knew who he was the day he came here with Ryan, didn't you? That's why you ordered for no one to touch him." I nod my head. "How did you know?"

"Because if you pull your head out of your ass for five minutes, you would see he looks exactly like you! He has your skin, and your hair with streaks of black through it. He has the same color eyes as both of us, but he has my nose. He has a sense of humor and a huge heart like you. And in case you haven't noticed, he has a gray ring around his pupils. Your wolf's eyes are gray."

CHAPTER 17
Dominic

I sit here in the middle of the woods, staring at the stream, Sophia's words playing over and over in my head.

"Your father is Dominic Silver, heir to the New York Pack."

I'm so angry at her. She had so many opportunities to tell me the truth. She has been lying to me for months! I asked her straight to her face who the kid was to me, and she lied. My heart is hurting. Lucian is seventeen—he's fucking *seventeen*! I missed out on all those years with my son because she ran and wouldn't let me explain why I had to reject her. If she wasn't so rash and took off, I would have known about my son. I could have raised him.

Branches snapping behind me pulls me from my thoughts. I turn back and see Nico, Jax, and Kai making their way over to me. I ran from the office after Sophia described how much Lucian looks like me, the guilt of not being able to figure it out sooner eating at me.

"Well, this feels like déjà vu." All four of us chuckle at Nico's insinuation; it wasn't long ago that Nico was in my place and Jax, Kai and I were the ones coming to comfort him.

"What are you guys doing out here? I thought you hated me

now Nicky boy?" Nico just shrugs his shoulders. The guys drop down beside me, and Kai hands me a bottle of whiskey. I tear the top off and gulp the liquid courage. I'm going to need it.

"Thank fuck you put clothes on before you came out." I chuckle at Jax; that fucking throw was making my balls itchy. We all sit here silently for a long while before Nico speaks.

"I don't hate you, Dom. I'm pissed as hell at you, but I don't hate you." I nod my head; I don't know what the hell to say to that. "Why didn't you come to me?" I take another gulp of courage before answering.

"How the hell was I supposed to come to you and tell you that in love with your sister? I didn't know she was my mate until a few months before she left; it took me months to try to build the courage to tell her. Then one day she surprised me and told me I was her *hugacko*. I remember the look on her face —she was so happy and giddy. She thought we could finally be together." I sigh and drop my head in shame. "We had been meeting up secretly for months. I couldn't risk anyone finding out what she meant to me, and I was scared that if the pack found out, they would kill her like they did my mom. I broke her heart that day. I told her she was my mate. She burst out into tears of joy and started to drag me back toward the castle so we could tell you. I panicked. I stopped her and told her that we could never be together, and I didn't want her as my mate. She fled the fae realm and that was the last time I saw the love of my life and mother to my child until she arrived here a year ago."

The guys hang their heads, no one looks at me or says a word.

"The day she gave birth to Lucian, I tried to break them out." I snap my eyes to Kai, glaring at the side of his head. I wanted to know how much he knew. Nico growls, clearly he forgot about Kai being with Soph, as I did. "She labored so long, it felt like days, and we didn't have any help. Sophia was amazing, she coached me through everything and–."

"Can I just butt in and say, out of the four of us, Kai has seen your *hugacko and mate's* vagina's, but not mine. Score to Jackson and zero to you two." Nico slaps the back of Jax's head, and I growl low in my throat. Jax rubs the back of his head. "The fuck was that for?"

"For being an ass, Jackson." We all turn around to see my dad standing behind us. We jump to our feet, but then no one moves or says anything. Dad sighs before he asks. "Why didn't you tell me Sophia Stone was your mate, Dominic?" I tense, but I don't want to lie anymore. I meet my father's gaze.

"Because I was scared she would end up like mom." Dad doesn't flinch or recoil, just nods his head in understanding.

"That, my boy, might be the wisest decision you have ever made." I gasp and look to my brothers to see they are all speechless as well. I never in a million years expected to hear that from my dad.

"Pardon me?"

"Oh, fuck off, Dominic, I have been trying for years to get you to use your manners, and now, of all times, you finally do?" The five of us break out into fits of laughter. Once everyone stops laughing, we all take a seat again by the stream, dad sits next to me sipping a bottle of whiskey Jax gave him. "So, who is going to tell me what happened this morning with Randall, and why a distraught Sophia opened a portal in the middle of my living room and told me my son needed me?"

We fill dad in about the drama with Randall, and Nico informs Dad and I both that before he, Jax, and Kai came out here, they opened a portal to send the armies back. Alex, Chase, and Mya opted to stay here another night and will leave tomorrow. Kai's staying as well, and in the midst of finding out I'm a father, I forgot about Randall and what he came for. Is he telling the truth? Will Lucian be consumed?

"Okay, so that answers the questions about Randall, but why did Sophia say you needed me, son?" I'm nearly out of my bottle of courage; I take a quick gulp and then answer my dad.

"Sophia admitted today that Lucian is her son."

"Took you all long enough to figure that out." The four of us turn to stare at my father in shock. He shrugs his shoulders. "What? It was pretty obvious." I glare at the old bastard. Well, now it's my turn to shock him.

"She came to get you because she just told me that I am Lucian's–."

"Father?" All four of us gape at him.

"How the fuck do you know that?"

"Watch your language, Dominic!" I throw my hands up in the air. Is he really going to worry about my language right now?

"How do you know, sir?" Jax asks, Dad shrugs.

"He looks exactly like Dom at that age, plus a dead give-away is the skin color, hair, eyes, and he also has a ring around–."

"Okay, okay, I get it, Dad. Why the hell didn't you say anything to me?" I'm getting pissed off right now; he knew this whole time and said nothing? Dad turns to face me, and so much wisdom shines in his green eyes.

"I knew Sophia would have had her reasons why she never told you. It is also not my place, son; that's between you and your mate." What a fucking cop-out.

"Bullshit! You let me get blindsided by her today! You could have told me, Dad." Dad reaches out and places a hand on my shoulder, but I shuck it off, glaring at him.

"Dominic you can be mad at me and angry all you want, but I didn't have any hard proof that he was actually yours. I suspected and thought as much, but didn't know for sure."

"You still could have warned me," I snarl back, and dad shakes his head and sighs.

"I hope to hell, now that you have a child of your own, that Karma will grant me my wish and come back on you tenfold." I scowl at the asshole. "Now why don't you tell me why you're hiding out here and not inside with your mate trying to fix this and find a way to build a relationship with your son?"

Old man has a point. Maybe I do need to sit down and have a calm, collected conversation with Sophia and hear her out.

CHAPTER 18

After Dom took off, I decided to go in search of Lucian. I searched the whole compound and couldn't find him. I'm about to give up when I wander around the back near where the chapel used to be and found him, Ryan, Alex, Chase, Mya, and Aurora sitting near the woods. I take a few deep breaths and give myself a mental pep talk before approaching the group. Ryan meets my gaze and gives me a sad smile.

"Come on, you guys, let's leave them to talk." She turns back to Lucian and clasps his hand in hers, giving it a reassuring squeeze. "We'll be in the mess hall if you need us, Luce." He nods, and she releases his hand and follows the others.

It's a beautiful afternoon. The air is still and the temperature mild. I sit down next to Lucian and stare out at the beautiful forest for a while. I want to give him time to come to me with any questions he might have. I know I have a lot to make up for, with not just him but Dom as well. I have fucked up a lot, and I want to try and make up for all my wrongs.

"Would you really have gone back to Randall for me?" His question surprises me, I didn't expect him to ask that, but I don't hesitate.

"Yes."

"Why?"

"Because you're my son, Lucian. I would lay down my life for yours in a heartbeat." He turns to look at me, and we sit here staring at each other.

"A part of me wants to wrap my arms around you and weep. I thought my mother and father were dead, and then here you are. The other part of me is so angry at you for your betrayal and deceit. I don't understand why you didn't just tell me."

"I was scared Dom—your dad—would reject you like he rejected me. I projected my own self-doubts onto you, and I shouldn't have done that. I need you to know that Dom had no idea I was pregnant. He just found out today, I swear."

"I get your reasoning and that pisses me off more. I'm so angry, Sophia, I feel like I have been living a lie." I reach over and grip his hand in mine.

"I am so sorry for all of this, and I will spend the rest of my life trying to make it up to you. I am so sorry we were robbed of seventeen years together." Lucian stiffens at my words. I know his whole world has just been turned upside down. I don't know how to make this situation right.

"You know, seeing Randall again today brought back so many of the nightmares I thought I had escaped. Just his presence alone reduces me to a scared child. That man has scarred me for life." My heart aches for my son; I know exactly how much of a monster Randall Cane is. He cares for no one but himself. The only person I thought he might actually love is Kai. It brought me joy today to see how disfigured his face is now; he may have escaped the battle, but he will always wear the reminder of what he lost that day.

"Believe me when I tell you that I know how much of a vile pig he is. I spent seventeen years as his captive, and every day was like living in hell."

"Will you tell me about it someday?" I thought about his question for a moment before answering.

"I will tell you some things but not all. It's too hard for me to relive. I'm not trying to be secretive; I just can't go back down that road again. I've moved past that." Lucian nods his head in understanding. We sit here for ages in comfortable silence, just gazing out at the scenery. It's a surreal feeling; I have been with Lucian for the past seven months, but not like this. There was always a tension between us before, because I couldn't build up the courage to tell him who I am to him. A feeling of peace settles over me. I never thought this moment would ever happen; I thought my son had died. Tears gather in my eyes, and I turn to Lucian so he can see the vulnerability in my eyes.

"Will you allow me to hug you?" Lucian looks taken back by my question, but after a moment, his beautiful eyes soften. He climbs to his feet and pulls me up. We stand there staring at each other for a moment, tension thick in the air. Now when he hugs me, he will know I am his mother. I know this is a huge step for Lucian. He opens his arms, with no hesitation I close the distance between us. We wrap our arms around each other, and I rest my cheek on his chest, tears flowing freely down my face. Lucian doesn't complain that my tears are wetting his shirt, he just grips me tighter and rests his chin on top of my head.

My baby boy is here, alive and well. This is the best moment of my life.

Dominic

The five of us make our way back toward the compound, thanks to being a shifter, I have a fast metabolism, so my buzz from the whiskey is already gone. As we near the compound, I catch her scent. She's outside. I pause and turn to the others, letting them know to carry on without me. I have a baby mama to sort shit out with. I take a few deep breaths and go in search of Soph. I round the corner and stop in my tracks. Standing by the trees near where the chapel used to stand is Sophia and Lucian, wrapped in each other's arms. A feeling of longing hits me in the chest. They are right there! Everything I ever wanted is right in front of me, and yet I can't seem to move my feet.

I have to return to New York. I still haven't been able to find out which one of those cunts is responsible for my mother's death. I can't risk Soph and Lucian coming with me, but I also can't leave them behind. What the fuck am I going to do?

The sound of rustling leaves behind me pulls my attention. I peer over my shoulder to see the three guys and my dad standing there, looking at me expectantly.

"What are you guys doing here?"

"You forget Dom, we know you. We also know the guilt will

be eating you alive, but you can't blame yourself brother." Fucking Nico, the ever-observant prick, who knows me to well. How did I not know Sophia was pregnant? We slept together *twice*, then she disappeared, and now seventeen years later, I find out I have a son. I have replayed those nights with Soph over and over in my head—they were the best nights of my life.

"Come on, son, I wanna meet my grandson." My dad's words pull me from my thoughts, and he claps me on the shoulder and pushes me forward. As we near them, Lucian lifts his head from resting on top of Sophia's and meets my gaze. I swallow hard. I hate to admit it, but right now, a seventeen-year-old kid has me shitting myself. Soph pulls out of Lucian's embrace and turns to see what has caught his attention. She freezes at the sight of us, and once we're to them, she subtly positions herself, so she is slightly in front of Lucian. I smirk. She's a lioness protecting her cub from the predator–me.

"What are you guys doing here?" Soph snaps. We stop a few feet away. Silence descends, and the level of awkwardness is excruciating.

"Well, since none of you kids want to talk, I will." Dad moves closer to Sophia and Lucian. He looks down and smiles kindly at Soph. "If you don't mind, sweetheart, I'd like to hug my grandson."

Sophia in shock, turns to look at me. I nod my head encouragingly, and she smiles up at my dad and then turns to see if Lucian is okay with this. When he nods, she moves to the side. Dad engulfs Lucian in a bear hug, and I hear the poor kid grunt. My father tends to squeeze the shit out of you. Dad pulls back and rests both his hands on Lucian's shoulders, smiling at him.

"I just knew it. You're way too good looking not to be a Silver." I roll my eyes and Soph grins. What can I say? I get my quick wit and sense of humor from my dad.

"Thank you, sir."

Dad tsks Lucian. "There will be none of that. You can call me Gramps, Pops, Grandpa or Your Greatness." Lucian snorts at the last part, and I scoff and shake my head, mouthing "No," at Lucian. We make eye contact for a second before we both dart our eyes away.

"How about *Poppy?*" Dad recoils and drops his hands to his sides. I'm starting to really enjoy this conversation.

"Why the hell would you call me *Poppy?* I'm a big burly man and I need a strong name, not a girly name. No offence, Sophia."

"None taken," Sophia snickers back trying to conceal her laughter.

"Well, I think it fits, because you remind me of a movie Smurf, and I watched. The main character has a big personality and is really kind." Dad seems a bit chuffed and even pushes out his chest a bit.

"What movie was it? *Die Hard, Fast and the Furious, Terminator–.*"

"*Trolls.*" Soph and I break out into uncontrollable laughter at Lucian's answer. I bend over, tears streaming down my face, and Soph is clutching her stomach from laughing so hard.

Dad turns and glares at me.

"Fuck up, *Branch!* I am not a fucking troll!" The look on dad's face is priceless and it only makes us laugh harder.

"Language!" I wheeze out between fits of laughter. Dad just narrows his eyes at me then turns to Lucian.

"I have prayed for Karma to bite him in the ass since he was young, and I hope you are the answer to my prayers. I hope you turn him gray and then make him worry for the rest of his days." I stop laughing immediately and scowl at my dad, who just smirks.

I march over to him, and shoulder check him out of the way then face Lucian–my son. The whole speech I have in my head dies as I stare at him. I see it. The hair, the eyes, the cheekbones. He looks like me. He is me—well, half me. No one speaks as Lucian and I just stand there taking each other in.

I have known this kid for months and never really taken the time to get to know him or ever truly look at him. Guilt weighs down on me. I could have been nicer. I could have done more than just ignore him. I drop my gaze from his and sigh.

"I'm so sorry. I should have known." I don't lift my gaze, but after a moment, when I see the tips of his shoes enter my line of sight, I lift my gaze to his, and he doesn't hesitate. He wraps his arms around me and hugs me, and I shake out of my stupor after a second and return his embrace. I'm.... I'm hugging *my son*.

I grip him tighter and pull him in closer. I don't cry—ever. I cried the day my mom died, and the day I told Sophia that I rejected her as my mate. But today will mark the third time I let tears fall from my eyes. I can't hold them back.

I have a son!

Lucian pulls back after a moment and I let him go. I smile at my boy and quickly wipe away my tears. Then, turning to the woman who gave birth to my boy, I close the distance between us and pull her to my chest. She returns my embrace.

"Thank you, thank you for giving me the greatest gift, little dove. I promise you I will fix this between us and be here for you and Lucian. I won't let you down again, Sophia!" I pull back and look down at her so she can see how serious I am. I will make this work for our son. I'll figure out a way. A throat clearing has us turning around to see Nico standing in front of Lucian, who is wearing a cheeky smirk. He is flanked by Kai and Jax.

"You do realize you shared a bed with your aunt for months, right?" Lucian's face morphs into one of pure mirth.

"You do know she isn't blood related to me, right? Only you

are." The smug look on Nico's face vanishes and is replaced by a sullen pout. Lucian has just one- upped the king of the fae.

"You little sh–."

Lucian cuts Nico off. "I'm kidding. I love Smurf." Nico growls. "Not like that! I'm glad we're officially family; maybe now you'll stop finding excuses to join Smurf and me when we hang out." Everyone chuckles at Nico's expense, but to his credit he takes it in stride. He claps Lucian on the shoulder and makes his way back inside.

"Well, kid, I like having you around, and I already consider you family. Finding out you *are* related is just a formality." Jax gives Lucian a hug and retreats to the compound, leaving Kai, Soph, Dad, Luce and I standing in tense silence.

CHAPTER 20

Sophia

Tension is radiating off Dom and Kai. Mr. Silver seems to sense the delicate balance and moves closer to the guys in case he has to intervene. The silence stretches, and it's becoming uncomfortable. I start scuffing my feet along the ground to give me something to focus on.

"You boys need to sort this out. You have been friend's way too long."

"He hid the fact my *mate* gave birth to *my* kid, Dad," Dom hisses. I feel a rush of anger surge inside me. How dare he? He has never once referred to me as his *mate*, and now all of a sudden, he wants to acknowledge me? Yeah, nah!

"You have no damn right, Dominic! You do not get to play the *my mate* card. Kai didn't do anything wrong." Dom turns angry eyes to me, but I stand my ground.

"He is supposed to be *my* best friend, and he should have come to me and told me, Sophia. Do not stand there and defend him!"

"Fuck you! You do not get to be angry at me—."

"YOU HID MY KID!" Dom bellows, and I flinch at the anger in his tone. His eyes change to the color of his wolf. So much for making this work between us. "You don't get to turn this on me Sophia. I lost seventeen years with my son. Kai could have told me, I–."

"You would have what, Dom? Tried harder to find me?" I scoff. "I told Kai not to say anything. I thought *my* son had died. Do you have any idea what that is like? No, you fucking don't. It was hell! Kai was there to help me through the hardest times of my life."

The anger doesn't diminish from his eyes; it intensifies. Mr. Silver moves to stand closer to Dom and I, and Lucian takes a step closer to me. Lucian wanting to protect me, warms my heart, but I won't let him get in the middle. He is the biggest victim after all. Dom narrows his eyes and glares down at me, and the look on his face sends a shiver down my spine.

"I searched for you every goddamn day. From sunup to sundown. I never gave up on you Sophia. Ask Nico what I just about started; I nearly cost you your life, because I wouldn't turn my back on you."

"Son, that's enough!"

Dom didn't take his eyes off me as he answers his father.

"It will never be enough, Dad. You can hate me all you want, little dove, but I never gave up on you." Dom turns to Lucian next, and once his gaze lands on our son, all the anger flees from his body. "I have to return to New York tomorrow."

"I know."

Dom swallows loudly then turns to his father. "Do you swear on your honor that you will end any of them if they try?"

"You have my word, son. I will kill them with my bare hands if they even *think* it." *What the hell were they talking about?*

"Lucian, I would like for you to join me in New York. I'd love to spend some time with you—if you want to, of course?" I can hear the slight tremble in Dom's voice. He's extending an olive branch to Lucian. I can tell from his body language that he's nervous.

"I...I..." Lucian looks to me, and I smile at him, letting him know that I will support whatever he decides. He releases a long exhale before answering.

"I have never been away from Smurf, what if she needs me–."

"Don't you dare, Luce!" We all turn to see Ryan, Mya, Aurora, Chase, Alex, Nico and Jackson loitering behind the side of the building. They have no shame! They know they have just been caught eavesdropping and don't give two shits.

"Smurf, what are you doing?" Ryan pushes off the side of the building and makes her way over to us, the rest of the crew following her. When she nears Dom and Mr. Silver, they step back so she can get to Lucian. She clasps both his hands in hers and smiles up at him.

"If you want to go with Dom–your dad—go. I will be fine, I swear. Nico and I are going back to the Knox coven for a few days anyway." Lucian cocks his head to the side.

"Why?" We all waited for her answer.

"Because we have to speak to my uncle and find out how the hell Randall managed to get his grubby hands on the moonstones." I forgot about that. I was too distracted with Lucian learning the truth. Today has been such a clusterfuck. I never thought Randall fucking Cane would ever show his face again. I won't lie, seeing him today in the clearing was one hell of a shock, and I have this sinking feeling that we're missing something. A part of me has a horrible feeling that Randall is telling the truth.

CHAPTER 21
Dominic

After a lot of reassurance from Ryan, Lucian agreed to come to New York with me and my dad for a few days. I am elated to get a chance to get to know him, but I am shit-scared at the same time. I have no idea how to be a father. What if I fuck it up?

These types of thoughts have been plaguing me since I decided to call it a night and head to bed.

Dad, Lucian, and I will return to New York tomorrow. I fucking hate that place. If only I didn't make that stupid fucking vow.

"Arrgghhh," I groan out loud. I needed to get out of my fucking head. So much shit has been running through my mind all day. I need a distraction. Before I can think on it more, a knock sounds at my door. I throw the covers off and head to answer the door, stunned at my caller.

"Yeah, I know, not who you expected to be knocking on your door at midnight."

I grin. "Well, you know me, I'm always down for a booty call babe." She glares then her eyes land on my naked chest, I see her gaze glide down further to my briefs as she hitches and swallows loudly.

"Like what you see, little dove?" She snaps her eyes back to mine and blinks a few times, her cheeks tinged the slightest shade of red. I hold my laughter in. She's embarrassed she got caught checking me out.

"Can I come in?" I step aside, and after closing the door I turn and lean back against the it, crossing my arms over my chest. She stops at the foot of the bed and turns to face me. I can see a slight twitch in her eyes, almost as if she's trying to stop her eyes from wandering. I, on the other hand, don't give a fuck. I blatantly check her out. She looks stunning: long black hair still damp from her shower, big violet eyes, and the cutest button nose you will ever see. She wears a thin, cream-color spaghetti strap camisole and matching sleep shorts. She looks like a fucking snack, and I want to take a bite.

The silence stretches between us, but the sexual tension ramps up tenfold. Sophia and I haven't been alone like this since she came back from Randall's; being alone with her is dangerous. I want inside her tight little body. I'm not the only one with my mind in the gutter, either—Sophia's nipples are poking through her camisole. Because I'm a sucker for fucking punishment, I scent the air and growl low in my throat. My wolf is fighting for control. I close my eyes and try to wrestle my wolf back. The scent of her arousal is driving him insane.

"Unless you want me to claim you, little dove, you need to say what you came here to say to distract me," I gri out.

"What? Why does your wolf want to claim me now?" I can hear the shock in her voice. I snap my eyes open and see the confusion on her face.

"Because I can smell your arousal from here, babe, and it's driving my wolf crazy!" I explain through clenched teeth.

"Maybe this isn't a good time, I'll come back tomorrow." She takes a step forward and I growl.

"If you try to leave now Sophia, you will entice my wolf, and he will chase you down and mark you." She cocks her head to the side and places her hand on her hip.

"Him or *you?*" Now isn't the time for one of her mind-fuck games; I'm hanging on by a thread. I can feel my vision changing from my eyes to my wolf's. I stop breathing through my nose and start breathing through my mouth because her scent is a drug. Luck hasn't been on my side with my wolf since Soph's return, but after being apart for seven months and then seeing her again, my wolf wants her...bad. Fuck, I want her bad.

"Both!" I growl. She drops her arm to her side and straightens up, and it takes all my willpower to focus on her eyes and not let my gaze stray. She looks smug, and proud that she manages to get me to admit that it isn't just my wolf that wants her.

"What do you want, Sophia?"

"I want to come to New York as well." I reel back so fast I smack the back of my head on the door. Pissed off that she caught me off guard, I don't rub my head and give her the satisfaction. I can see she wants to laugh—the corners of her eyes crinkle—and I scowl.

"Why the change of heart?" Her expression changes within a second, the laughter is replaced by annoyance.

"Because my son happens to be going there." I close the space between us, my need to claim her long forgotten. My anger is riding shotgun now. I glare down at my deceitful mate.

"He is *our* son, Sophia. You may have carried and gave birth to him, but you sure as fuck didn't fuck yourself to make him. If I recall, my dick had a hand in making him." As if she has no control over her eyes, they trail down my naked torso and land *said* dick in question. I stand there proudly in my black briefs. After a few seconds, she snaps her gaze back to mine and glares up at me. I smirk.

"Fuck you–."

"Name the time and place, little dove."

"You're a fucking pig!"

"And you're a pain in the ass, but I still want to fuck you."

"How about you go fuck yourself, Dominic."

"How about you get on your knees and suck my cock and make it up to daddy, then maybe I might be swayed into forgiving you for hiding my fucking kid!" She doesn't flinch or recoil, instead she closes the slither of space between us. In shock, I stand there as still as a tree. She runs a finger down my chest and slowly traces my abs. My dick is rock fucking hard, and the lower she traces the harder I get. This is like fucking torture. I can feel her tits pressed against me, and her arousal clouds my senses again. My wolf is more interested in our mate sucking my cock right now than claiming her, so he isn't fighting for control. But I'm fighting not to fucking come in my pants like an amateur. It has been so long since I felt a woman's touch.

"You want me to suck your cock, baby?" Her voice is low and husky, and I groan and loll my head back. She starts to pepper kisses all over my chest, her hand finally reaching the band of my briefs. I hold my breath in anticipation as she reaches up with her free hand and grips the back of my neck, pulling my head down to hers. I'm a hair's breadth away from claiming her lips, jutting her tongue out to moisten her lips. My eyes follow the movement; I want that tongue lapping at my hard cock.

Her hand slides beneath my briefs, and she palms my aching cock. I hiss and close my eyes as I relish in the feeling of her hands on me. She holds my cock in her palm and then leans forward to start licking and suckling on my neck before she starts to pump my cock.

Fuck me!

She only pumps my cock twice and I'm nearly ready to blow my fucking load like some prepubescent fucking teen.

Two more strokes, then she bites the side of my neck and I moan ...loudly.

"Fuck, Soph. That feels so good, baby."

"You want me to make you come?"

"Yes."

"You want me to kneel before you and suck your *huge* cock?" I groan at hearing the word *cock* come out of her mouth.

"Yeeeessssss." She stops licking and sucking my neck, and her hand stops stroking me. She rips her hand out of my pants and pushes me back. I stumble back a few steps, in shock.

"Pathetic!"

What the actual fuck just happened? I'm standing here, gaping at her, fucking confused as shit—and hard as fuck, I might add.

"What the hell, Soph?"

"You're pathetic, Dominic. Go find some loose bitch that'll kneel for you." She brushes past me as I stand here with my mouth in an O shape. She opens the door, and just before she leaves, she turns and says, "You know when I said you had a huge cock?"

I nod my body on autopilot.

"I lied."

CHAPTER 22

Sophia

I wake the next morning feeling like I haven't slept a wink. Thoughts of Dom's body and his cock plagued me all night. I am woman enough to admit that I came back to my room and jumped in the cold shower, trying to get my libido to settle the fuck down. Well, that didn't happen, so I pulled the detachable shower head off the wall, spread my legs, and let the hard pressure of the water hit my clit. I climaxed with Dom's name on my lips. Even after climaxing by my own hand, I still felt hot and needy.

I never should have let Dom get under my skin last night; the only way to even the playing field with that man is to beat him at his own game. I admit I would have sucked his cock gladly, until he told me to get on my knees. That triggered memories I wish I could erase from my mind.

I will kneel for no man.

I feel my power rush to the surface at the sudden anger coursing through my veins. I close my eyes and take a few calming breaths. It starts to work until my bedroom door slams open. I bolt upright in bed. When I see who it is waltzing into my room and kicking the door shut on their way to my bed, I glare.

Dominic makes his way to the vacant side of my bed and drops down, crossing his legs at his ankles and putting his arms behind his head. He turns and smiles up at me. That smile does things to me, so I avert my gaze. I should have just dealt with the fucking smile. Now I can't seem to pull my eyes away from the exposed skin on his abdomen; with his arms stretched behind his head, his shirt rides up. His jeans are low on his hips, and the bottom of his six pack is on display. I groan then slump down in the bed and bang my head against my pillows a couple times.

"Feeling a bit strung out, babe?" I don't even look at him let alone acknowledge what he says, which just causes him to chuckle.

"What the hell do you want, Dom?"

"You." I snap my gaze to his so fast I crack my neck. I expect to see laughter or some form of humor in his expression, but all I see is seriousness and longing.

"Your mood swings are giving me whiplash. You want me, you reject me, you want me, you don't, and now you want me again." I roll my eyes at him and then turn so I'm looking up at the ceiling. We lay there next to each other silent for a long time, though the silence isn't uncomfortable. Dom releases a loud exhale before he speaks.

"You know the day I told you I couldn't take you as my mate?" He pauses, waiting for me to answer, and I grunt instead of using words. That's not a day I like to think about; it's the day the boy I had a crush on my whole life broke my fucking heart.

"I wish I had of done things differently that day. That day has played on repeat in my mind every single day since. I was a coward. I didn't want you to end up like my mom; I thought I was protecting you. How fucking wrong was I though, huh? If I had of claimed you, maybe things would be different, and we would have gotten a chance to raise our son. Instead, you spent seventeen years as a prisoner because your *hugacko* was a fucking coward." Tears fall from my eyes. I can't stop them from sliding down my face. Everything he just said hits me right in my heart. I would give anything to go back and change that day.

After clearing my throat a few times, I answer Dom.

"I can't think like that. I went through all of the shoulda, coulda, wouldas for years. All that did was put me in a dark hole that I needed help to climb out of." Dom rolls on to his side and faces me, but I won't meet his gaze—I can't. He reaches over and rests his hand on my stomach, and I tense. He doesn't move his hand, though the heat from his hand is making my blood boil.

"I know we're both still angry as fuck at each other Soph, and I know we have a lot to work out. I want us to sit down in the next few days and talk about things. I don't like it or even think it's a good idea, but if you want to come to New York–."

"Yes, I do!" I blurt out before he can finish what he is saying. I turn and look at him to find he is smiling wide. "Why are you looking at me like that?"

"Because I knew even if I said no, you would siphon my power and open a portal of your own to follow us." Now it's my turn to grin.

"How long have you known I could siphon your power?"

"Since the day Ryan erected the dome in the clearing. My magic was low when I returned with Mya and the boys, but once at the compound, I felt this pulling sensation in my gut. I traced that feeling and followed it. When I got to the clearing, Nico thanked me for sending you ahead. I asked what he meant, and he said he knew it was me that sent you because the portal was yellow and not purple like the other fae." I bite my bottom to stop myself from laughing, and Dom's gaze drops to my mouth. His pupils dilating, and I hear low growls coming from him. I know his wolf is close so I grip his chin in my hand and lift his gaze back to mine.

"My eyes are up here." Dom's eyes change to the color of his wolf's, and I move my hand from his chin to the back of his head and stroke his hair. I have always loved the strange silver color of his hair. I mean it was quite weird to have silver colored hair and your last name is Silver as well. Dom's eyes close as I continue to stroke his hair; he scoots down the bed and gently puts his head on my chest...I still.

"Don't stop touching me, Soph, if you do, I will lose control." So, I carry on running my fingers through his hair. His hand that rests on my stomach slides beneath the covers and he places it on the top of my thigh. I suck in a sharp breath.

"Relax babe, I'm not the type to get you horny as fuck and then get you so close to exploding and fucking leave!" Laughter burst out of me; I can't stop it. Dom moves and looks down at me with confusion.

"You seriously think, me having fucking blue balls is funny?" More laughter burst out of me, but my laughter dies in my throat the moment Dom's hand slid beneath the cover again and cups my sex. My eye wide as I gasp. I lock my gaze on his and see a sexy as fuck smirk on his gorgeous face. "Don't stop laughing on my account, babe."

"Dom." I'm not sure whether I say his name in warning or begging. I have no fucking idea what I want right now. Him being this close to me short-circuits my brain.

CHAPTER 23
Dominic

Hearing my name on her lips like that is the best form of torture. I can see in her eyes that she wants this, but isn't sure. Last night when she left me high and dry, I swore I would stay away from her and continue to fight this mate bond. This morning I planned to come here and tell her she could come to New York and then leave. As soon as I saw her lying in bed, my plan went out the fucking window.

I feel the heat from her core against the palm of my hand. I close my eyes and relish in the feeling of her heat. Fuck it, I'm going in.

Opening my eyes, I stare down at her as I slip her sleep shorts to the side. I groan. She isn't wearing any panties, and her arousal coats my finger as soon as I slide it between her folds. I run my digit up and down her sweet pussy, and she lets out a breathy moan and throws her head back. I withdraw my hand and move down the bed, she jerks up on her elbows, narrowing her eyes.

"Seriously?" I smirk as I throw the covers off her legs and settle myself between them. "Oh…"

I don't respond, instead peeling her flimsy sleep shorts from her body and chucking them over my head. I suck in a sharp breath at the sight of her bare glistening pussy, my mouth watering in anticipation. I bury my face between her legs and begin to lap her sweet pussy, and she moans so fucking loud when I circle my tongue around her clit. I lick from top to bottom, and once the taste of her wetness coats my tongue, my wolf surges forward. I push him back down. I won't mark her—not yet. I insert a finger inside her as I circle her nub with my tongue.

"Oh fuck, Dom!" Her pussy is so fucking tight! My dick is straining against my zipper. The taste of her and the feeling of having my finger inside her is making me crazy. I pump my finger in and out of her, picking up the pace the louder she moans. I can feel she's close when she starts gripping my finger.

"I'm...Oh fuck Dom, I'm gonna come!" I suck her clit into my mouth and quickly add another finger, never slowing my pace as I pump her. Two seconds later she's screaming my name as she comes all over my fucking hand.

I slow my pace and gently lap at her clit as she comes down from her orgasm.

I sit back on my knees and look down at her, all rosy cheeks, glassy eyes, and messy hair. Her legs are wide open with me seated between them. It wouldn't take much; all I would have to do is pop the button and lower the zipper on my jeans and then I would be inside her. She meets my gaze, and the look in her eyes makes the decision for me. I lean down and place a soft kiss on her lips before drawing back. She looks utterly baffled. I try smile a reassuring smile, but judging by the look on her face I fail, so I go with words.

"Don't overthink this little dove. We'll talk about it when we get to New York. You should get ready and pack."

"W-what about you?" Her gaze lowers to my hard cock that is currently tenting my pants. I shake my head.

"This is about you, I'll be fine after a cold shower." She giggles, and that sound causes a thousand different feelings to swirl inside my chest. Reality hits me like a ton of bricks. What the fuck did I just do? I jump from the bed and quickly leave the room. I know I'm a fucking asshole, but I never should have done that. This bond and my feelings for her are clouding my judgment.

"Fuck!" I'm such a stupid fucking asshole who has to learn how to think with his brain and not his other fucking head.

After saying goodbye to everyone, Sophia, Lucian, Dad and I all left through a portal I opened. Emerging from the woods at the back of Dad's house, we lead Soph and Lucian to the house and show them to their rooms. Dad told us all to unpack and get settled while he makes us some supper. Lying here in my bare-ass room, I flop down onto my bed and stare up at the ceiling, but not really seeing shit. This morning's events are playing on repeat in my head. I can still taste her on my tongue, her scent clinging to me, and it's doing my head in.

What if I take Sophia as my mate and something happens to her? What if I don't take her as my mate and live the rest of my life miserable? We have a child together., I don't think it matters what I choose now. Sophia will always be a target because she is the mother of the future alpha. Lucian has no idea about that; he doesn't realize that being my son means he will be expected to lead this pack after I step down or die. I don't want that ball and chain for him. I want him to be able to choose his path in life. I'm so lost in my own thoughts I don't hear her enter.

"Lucian and I are gonna take a walk." I bolt off the bed and stare at her in shock. Has nothing I've said to her registered inside her brain? "Why are you looking at me like that?"

"Has nothing I have said sunk in?"

"Uh, maybe?" I growl at her blasé tone.

"You have no fucking idea the danger you are in by being here. I rejected our bond to keep you safe, but now it seems I did that for nothing."

"The fuck are you on about, Dominic?" Lucian walks through the open door and looks between us. The tension is thick enough that I know he can sense it.

"Answer me, Dom." My attention snaps back to Sophia. I won't lie.

"Me rejecting you means nothing now Soph; everyone will know you're Lucian's mother and I'm his father." God that felt weird, saying I was a father out loud. "Which means in order to get to me they can now go through you or my kid."

"Why would they want to harm us?" I turn to Lucian, so many questions swirling in his strange eyes. I release a long sigh, but it isn't me who answers.

"Because your mother is a half breed and so is your father. The pack don't take kindly to half-bloods." All three of us look to my dad, who's leaning against the open door.

"Mr. Silver, what does that have to do with anything?"

"Sophia, my dear, there is so much you don't know. Come down for supper and I will explain everything to you both."

We all sit the small circular wooden table, but no one utters a word. I feel like whatever Dom's dad has to say is going to change everything.

"Oaky, here's the deal I'll talk as long as you all eat." We nod so he continues. "Dom's mother was a fae, the most beautiful fae I have ever seen. We weren't mates, but that didn't matter to me. As soon as I laid eyes on her, I just knew she was going to be it for me. She turned me down, you know. I asked her on a date and she straight up said '*not in this lifetime.*' I was shocked by that. I never gave up trying, though." I could hear the longing in his voice, but I could also see happiness in his eyes as he speaks about his late wife. Dom doesn't utter a word.

"Anyway, finally she agreed, and we fell in love—well, she did. I was already in love with her. Not long after, we decided to get married. A few months after our wedding, my father passed, so I had to return to New York and assume the role of alpha. The pack was in tatters after their alpha died, so I had my work cut out for me."

"Do we really have to talk about this?" Dom grits out, his gaze focusing on his plate, like it's so interesting.

"They have a right to know son—she has a right to know why you did what you did." Dom snaps his gaze to his father in shock.

"How?"

"You're my son, Dominic, you don't need to say it with words. I can see it in your eyes."

Lucian and I look between Dom and his father, confused as fuck.

"Let me carry on. It took years to get the pack back in order, and when we did, the pack still had a lot of tension among them. It took me longer than I would like to admit to clue in. The problem wasn't the pack; *they* had a problem with their alpha being married to a fae and not a wolf. They demanded that I divorce her and find a shifter to marry and have children with."

I see Dom tense out the corner of my eye. He is gripping his fork so tight I think he might bend it. I reach under the table and rest my hand on his thigh. I feel him tense and then relax when he registers it's me touching him.

"I refused, of course, and a few months later, we found out Monica was pregnant. We were overjoyed. The pack wasn't. They wanted the child aborted. Fast forward, Dom came along, and we were so happy for many years. I noticed as the pack started to take up more of my time, I would get home late and find out that Mon didn't send Dom to school again, or she hadn't left the house. This went on for months, until I confronted her, and she finally told me she was scared to leave the house."

Oh my God, my stomach just dropped. Dom places his hand on top of mine under the table and squeezes. Dom still won't take his eyes off his plate and Lucian is looking very pale; he knows where this story is going as well.

"I-I tried to reassure her that nothing would happen to her or our son. But she wouldn't hear it. She said I was delusional because I couldn't see how she and Dom were being treated behind my back. Monica told me that one night when I had to go away for pack business that she and Dom were the targets of abuse. One member of the pack even assaulted Monica; he punched her in the face." Dom starts shaking next to me, and I can see ripples of fur running down his arms. Fuck, he's losing control! This story is clearly a trigger for him. Lucian reaches over and places his hand on Dom's shoulder. Dom stops shaking and snaps his gaze up to our son, who smiles reassuringly.

"I am so sorry for what happened to you and your mom–."

"We haven't even gotten to the best part yet. Just wait, there's more." Lucian reels back, in shock at Dom's bitter tone.

I snatch my hand back and say, "Don't talk to him like that, he is just trying to comfort y–."

"I meant it! You have to hear the best part Sophia, so then you will understand why the fuck I rejected you! Neither of you two should be here. I was stupid for fucking inviting you here. You both need to leave now!"

Dom pushes away from the table and storms out of the house. I turn to Lucian. We are both in shock by that outburst, and his words hurt. He throws around the word *rejected* like it holds no weight.

Ian reaches out and places one of his massive paws on each of our shoulders and says.

"Let me finish, then you will understand why he just stormed off. Please just know he has every right to be angry. I didn't listen, and I cost him his mother, who was the love of my life." Luce and I both nod our heads at Ian's ominous words.

"After I returned, Monica told me what happened. I banished that pack member and punished any of the wolves involved in abusing my family. Things were fine for a while after that, but every time I had to go away, it would start up again. Things got worse when Dom came into his powers. He was the first hybrid."

"I thought Smurf was," Lucian said, and Ian turns to his grandson and grins.

"She is the third." Ian's gaze slides to me then back to Lucian. "Dom is the first, then Sophia, then Ryan. Dom is an oddity; people feared him. When he shifted, he was double the size of boys his age in wolf form. When Dom was sixteen, things turned for the worse. Dom and Monica stopped sharing what would happen to them while I was away. I noticed Dom was training more with his magic, but I just thought he was trying to master that side of him. What I didn't know was Dom was pushing himself so hard because when I was away, he wanted to make sure he could defend his mother. Monica was the target of so much hate, I should have known when she wouldn't leave the house anymore or she looked tired and withdrawn. I had no right chasing after that woman and making her come here!"

Mr. Silver is vibrating with rage, his fists clenched on top of the table. I had no idea what the hell to do. Lucian places a hand on his grandfather's forearm, but he doesn't say anything. After a few tense moments, Ian gets himself under control and then continues.

"Dom met Nico, Jax, and Kai by this time. He went to visit the boys in Wonder Lake at the local pub. He and Jax had always been tight, as Jackson's father and I were great friends. So, whenever I was home, he would leave and go visit his friends; his mother taught him how to portal. While Dom was away an emergency came up and I had to leave. I asked Monica to come with me, but she refused. She told me she would be fine, and Dom would be back in the morning. I had a gut feeling that something was wrong, but she assured me she would be okay, so I left."

I can see tears gathering in Mr. Silver's eyes. His shoulders droop, and he hangs his head, his chin resting on his chest. Out of nowhere, a hand appears on his shoulder and I'm surprised to see it's Dom. His face is contorted in pain and anger. Mr. Silver reaches up and covers Dom's hand with his.

"When I got home the next morning, the house was empty. I didn't know Dad had gone, so I thought he and mom were out on a walk or something. I decided to head out back and do some magic training and try out the new chants Nico had taught me. As soon as I exited the back door, I found her. Those cunts had stripped her naked and hung her from the tree out back."

I gasp and cover my mouth with my hand, tears leaking from my eyes without my consent. My heart is breaking for Dom. I can hear so much heartbreak in his voice, Mr. Silver's shoulders are shaking from his silent tears. I peer over at Lucian to see his eyes clenched shut and his hands glowing yellow atop the table.

"I went to cut her down and that's when I noticed the scents clinging to her. They didn't just kill my mother—they raped her, beat her, and then killed her. All because she wasn't a fucking wolf! I fucking hate this pack. Killing each and every one of those cunts that hurt her wasn't enough." Dom turns his angry eyes to me, but I know his anger isn't directed at me.

"I rejected you Sophia, because I don't want to be Alpha. If I had accepted you, my dad would have had to step down and let the mated heir rule. I don't want you to end up like my mother. You never gave me a chance to explain before you took off."

CHAPTER 25

Dominic

I see a look of understanding and regret cross Sophia's face. I tear my gaze from her to look at my son. I see anger swirling in his eyes—he's so tense, and his hands are glowing. It makes sense now why his power is yellow, like mine and Sophia's. Soph's power changed from purple to yellow the day I told her she was my mate.

"I never should have brought you here, either of you. I was stupid to think I could have my cake and eat it too. I think it's best you take your mother and leave, Lucian." He pushes back from the table and stands, glaring at me. I move from behind my dad and stand in front of Lucian, meeting his heated glare.

"You do not get to tell me what to do," he grits out.

"I'm trying to fucking keep you alive Lucian!" I snap.

"I've survived this long without you." Wow, that hurt.

"I may have just found out who you are Lucian, but losing you would destroy me. You are my blood; my job is to protect you."

"Protect me from what?" he yells.

"From this fucking pack! We have been trying for fucking

years to find out who ordered the attack on my mother. We are still no fucking closer."

"I can help."

"No, you can't!"

"How do you know?" He screams in my face.

"Because I couldn't even save my own fucking mother from these cunts! I won't lose you to them as well!"

Everything goes silent. I can't believe I just blurted that out. Sophia rises from her chair and comes around to stand beside Lucian and me.

"Why do you both stay here then?" she asks.

"Because aside from Dom, revenge is all I have left." Sophia's eyes soften at my dad's admission.

"I'm not leaving. I may not know who she was, but she is a part of me as well, and I will see to it that justice is served for her." I felt like a part of my heart has just been put back together at Lucian's words.

"I'm staying as well." I look to my dad, and he shrugs his shoulders, meaning the decision is mine to make as to whether or not Sophia stays. If I tell her to leave, I know she'll go Hurricane Sophie on my ass, but if I let her stay... What if something happens to her? I can't lose her, not again. Sophia is everything to me. I just have to man up and make a decision. I can't keep playing hot and cold with her emotions. I take a deep breath and turn to face the only person in this world that can make my nuts shrivel up like no other.

"If you stay—." She opens her mouth, and I narrow my eyes, so she quickly closes her mouth and glares. "You do not under any circumstances leave this house without me or my dad. I mean it Sophia; I don't give a shit if the bathroom is backed up, you piss yourself if you have to. Am I clear?" I see Lucian try to hide his smile. Maybe I went too far with driving my point home, but fuck it. Soph looks from me to my dad then finally settles her gaze back on me. To my utter shock, she closes the space between us and wraps her arms around me, resting her cheek against my chest. I stand there stunned for a moment before I return her embrace.

"I promise Dom." Relief flows through me at her words. "I-I am so sorry about your mom. I promise to help in any way I can; you know my brother and the others will help as well."

I deflate in relief, resting my chin on top of her head. She has no idea how hard it is for me to let her in and allow her to know about my mom. I haven't even told my brothers that story —all they know is that my mom was killed.

"I can't see him rejecting her much longer *Poppy*." Dad breaks out in laughter, and I feel Soph start shaking in my arms with silent giggles. I lift my gaze to Lucians and see him smiling wide, and I grin.

"You know you get your sense of humor from me, right?" Lucian rolls his eyes. "You also get your good looks from me too." Sophia pulls out of my embrace and glares at me. I smile down at her. In 3...2....1...

"You're such a dick!" There it is.

"Babe, you know it's true." She scowls.

"Let's just hope he takes after his mother in the department of being able to keep his mouth shut and not spilling secrets over town." Lucian and Sophia burst out laughing. I turn and glare down at my dad.

"You're a fucking traitor!"

"Dominic–."

"Language," Lucian finishes for him. I growl at my kid.

"You're gonna be a real pain in the ass, aren't you?"

Dad stands and claps me on the shoulder.

"Thank you, Karma," he says as he blows a kiss to the heavens. Fuck me in the ass, this whole kid thing is going to be a real bitch.

We have been in New York for two weeks now. Lucian is determined to stay and help Dom and Ian. Ryan and Nico have visited a couple of times. I know it's hard for Lucian to be away from Ryan. He is handling the distance between them better than I thought. Now that Ryan has more control over her power and isn't so reliant on Lucian, it's a bit easier for them to separate. Nico and Ryan are still chasing a lead on Randall. We don't know yet if what he said about Lucian is true. We have been keeping an eye on him to make sure, and Aurora and Mya have been trying to bring on any visions they can about Lucian's future. Ian had his pack doctor run blood tests, but all tests have come back normal.

Dom spends most of his day with his father, learning how to run the pack. When he returns, Dom, Lucian, and I sit down and talk for an hour or so each day. We're all trying to get to know each other better; I still refuse to talk about my time with Randall. Dom wants me to see a therapist, but what he doesn't know is I have been seeing the same healer as Nina. Nina and I have formed a bond, I guess you could call it. We understand each other and the trauma we have both been put through at the hands of another.

Dom and his dad are hosting a pack party in a couple of weeks. Dom thinks it would be a good idea to have all the pack together and get Jackson out here so he can help pick up on lies. I'm not sure what Dom and his father are hoping to find, honestly. I know that they killed the six shifters involved in Monica's death. If you ask me, I think they're both holding onto their revenge, so they don't have to deal with their grief.

I'm still on house arrest. I can't leave the house without Dom or his dad. Dom even went as far as getting Alex and Chase to put a fucking tracking spell on me so he'll know where I am at all times. When I found out he went behind my back about this, I lost my shit and may have *accidently* kick him in the balls.

Dom and I haven't spoken about what happened back in Wonder Lake. I think it may be for the better though. I may not leave the house, but it doesn't stop this guy Louis from dropping letters off most days. I know what he is trying to do; he hates Dom, and is trying to turn me against him. The letter that he dropped off this morning, not long after Dom, Lucian, and Ian left, has put me in a foul fucking mood. I have no right to be jealous; after all, I did tell Dominic that I rejected him as my *hugacko*. I still didn't fucking expect him to do this.

By the time the three guys return home that evening, I have dinner plated and waiting on the table. I sit in my usual seat crossing my arms. All three men eye me warily as they take their seats. They thank me for dinner before they start to dig in. We have all gotten along so well—until now. I can't stop glaring at Dom. The thought of food sours my mouth. Dom breaks the awkwardness by speaking, but he doesn't look up from his plate.

"I can feel your laser vision burning a hole in my head, Superwoman, what's got your panties in a twist?" When I don't answer straight away, he finally lifts his head and meets my gaze.

"You got something you want to tell me, *mate?*" I spit the word at him like I have heard Jax do to Aurora. I know it pisses her off when he says it, so I'm hoping it will work on Dom, because I'm so ready to throw down with him right now.

"Calm the hell down Jackson Junior. Why don't you tell me what I have done now, so we can sort it? The last thing I need right now is for Nico to come back and threaten my dick... again." Lucian and Ian try to mask their laughter with coughs but fail–miserably.

"Am I invited?"

Dom scrunches up his face in confusion. "Invited to what, little dove?"

"To your wedding? I thought it only polite that I be there since you did fuck me, then reject me, and oh, wait.... I am the fucking mother to your son!" Dom pushes back from the table to stand, and I do the same. Lucian and Ian follow suit. They don't intervene, but I know if Dom and I go too far they will jump in and stop it.

Dom glares at me and growls low in his throat.

"How the fuck do you know about *that*, Sophia?" So, Louis *is* telling the truth! I won't give up my source.

"It doesn't matter how I know, all that matters is that I know. When were you going to tell me?" Dom averts his gaze to his dad then Lucian. Lucian won't meet mine or Dom's gaze. What the hell is going on there?

"Sophia, I think–." I turn to Dom's dad, and the look on my face has him closing his mouth. I turn back to Dom and drop the mask I had in place. I let him see my hurt, confusion, and anger all over my face. He closes his eyes and sighs as he runs his hand through his hair.

"Soph, it's not what you–."

"Save it, Dominic. I don't want to hear more of your bull-shit; just be man enough to own your shit. You want to know something really fucking stupid though?" Dom lifts sad eyes to me. "These past few weeks I felt we were becoming a family. I felt like we could maybe make this work. How dumb am I, huh? You were right that day, you know. I should have known since the first time that I met you that you weren't end game material."

I hear Lucian and Ian gasp, and Dom drops his gaze. "Well, consider me educated now: you and I will never be. We share a child together, and that is it. I wish you and your new wife well, Dominic." I turn to Lucian and see so much sadness in his eyes.

"I will return to Farrarie tomorrow. If you need me, that is where I will be waiting for you. Mr. Silver, thank you for having me and opening your home to Lucian and myself. I am sorry for my outburst and ruining dinner."

I give Dom a wide berth as I maneuver past him to head up to my room, where I can break down alone, where no one will judge me for being so foolish as to think I could have my family. My chest aches. I was so stupid! Yet again, Dominic Silver breaks my heart. When will I learn?

CHAPTER 27

Dominic

What the fuck just happened?

I turn to my dad and Lucian, both of them slack-jawed and just as confused as I am. I have no fucking idea how she got that information. I need to fix this; so much has changed for me in the past two weeks. Lucian and I are forming a bond. I *thought* Soph and I were getting closer and starting to let the past go—clearly, I was wrong.

"What just happened?" I shake my head. I have no idea how to answer Lucian. Sophia jumped to conclusions, like usual, and doesn't let me fucking explain.

"You need to fix this, son, or all the work you have done these past weeks will be for nothing." Nodding my head, I quickly exit the dining room and head up the stairs to Soph's room. I don't bother knocking, I just barge in and freeze at the sight in front of me.

"I will give you three fucking seconds to let her go. If you harm her in any way, I will fucking kill you, your mother, and your sister."

"Don't make threats, mutt. We will never follow you. Until

you learn this, you will always lose!" I take a step forward and he pushes the dagger harder against Sophia's throat until a trickle of blood runs down her chest. I don't move a muscle. I hear footsteps behind me and know that my dad and Lucian must have heard. A second later I feel Lucian at my side, his hands are glowing a bright yellow.

"Let her go *now*. He may not follow through on his threat, but I will. I won't stop at your family. I'll take your friends and their children or anyone they hold dear. I will take the whole fucking pack if I have to." As psychotic as it sounds, I am so fucking proud of my son right now. Louis stands there with a tear-stricken Sophia, her back to his chest, dagger at her throat. Louis smirks, a look on his face promises pain and heartache. I look to Sophia, and I see it in her eyes. Louis was the one to feed her all the lies.

"You three will all pay with your life!"

"Louis, you are not strong enough to take us all on. Let Sophia go now, and I will make your end quick." I can hear the fear in Dad's voice, this situation is triggering for him, too.

"I may not be, but he is." With his words a portal opens near Louis and Sophia. Fuck no!

"If you take my mother through that portal, I will hunt you down and kill you slowly." I can hear the growl in Lucian's voice, and I see out of the corner of my eye white hair sprouting from his arms. Holy fuck, can he shift?

"Yeah, you and what army, kid?" A slow, devious smirk graces Lucian's face.

"My best friend is the strongest supernatural in the world, and my uncle is king of the fae. One of my dad's best friends is king of the vampires and the other is king of the shifters. I have friends and family in high places, *mutt*. We will come for her, and then we will come for you, mark my words." The mask on

Louis's face drops for a second, but that's all I need. I can see the fear and uncertainty in his eyes.

He starts to take steps toward the portal, dragging Soph with him. Before they reach the portal, I move forward and raise my hand to blast the bastard. Louis must see me coming because in a lightning-fast motion he moves the dagger from Sophia's throat and lodges it in her stomach before ripping it out and holding it against her throat once more. Lucian tries to run at them, but dad quickly wraps his arms around Lucian to stop him. Sophia's eyes find mine, and I'm stuck rooted to the spot. I see so much blood seeping through her yellow shirt. The look of pain and horror on her face snaps me out of it.

"Run, Louis, and don't stop. I lost her once, and I won't lose her again. You tell Randall fucking Cane I'm coming for my mate." I see the shock on Louis's face. *Yeah, you fucktard, I know you're working with Randall.* Louis enters the portal facing his back toward it so he can keep his eyes on us.

"I'm coming for you Sophia!" A sad smile graces her face.

"I love you both!" And then she disappears through the portal.

I drop to my knees.

"MOM!" I snap my gaze to Lucian. He's vibrating with rage, white hair breaking out over his arms and legs. Tears run down his face. "We have to go and get her, NOW!"

Dad snaps his eyes to me.

"Get up and be the father he needs Dominic!" Like I'm on autopilot and have no control of my body, I move to stand in front of Lucian. I gasp at the sight of his eyes shining a vibrant bright purple. His wolf is riding him hard and trying to break free. Has he ever shifted?

"He is not mine to control Dominic." I look over Lucian's shoulder to my dad, confused as fuck. "You need to be his alpha Dom, help him. He needs you to help him son."

I look back to Lucian and see the torment and struggle in his features, then I hear a bone snap and he screams. Fuck, he's shifting. I place my hands on either side of his cheeks and force his gaze to mine.

"Stop." But he doesn't; he keeps shaking and thrashing against my father's hold, and I hear more bones cracking. Lucian's screams fill the room.

"Dad, I don't know what to do!"

"Accept that you are an alpha Dominic. If he shifts too fast, he will fucking die, now save your son!" That snaps something inside me, and I feel my wolf rise up and I let him out a little, my vision shifting to my wolf's.

"Stop! We will hunt, and we will find our mate. I will bring your mother back to you Lucian. I swear on my life that I will bring her back. You will not lose her." I can hear the rasp in my own voice. I have never allowed my wolf to take over so much that he is able to speak through me. Sophia being taken again is causing my wolf to fight against my hold. Lucian's eyes go wide and then minutes tick by as his bones start to knit themselves back together.

Once he is under control and not fighting against my dad, I nod my head at dad to release him. Lucian falls forward and stumbles into my arms. I wrap my arms around him and stroke the back of his head. Tears fill my eyes. This is the first time I've held my son.

"I promise you; we will get her back. I won't stop, I won't rest, and this time I will make sure that scar-faced bastard dies." Lucian wraps his arms around me and nods into my shoulder.

"I can't lose her. I just got her back, and I won't let her go. We have to save her...Dad." I still, and my dad's eyes go as wide as a dinner plate. Lucian has never called Sophia or I by our titles. A feeling I can't explain enters my chest. *My kid just called me "dad."* A tear slides down my cheek, and I tighten my hold on my son.

I will make Randall pay, for what he did to my mate; I will make him suffer for what he did to my son. I will kill that fetid lump of flesh slowly. I pull away from Lucian and rest both my hands on his shoulders and look him in the eyes.

"What now?"

"Now son, we go to war."

CHAPTER 28
Dominic

When we step through the portal twenty minutes later, Jax, Aurora, and Kai are all standing in Jackson's office. Jax looks concerned, and Kai looks on edge, and Aurora looks scared.

"Okay, by the looks on your guys' faces, something has happened." Before I can answer, the office door swings open and an angry king of the fae barrels into the room with Ryan hot on his tail. Alex, Chase, and Mya trail in after them.

"Where the fuck is my sister, Dominic?" My gaze strays to Mya's; I can see by the look in her eyes she had a vision. That would explain why they're all here; I only had time to call Jax before Dad, Lucian, and I opened a portal to Jackson's compound. I didn't know Kai was here already. I was going to call the rest of them once we got here.

I must have taken too long to answer, because Nico makes his way over to me. I can feel the anger radiating off him when he stops a foot in front of me.

"Where is she?" he yells. Ryan is trying to pull him back by his arm, but he shakes her hold and grips the front of my shirt, pulling me to him, until we're nose to nose.

"Let him go!"

"Stay out of this boy!" Nico snaps back at Lucian, and the way he just spoke to my son shakes me out of my stupor. I grip his hands and pry them off me, pushing Nico back. He recovers and tries to come back at me, but Lucian quickly steps in front.

"Nico, stop!" Ryan shouts at her husband.

"You touch my dad like that again, uncle or not, and I will put you down Nico." Nico pauses and gasps ring out around the room. Given the situation, I shouldn't smile, but I do. I'm not sure if they're more in shock at him calling me "Dad" or him threatening Nico. Ryan releases Nico and shoves him out of the way to get to Lucian.

"Luce, can you tell us where Sophia is, please? Mya had a vision that something bad happened to her and said we should all meet you here." Lucian looks over his shoulder at me. I nod my head, and he turns back to Ryan.

"My mom was taken, and we need your help." Growls and shouts fill the room, and Nico side-steps Ryan and comes to stand in front of me. We stand there glaring at each other. He's my best friend, and I know him better than anyone. He blames me for his sister's disappearance.

"What. Did. You. Do?"

I growl low in my throat. "She may be your sister Nico, but she is my fucking MATE!" I yell.

"You're supposed to protect her! This is the second fucking time my sister has been put in danger because of you." I snap, reel my arm back, and clock my best friend square across the jaw. He stumbles back a few steps, rubbing the side of his jaw, and then he comes back to me. Before he can reach me, Lucian is in front of me again, glowing yellow and growling. Fuck, he needs to shift soon. White fur is breaking out again on his arms and legs. I look around the room and see looks of awe on everyone's faces.

"If you touch him again or accuse him of hurting my

mother, I will be the one you deal with." Kai cuts across the room and blocks Nico from Lucian's gaze, a look of wonder and awe on his face.

"She always knew you were special. Now I understand Tyler's nickname." I cock my head to the side, confused as fuck at Kai's words. "He called you *trifecta* because you are part warlock, fae, and shifter. You are the *trifecta,* Lucian." Well, now that Kai says it, it really does make sense. Lucian stops growling and pulls his power back.

"Sophia was taken by one of my pack members. We've been tailing him and found out he has been working with Randall Cane. We had planned to have a pack meeting tonight after dinner to arrest Louis and bring him before Jax and the council, but he ambushed Sophia in her room–."

Chase cut my dad off.

"Why didn't you stop him?"

I drop my head in shame. I did try.

"Dominic tried to stop Louis, but someone opened a portal for him to escape. When Dom tried to stop him, he—." Dad couldn't finish, so I did it for him.

"He had a dagger to her throat, and when I tried to stop him, he stabbed her in the stomach. There was so much blood...I...I froze." I hear a thump and lift my gaze to see Nico had dropped to his knees, his head clasped between his hands.

"Is...is...she...is my sister alive?" Nico's tear-filled gaze lifts to mine, and I can't lie to him.

"I don't know Nico, there was so much blood. We never consummated the mate bond, and I haven't claimed her, so I can't feel her." I growl out, pissed at myself for not claiming her when I had the chance.

"We have to locate her now! If she is injured, she'll need our help. Aurora, have you seen anything?"

"No, Jax, I haven't. I'm sorry Dom, I have been so focused

on trying to see Lucian's future that I've kind of blocked myself off to other visions." Fuck, I was hoping Aurora would be able to help.

"We can try a locator spell. I can use Nico's blood to help the search, that way it will only link to familiar lines." We all nod our heads and do as Mya asks. Nico doesn't hesitate to slice his palm and offer his blood.

Nothing happens.

We try so many times that I lose hope.

"Wait, what if I do it? I am her son. Wouldn't I be a better link than Nico? No offense, but you're only her half-brother." Nico looks like he wants to argue but in the end, he knows what Lucian says is true. Lucian is our best shot. I stand and leave Lucian, Mya, Alex, Chase, Aurora and Ryan to it while Dad, Kai, Jax, Nico, and I walk to the other side of the office.

"I need to say this, and I want you four boys to hear me." We all nod our heads. "Okay, this is going to be hard to hear, but if we find her and she isn't okay, we have to get Ryan to subdue Lucian. He will lose control, and if he shifts, he will go nuts and none of us will be able to bring him back." I know Dad is right; Lucian is an anomaly. On top of that, he's a shifter without an alpha, and he is fucking powerful.

"I will let Ryan know sir." I appreciate Nico's cooperation. Nico turns to me next and says, "*When* we get my sister back, you have to decide. You either claim her as your mate or you let her go. Do you understand?" I growl; I fucking hate being told what to do.

"Dom?" I pull my gaze from Nico to look at Jackson. "I'm going to do a full pack recall and investigation into the New York pack. Your dad has granted me access. I don't know the full story, but I know enough. I can't let you out of your vow, but I can remove pack members."

I get what Jackson means; he is willing to get rid of anyone in the pack who I thought had anything to do with my mom's death. I turn to my dad and see the truth in his eyes. He has told Jax some of the story about my mom. I can't think about all that right now, I have to keep my head in the game.

"Thank you Jax, I'll deal with all of that later." I turn to Nico next. "One, stay the fuck out of my relationship with your sister. Two, I claimed your sister a long fucking time ago, I just need to do it properly now. I'm pretty sure I have a lot of fucking groveling to do, though." The five of us chuckle.

Two hours later, Lucian shouts out.

"I got it; I know where she is!" We all crowd around Lucian and the map with his blood on it.

I'm coming for you little dove.

CHAPTER 29

Sophia

I'm so cold.
I'm in so much pain.
I can't move.

I come to and blink my eyes open slowly, groaning in pain. I try to lift my hands but I can't. I turn my head to see my wrists are cuffed to the sides of the metal bed.

Where am I?

I close my eyes and try to recall what happened, and after a moment it hits me. I was ambushed in my room and then taken. The pain in my stomach registers. I was stabbed! What the fuck is going on? Dread pools inside me. Was Dom right? Did that Louis guy bring me to Randall? Tears gather in my eyes. I will not live like that again.

A sound disrupts me from my thoughts, and I turn my head to see a door opening. Light spills into the room from the open doorway. I can only make out a body shape, I can't see the person's face. A light turns on and I slam my eyes shut at the shock of the brightness. A moment later I open them, and the figure is clear now—it's a man.

"Who are you?" I rasp out, my throat sore. I need water. He narrows his muddy brown eyes at me.

"I'm here to do your final check before your rescue party gets here." What the fuck does that mean?

"W-what rescue and what checks?" He smiles down at me darkly but doesn't say anything. I have a sinking feeling that something bad has happened. The man lifts the blanket covering me and I notice then that I am in a hospital gown. What the fuck? He lifts the gown and I attempt to close my legs when I feel a whoosh of air hit my thighs. My ankles are cuffed as well. No God, please, no.

"Stop moving!" the man snaps.

"If you fucking touch me, I swear to God, I will fucking kill you!"

"Shut up, bitch, you're in no position to make threats." The blood in my veins turns to ice. I can't do it. I would rather die than have this happen again. I struggle against my restraints as the man climbs on the bed and kneels between my legs. I see a look of lust in his eyes. I trail my gaze down his body to see his hands are undoing his slacks. Tears stream down my face. *No, no, no, not again.*

The fucker shreds the gown from my body, and I whimper. I'm cuffed to this bed, naked and chained like a fucking dog. I try to access my magic to blast the fucker off me, but I can't. Something is seriously wrong; I can't even feel a flicker of my magic. He smiles evilly at me; my skin is crawling with disgust. He captures one of nipples between his teeth and bites down hard. I scream.

"No! Stop! Get off me!"

I don't question Lucian; as soon as he gives us the location, we open a portal to Brownsville, Pennsylvania. Lucian says there is an abandoned hospital there where Sophia is being held. Eleven of us exit the portal in Brownsville and we stand outside the massive abandoned building that was closed down thirty years ago. It's an ominous looking building. I strain my hearing and scent the air. I can only detect two heartbeats. Then I catch her scent. I bolt into the building and follow my nose. Her scent is all over this place. As I round the corner of the hallway, I pause. Her scent has changed from calm to panic and then fear.

"No! Stop! Get off me!" I hear her scream, and my blood boils and I take off. I hear the others behind me. I can tell I'm getting closer; her scent is getting thicker the closer I get.

"I will fucking kill you! You're a fucking dog!"

"Do it then you little bitch! Fucking do it!" I don't stop, I don't hesitate. I know she's behind the door at the end of the hall —light is spilling out from beneath it. I launch a yellow energy ball at the door, and it explodes. I run into the room and freeze. Sophia is cuffed to the bed, naked. Her gaze turns to me, and a sob breaks free, tears streaming down her beautiful face. There's a man on top of her with his pants undone, and his dick is hard. I see red, I don't fight it. I let the change wash over me and in two seconds I'm on four legs and running toward the guy. He tries to shimmy off the bed, but he's too fucking slow. I smell he isn't a magic user—he's a vampire.

I launch at him; we land on the floor. I don't fuck around—I go for the kill shot, clamping my jaws around his neck and shaking him like a doll. The metallic tang of blood fills my mouth and coats my tongue. I stop shaking and look down at him. I can see in his eyes that he knows he is going to die. I pull back and rip his fucking throat out.

Tossing his body aside, I quickly change back to my human form. Once again, my wolf doesn't fight me; his biggest concern right now isn't claiming our mate but making sure she is okay. When I turn to look at her, I see Nico covering her with a blanket, Alex and Chase casting a spell to release her of the cuffs. Lucian is at her head, stroking her hair. The others stand around looking shellshocked. Her small whimper spurs me into action. I move toward her and push my way past the others. Alex has just undone the last cuff. I scoop her into my arms, and she hisses in pain. She wraps her arms around my neck and breaks down on me then buries her face in my chest. Fuck!

"Portaly openinga compundy awa." Yellow magic swirls in front of me as I open a portal back to Jackson's compound, and I don't wait for the others as I enter.

I close the portal behind me. Nico will bring the others back. Right now, Sophia needs me. I make my way to the room I always use when I'm here. She's still sobbing in my arms as I kick the door open to my room and use my magic to shut and lock it. I walk straight past the bed and head to the bathroom. I place Sophia gently on the vanity bench and turn to start the shower. I keep my gaze on hers the whole time I'm pulling the blanket away from her; this isn't about sex this is me needing to wash the scent of someone else's arousal off my mate and making sure she is okay.

Once I see steam billowing out from the shower, I scoop her up and walk into the massive shower. I place her on her feet but keep my hands on her waist, not ready to let her go.

I feel her start to tremble in my arms.

"Dom, I...I need Kai." I reel back, shocked, my grip on her tiny waist tightens and she flinches. I look down then and see bruises and teeth marks on her perfect tits as well as stitches across her abdomen, bruises in the shape of handprints across the top of her thighs. I know what that means. I hang my head in shame; this is all my fault. A sob burst out of her. I wrap my arms around her and pull her to me. Tears leak from my eyes. My beautiful, strong mate.

"I will kill them all, Sophia." She doesn't answer, just sobs harder.

CHAPTER 31

After Dom washed and dried me, he dressed me in some of his sweats that I had to roll three times just to fit me, and he put me in one of his shirts that hangs down to my knees. After he dressed me, he scooped me up and laid me under the covers of his bed. He then gave me some painkillers and a glass of water. We haven't spoken; neither of us know what to say to the other. So instead, he jumps in beside me and just holds me gently. I don't know how much time passes, but a knock at the door pulls me from my thoughts. Dom doesn't move, just flicks his wrist and the door opens.

I rise to see Lucian standing in the doorway with the others behind him. There are so many emotions running across my son's face. I scoot back to sit up, and Dom helps me by placing some pillows behind my back. Once I'm sitting up, I pat the side of the bed and Lucian comes barreling over. He sits beside me, and we just stare at each other. Tears gather in not only his eyes but my eyes as well. I open my arms and he flops forward to grip me in a hug, his large body shaking in my hold.

"Mom." Hearing him utter that one word has me breaking

down as well, and we cling to each other, I thought I would never see my son again.

"Shhhh, it's okay. I'm right here."

"I...thought I...lost you." He hiccups each word, he buries his face in the crook of my neck. I see Kai making his way over to Dom, and he hands him something. Lucian and I pull away from each other and I smile at my beautiful boy. I drop my hands into my lap, Dom leans across and grasps one of my hands in his, Lucian does the same with the other. I smile at both of my boys. Dom and I still have a lot to work out, but I can tell in his eyes he's ready to try and make this work. First though, I have to find out if this marriage thing is for real.

"You know, they really do make a good-looking family." We all chuckle at Alex.

"That's got to suck *Tink*, that your best bro is banging your sister behind your back." Everyone turns to glare at Chase. I'm waiting for my brother to slap him or blast him or something.

"You know what *Brina*, it sucks just as much as me banging your cousin in your house each night. Or how about when we watched that movie? Ryan sure as fuck wasn't screaming because she was scared, she screamed because I made her come all over my fucking hand while you were sitting right next to her!" I look at Ryan and see she has turned beet red, her mouth opens in shock. Chase looks from Nico to Ryan and then pales.

"Oh my God, I think I'm going to be sick!" Chase races from the room with a chuckling Alex behind him. Mya and Aurora both offer kind words before they leave. Now it's just Nico, Jax, Kai, Mr. Silver, Ryan, Lucian, Dom, and I. It's quiet for a moment and then Ryan breaks away from the guys and crawls from the bottom of the bed up to the top, knocks Dom's hand away and pushes him over so she can slide in for a hug. I return her embrace.

"We'll find them Soph; we'll make each and every one of

those fuckers pay for what they did to you." She tightens her hold around my waist, and I flinch. Dom catches my gaze over the top of Ryan's head. He pats her gently on her shoulder to get her attention.

"Ease up love, Soph is…injured." Ryan pulls back and stares at me with concern in her eyes.

"Where, what happened? Jackson, get the doctor!"

"NO!" I shout, and all eyes turn to me, confused.

"So-So, if you're hurt, let Doc take a look at you." Nico pleads. I turn to Dom and implore him with a look not to let the doctor come. I don't want the others to know. He reaches over and puts a vial of blood in my hand.

I stare at it, then turn to Kai. "Thank you." I pop the top and drink Kai's blood. It may not dull the pain, but it will heal my surface injuries. I down the blood then pass the empty vial back to Dom. I feel a pinch where the stitches are, and I know I'm healing already. It won't erase the bruises that mar my skin, but it will help them to fade quicker.

I can feel everyone's eyes on me, and I see Dom turn and throw his legs over the side of the bed. He hunches over with his hand covering his face. The silence is deafening. I'm not in the mood for twenty questions, so I do the only thing I can think of and make small talk. I lift my gaze to my son's and smile softly. He tries to mimic me, but it doesn't reach his beautiful eyes.

"That was an epic speech you gave back there." He releases a loud exhale, and this time the smile does reach his eyes.

"What speech?" My brother asks.

"He threatened Louis and told him his uncles were kings, and his best friend is the most powerful supernatural in the world." I see shock and pride war on the three guys faces, and Ryan hums her approval. My gaze lands on a stoic Mr. Silver. He won't meet my gaze.

"Are you okay Ian?" He lifts sad green eyes to mine, and there is so much guilt shining in the depths of his eyes.

"No, Sophia, I am not." I look around the room to see everyone looking just as shocked as I am—even Dom is staring at his dad.

"I am so, so sorry my dear–."

"Dad, it wasn't your fault." He snaps angry eyes to Dom, but he isn't angry at him. He's angry at himself.

"If I had of listened to you years ago Dominic, your mother would still be here. Your mate wouldn't have the scent of other males on her." I recoil at his words, and Nico's gaze darts to me as he narrows his eyes. I avert my gaze to my lap.

"What the fuck does that mean Sophia?" I don't have it in me to answer him; I'm too ashamed. "Answer me!"

"Don't fucking talk to her like that!" Dom roars, and I lift my gaze to see Dom is now on his feet and he and my brother are having a stare off. I don't want them to fight. I turn to Ryan, begging her with my eyes to calm my brother down, and she nods and jumps off the bed, making her way over to my brother. He deflates the moment she wraps her arms around him and hugs him.

"So-So?" I turn and look at Kai, and I see the question in his eyes. I can see how tense he is; his fists are clenched at his side. I shake my head, and Kai lets out a whoosh of air. Dom looks between us.

"What the hell are you two not telling us?" I can hear the mistrust in Dom's voice; he hates not knowing the full story. I look around the room and see the worry on all my friends faces. I turn to Lucian, and the look on his face is my undoing. A sob breaks out of me. Lucian leans forward and wraps his arms around me, and a moment later I feel the bed dip and another set of arms wrap around both Lucian and I. I don't need to look to know its Dom. I don't want this moment to end; this is the first time we have ever held each other like this, like a family.

"Sophia, I need to know what happened. My mind is conjuring up so many different things right now, and I know this bastard knows more than he's saying as well." I pull back from Dom and Luce and smile at both of them. Dom scoots over and then pulls me onto his lap, resting his back against the headboard. Lucian moves over to us as well and sits in front of me, clasping one of my hands in his.

"Soph?" I lift my gaze to my brother's and sigh. Dom starts to rub his hands up and down my arms, offering me his silent support.

"Can you stop fucking doing that!"

"Doing what? Touching my mate?" To drive his point home, Dom leans forward and starts to kiss my neck, and it takes everything inside me not to moan and tip my head to the side to give him better access. Nico steps forward but stops when Jax places his hand on his chest.

"Dude, seriously?"

"Fuck off, Jackson she's, my sister."

"And she's his baby momma and mate, so he trumps you, big guy." All eyes turn to Ryan, and she shrugs her shoulders. "What? It's true, Nico just has to learn how to master his control freak issues and realize Sophia isn't a little kid anymore. She is a mother and a mate; she can hold her own." I smile at my sister-in-law and mouth a silent *thank you.* Nico glares down at his wife, and she smiles up at him and blows him a kiss.

I turn to Mr. Silver to see a small smile on his face; he's smiling at Dom.

"Ian?" He turns his eyes to me and shame colors his features. "None of this is your fault. I knew Randall would come back for me. I just didn't realize he knew where I was. I assumed he'd think I was here or in my realm. Please don't blame yourself." Ian doesn't reply, just nods his head. It's going to take a lot of convincing before he actually believes me.

"You saw it, didn't you?" I look to Kai and nod. "How long?"

"Three days."

"What the fuck are you two on about again? Fill the fucking rest of us in. I hate to fucking admit it, but I'm starting to realize why Nico wants to constantly punch you in the face Melakai!" Nico breaks out into laughter at Dom's outburst, clutching his stomach and pointing at Dom.

"Now...you...know." I hear Dom growl behind me, and Ryan is glaring daggers at my brother.

"Know what, asshole?"

"What jealousy feels like. It fucking burns, doesn't it?" Dom wraps his arms around my waist and pulls me closer into his chest then buries his face in the crook of my neck.

"Fuck you, Nicky boy. Soph, your brother's being mean to me." Everyone is in hysterical fits at Dom's comment, even Lucian is wiping tears from his eyes.

"Whose fucking side are you on kid? The dickhead king of the fae or your cool as fuck DILF of dads side?" Lucian recoils and scrunches his face in disgust. I feel Dom tense beneath me.

"One, eww. Two, you are so not a fucking DILF, my man."

Dom growls.

"Soph, tell that little shit of a kid we share DNA with that I am a DILF." I clamp my lips shut to keep from laughing at Dom's childishness.

"What in God's good name is a DILF?" Ian asks.

"Dad I'd Like to Fuck!"

"Dominic–."

"Language!" everyone says in unison, with laughter that follows.

CHAPTER 32

Dominic

"That is the most stupidest idea I have ever heard, love."

"Don't be a party pooper Dom."

"Why the hell do you all want to sleep in my room?" Ryan turns her gaze to Sophia and then back to me as she raises a brow.

"It's for one night," Jax whines.

"Don't you have a mate to bang, and don't you have a husband to blow?" I hear a growl and then a slap on the back of my head. I whirl around to see Nico glaring at me. Nico fucking hit me, the asshole! I'm about to wipe that smirk off his face in three seconds.

"Plus, I kind of have a mate that needs an oral exam, if you feel me." Nico pales and stumbles back, and I hear Sophia groan behind me.

"You're a real fucking dick, you know that? Stay away from my sister and keep your fucking pin dick in your pants."

"Dude, you do realize the only reason you're an uncle is because he didn't keep his dick in his pants, right?"

"I am aware, fuck you very much Jackson! Now if you'll

excuse me, I have to go and bleach my fucking eyes and ears now, to rid myself of that mental picture!"

"You're one to talk," Sophia scoffs. "You fucking defiled our kitchen, library, throne room, and my fucking childhood tree hut! Your naked ass is burned into my mind's eye. I've seen Ryan's tits more than I've seen my own lately." I choke on air and everyone laughs. Ryan is the color of a tomato and glaring at her husband. Nico, on the other hand, puffs out his chest and holds his head high.

"What can I say, I have needs." Ryan sighs and shakes her head. She knew what she was getting into when she married the bastard.

Dad leaves the room after bidding Soph a good night. Nico, Ryan, Kai, Jax, and Lucian hang behind. I'm in no rush to get rid of my son, but I am keen for the others to fuck off.

Soph, Ryan and Luce sprawl out over the bed, the guys and I sit on the couches as we stare at the three of them on the bed. A smile graces my lips; my whole world is right here in this room.

"What are we gonna do now?" Jax asks.

"Sophia and Lucian will not be returning to New York. They will go back to Farrarie and stay there until I have dealt with the pack, and then we take Randall out."

"What. The. Fuck." All four of us turn to Lucian. If he was Superman, I would be burnt to a crisp right now from his laser vision.

"Luce, he's only trying to–."

"I don't give a shit Smurf, I'm not being left out of this, and you can't make me. I'm old enough to make my own choices!" I smirk.

"Technically you're still seventeen, so what I say goes." The little asshole smirks right back at me, and I can tell from the look on his face that he has a comeback.

"Produce a birth certificate that has your name on it." My mouth drops open. That little...

"He's right, we will not hide, and be real Dominic. If Ryan is fighting, she needs him with her." Lucian full-on fucking smiles at me, and places a quick kiss to Soph's cheek. I glare at the little bastard.

"You know you may have won the race of your life to get from my sack to her egg, but I will still beat your ass boy!" I jerk forward and rub the back of my head. "The fuck did you hit me for, you wanker!"

"That's my fucking sister you're talking about, and I don't want to hear her name and your fucking scrotum talked about in the same sentence again." Lucian and the others chuckle I turn to Sophia and pout. She rolls her eyes and smiles, patting the space next to her on the bed. I stand and wink down at Nico, as I make my way over to Soph and cuddle up beside her, just to rub it in Nico's face more, I say, "Ry, why don't you come lie on my other side love. Soph doesn't mind." Ryan doesn't even get a chance to answer before Nico stands, snatches her off the bed, flings her over his shoulder caveman-style and stomps out of the room. mumbling under his breath about me being an asshole, and how he's going to kill me one day.

"You know you're gonna push him to far one day." I just grin at Jax.

"Out of all the people in the world, the one person who pushes his buttons like no other, ends up being his sister's *hugacko*. That is Karma at its finest." We all laugh; Kai isn't wrong. I to wind Nico up; it gives me so much joy to piss him off.

Sophia yawns and stretches but then flinches, and Kai moves toward the bed.

"Do you need more?" he asks Soph.

"No, I'm okay, it's just tender."

"Did you see him?" Kai asks.

"No, when I came to, I was alone in that room. The only person I saw was..." Sophia doesn't finish; we get what she means.

"If he took you, why not ward your location? He is up to something, and he will come for you again, Soph."

"I know, he's already planning it." I reel back in shock.

"How do you know?"

"I can see people's love lives, remember? I can see Randall's. He thinks he's in love with me." I feel her shudder at the thought, though I hope we can use this to our advantage.

"Are you sure?"

"Yes, Dom, I'm sure."

"Good, now we make a plan to use his love for you against him and make sure he can never harm another person again."

CHAPTER 33

Sophia

Lucian and the guys left after we discussed a plan. I'm wiped out and tired as fuck. I know Dom and Lucian haven't slept since the day before. I brush my teeth and relieve myself, then make my way back to bed, where a shirtless stud is lying under the covers. I stand there and stare at the most beautiful man I've ever seen. Dom's whole body is solid muscle. His body is a work of art; there's not an ounce of fat on him. His beautiful silver blond hair is a tousled mess. He has one of his arms resting behind his head, and his eyes are closed. The eye-fucking details when his eyes pop open. I make my over to the bed and hear him swallow loudly as I slip under the covers.

I pause before scooting down the bed and turn to him.

"Why are you looking at me like that?"

"You don't have any pants on." I feel my cheeks heat; I've never been able to sleep in underwear, but I didn't think he would notice, since his shirt covers my lady parts. Ryan said she'll drop me off some clothes in the morning, so I'll have to go commando tomorrow as well. I draw the line at borrowing a pair of my sister-in-law's panties.

"I-I can't sleep in them. If it bothers you, I can sleep on the couch?" When he doesn't answer, I sigh, and throw the covers back so I can slip off the bed. I don't make it an inch before his arm snakes around my waist and pulls me back against his chest. I squeal in surprise. Kai's blood has done the trick; I still feel a small amount of pain, but it isn't nearly as bad as before. I can feel he's only in briefs; the heat of his thighs are burning the back of mine. Dom keeps his arm around my waist as he nuzzles his nose against my neck. I still in his arms. After everything that happened to me today, how can I be turned on right now? I should be repulsed by the idea of sex, but instead I'm shivering with need. What the hell is wrong with me?

"I promise to behave, little dove. I just want to hold you, if that's okay?" I can't answer past the lump in my throat so I simply nod. We lie there for so long, our breathing is the only sounds in the room. I thought Dom fell asleep hours ago, I'm too scared to close my eyes incase the nightmares come. I don't want Dom to know how damaged I still am after everything with Randall.

"Wanna talk about it?" His question gives me a fright. I thought he was asleep.

"I'm scared." I admitted. I feel Dom tense behind me, and his arm around my waist tightens.

"Scared of what, love?"

I take a few deep breaths before answering. "Scared of what you will think of me when you know the truth."

Dom peppers kisses all over the side of my neck. "I will never look at you any differently Sophia. You are and always have been the apple of my eye. You had me wrapped around your little finger from the first day I met you."

"Then why didn't you tell me why you rejected me?" Dom groans behind me.

"You took off before I could even explain—just like yesterday. As soon as dad found out that you are my mate, he told me it was my choice. I cancelled the engagement with Sienna and told him I want you. I've *always* wanted you Soph. I was just so scared of you getting hurt because of me, and now look how well that turned out."

I roll over so we're facing each other, and thanks to the bedside lamp, I'm able to see Dom clearly. I have never seen Dom look so vulnerable—the uncertainty and grief is plastered all over his face. I reach up and stroke his cheek, his stubble scraping pleasantly against my palm. His eyes close and he nuzzles into my hand.

"I'm sorry." Dom's eyes pop open and he stares at me like I'm a fucking unicorn. I huff in frustration as Dom's eyes fill with humor and his beautiful full lips stretch into a wide smile. I playfully narrow my eyes at him.

"Babe, come on. You never say *sorry*. Even when you're wrong, your right." Now I grin. What can I say? He knows me well.

"At least now you're starting to get it." We both chuckle.

"Can you tell me what happened Soph, please?" I release a whoosh of air. I want to unburden myself by having someone else share this weight with me, but I'm scared shitless that Dom will think I'm disgusting. He grips my hip and squeezes.

"I'm not going anywhere Soph. I want you, and I want this to work. In order for us to move forward, we need to have no secrets between us." I swallow loudly, tears gathering in the back of my eyes.

"C-can you turn the light off, I-I won't be able to tell you while you're looking at me." He doesn't hesitate; he releases my hip and turns to flick the light off. I'm scared of the dark all the time now, but with Dom beside me, it's not so suffocating. Dom wraps his arm around me and pulls me in close, and I turn my head and rest my cheek against his naked chest. Dom rubs my back, and the motion is so soothing I start to relax.

She takes a deep breath then sighs before she starts to tell me her story. I know this story is going to destroy me, but I need to hear all the details.

"In order for you to understand, I need to start from the beginning, okay?"

"Okay."

"The day in the meadow, when you rejected me, I acted out and took off to the Earth realm. In the time I was there, I learned that I was pregnant with Lucian. I knew, no matter what whether you wanted me or not, you had a right to know you were going to be a father. What I didn't realize was that in the time I was there, Randall had spotted me and was following me. When I tried to return home to tell you the news, he captured me and took me prisoner.

"I was chained and starved for weeks. I had no idea where the hell I was. I was so scared, and I just wanted to go home." I try so hard to hold my growl inside me, but it slips out. Sophia doesn't pause or stop.

"After what felt like months, a man came down the stairs

and unchained me and then took me to Randall's mansion. My stupid ass thought I was going to be rescued. How fucking wrong was I? I was scrubbed and primped like a prize pony then dressed and dragged down to the dining room to join the *king* for dinner. Once I realized I wasn't getting rescued, food didn't seem appealing, but I knew I had to eat for the baby. I wasn't allowed to feed myself. I was only allowed to eat from Randall's sick fucking hand. I was locked in my room every day until Randall demanded my presence. After a few months I started to worry–."

"Why?"

"Because I was starting to show, and Randall had made it clear that I was his *treasure,* and only he was allowed to play with me." My grip on her waist tightens, my wolf warring inside me for control. He wants Randall's blood coating his tongue.

"One night at dinner he noticed that the dress I was made to wear was tight around my midriff and he questioned it. I knew I couldn't lie. My belly was only going to get bigger. When I told him I was pregnant, he went into a fit of rage and struck me." I bury my head in her chest and wrap my arms around her, and she begins to stroke my hair as she continues. "Anyway, he went off and banished me to my room for a few weeks. By that time Kai had learned I was being held at the mansion, and he was trying every day to get to me.

"One night I heard my door open and bolted out of bed, expecting it to be Randall but it wasn't. Kai was such a sight for sore eyes. I broke down and told him everything. He stayed with me that night, and it was the first time I had slept properly in months. Every night after that, Kai would come to me and stay, so I could rest. I asked why he was suddenly allowed to visit me, but he would never tell me. As the last trimester of my pregnancy was coming to an end, Kai and I tried to form a plan so I could escape. I knew Kai couldn't come with me because of his stupid fucking blood oath, but he promised to get me out."

"Why didn't Kai come to us?"

"Because he was made to enter another blood oath; he was allowed to continue to be with me each night if he bound himself to Randall. Kai did that, so he could make sure me, and the baby were okay. Part of the deal was that he could never speak about anything in regards to me and the baby, so he could never come to you."

"So you told Kai and Randall that the baby was mine?"

"No, not at the start." I tense. Why the fuck did she hide it?

"Why?"

"Because I was scared that my baby would be used as a tool against you and my brother. I told Kai the truth but not Randall."

"Why did he keep Lucian Soph?" She released a long breath before continuing.

"The day I went into labor was the day I was supposed to escape. Randall was out of town, and it was the only chance we had, but then Lucian decided it was okay to come two weeks early. Kai helped me through the birth and everything. No sooner had Lucian come out of me, Randall whisked him away. One of the staff had alerted Randall that I was in labor, and he came back straightaway. When he returned with the dead baby, I broke Dom. Something inside me shattered. I cursed him to hell and told him that when my baby's father found out what he had done, he would kill him." I smile into her chest; she isn't wrong. He will die for what he did.

"Then what happened?"

"He asked me why a one-night stand would care about their dead bastard kid. I told him that it wasn't a one-night stand like I had led him to believe. I told him the father to my baby is my *hugacko* and then told him you were the father. He saw red and tried to come after me. I won't lie. I wanted him to kill me, I thought I had just lost my son, and you had rejected me. I didn't want to live in a world where my son didn't exist. If it wasn't for Kai intervening, I honestly think Randall would have killed me."

"I will fucking kill him Soph, for what he did to you and for what he did to *our* son."

"I know you will."

"What happened after that?" She sighs loudly.

"Don't interrupt, just listen, or I'll chicken out." I nod against her chest and brace myself for what I'm sure is going to be a fucking horrid tale.

"I fell into a dark hole—refused to eat, shower, or change. Kai tried to help me; he thought burying the baby would help, but it didn't. Every time I closed my eyes all I could see was my son's lifeless body. It was like my mind checked out, but my body remained. Randall called on me daily; servants were sent to bathe and dress me then I would be fed dinner by Randall, then banished back to my room. That went on for months, but Randall grew tired of my ungratefulness. He said if I wouldn't snap out of it, he would beat it out. He made Kai watch as he beat me the next night. That happened every second day for three months. Even through all the pain, I still couldn't find the will to live. I lost my son and I thought I lost you. I was a shell, Dom, you have to understand that. Please understand I was broken; I had no fight left." I feel her tears hit the top of my head.

"I've got you little dove, I will never let him take you."

"You don't understand; what happened today is just another one of his games. He just wanted me to know that he could get to me whenever he sees fit. He had me stitched instead of giving me vampire blood, so I would know that he is the one in control. Randall will come for me again Dom. He really thinks he is in love with me, and he won't stop until I'm by his side." I growl, and I can feel the hairs on my arms lengthening. My wolf is pissed at the thought of someone taking his mate from him.

CHAPTER 35
Sophia

I suck in a breath. I have to tell him the truth now or I never will.

"Randall found out that Kai was sneaking small amounts of his blood to heal the worst of my injuries. One night he followed Kai into my room and caught us. He had his men hold Kai down and they all beat the shit out of him while I watched. I couldn't do anything to help him. I screamed for them to stop but they didn't listen. That was the night it all changed. Randall had Kai strapped to a seat in my room, and when Kai finally came to, Randall told him that because of his disobedience, I would pay the price. He made Kai watch as he…."

I took three deep breaths. Dom is stiff as a surfboard in my arms. He knows what's coming but doesn't say anything. He wants me to say it.

"Randall made Kai watch as he raped me. This went on for years. Every time Kai would try to help, Randall would have him strapped to a chair while he defiled my body. After four years of trying to help me escape, I begged Kai to stop. I begged him to stay away from me. I knew I was wrong to push him away, but every time he stepped out of line, I paid the price.

That is why Kai would never risk coming to you. When he finally found Ryan, things changed. He spent more time focusing on her which caused him to stop trying to save me. I was fucking grateful."

"Soph—."

"Shhh, I'm nearly done, I swear. One of the last times Randall came to my room, he told me that he and I would be married the next month. I swear to God, I nearly threw up all over him. I was lucky as fuck, though—Kai set me free before that could happen. I wanted to take Kai with me, but I couldn't carry him Dom, I want you to understand, that Kai saved me in so many ways. He never gave up trying to free me, so please don't be mad at him."

"Can I turn the light on?" Shocked at his random question, I nod, and he moves to turn the light on and he sits up, so he's resting against the headboard. Before I can comprehend what's happening, he grips me by my hips and lifts me so I'm straddling his thighs. We stay in that position for a few minutes just staring at each other. I could get lost in his beautiful violet eyes. He cups my cheeks, pulling my face down so our foreheads rest against one another.

"I just have one more question Soph." I nod. "The day Ryan came back, how did you know Lucian was the baby you thought you lost?" I smile and pull back, his hands drop to my hips.

"He looks exactly like you, but not only that. I can't see my own love life, I never have been able to, but that day, I had a quick flash of a vision, and I saw Lucian as a baby after I gave birth to him. When I looked into his eyes, it was like the broken part of me mended, and I was whole again. That's when I knew he was my baby, he was our son." A sad smile graces Dom's face, I know he is hurting. "I'm so sorry for not telling you sooner. I know I should have told you that day, but I was in shock. I thought a part of me just wanted to make that vision real. Then when I asked him how old he was, I knew. Lucian's birthday is the seventh of August, he is seventeen now." Dom's eyes soften, he cups my cheeks again and rests my forehead against his.

"You Sophia Stone are the strongest woman I know. You protected our son with your life, and even when I didn't deserve it, you still protected me by not giving me up as the father. I don't deserve it Soph, but I am asking you to give me another chance. I'm gonna fuck up, that's inevitable, but I'll always try to be better." I open my eyes in shock, so much longing shone in Dom's eyes.

"After everything I just told you, you still want me?" He doesn't have to use words; instead, he smashes his lips against mine. I gasp in shock, and Dom uses that to his advantage and slips his tongue inside my mouth. I moan at the feeling. God, he tastes so good. I began to explore his mouth and let my hands roam all over his naked chest and down his arms. Dom's hands grip my hips and pull me forward, so I'm sitting on top...Oh, fuck me, I'm sitting on top of his cock. I can feel the heat of it through his boxers, and a gush of wetness begins to gather between my thighs. What an amateur! All he has done is kiss me, and now I'm wetter than fucking Niagara Falls.

As if my body has a mind of its own, I begin to rock my hips back and forth across his hard bulge. A hiss escapes Dom, and I smile triumphantly. I capture his lips again and wrap my arms around his neck. Dom runs his hands under my shirt and pauses on the scar across my abdomen. He pulls back and looks up at me with lustful eyes.

"We should stop, you must be sore." I can hear the strain in his voice.

"Kai's blood has done the job. I want you to replace all of the bad memories with good ones. I want this Dom. I want you."

That is all he needed to hear. Dom rolls us, so I am now on

my back. He gathers my shirt in his hands and then tears the fucking thing from my body and chucks it to the side.

"Clothes are overrated anyway," Dom murmurs, and I laugh softly. He can always ease tensions with his wit. I won't lie; I am fucking nervous, but I want Dom to take away the bad memories and replace them with loving and beautiful ones.

He stares down at my naked body in awe, and I start to feel self-conscious about the bruises on my breasts and thighs. I wrap my arms over my chest and try to close my legs but I can't because he's kneeling between them.

"Don't hide from me, Soph."

"Then stop looking at me like that!"

"Like what?"

"Like I'm some strange being." Dom smiles and shakes his head.

"I'm looking at you because I hate the fact, I never got to see your belly grow. I never got to feel my son kick or talk to him. I'm looking at you because you are fucking extraordinary Sophia. You have given me the greatest gift of all, a child. I will never be able to gift you anything of that magnitude." I feel a tear leak from my eye as I reach up and cup his cheek.

"Just give me all of you and then we're even." His eyes open wide, and a devilish grin breaks out across his face. He leans down and captures my lips in a kiss that has me seeing stars. Kissing Dom is like floating on a cloud. He has always been the forbidden fruit that could never be obtained. But here and now, in this moment, he is mine to claim, and I am his. My heart has always belonged to Dominic Silver. Fate cemented my love for him when I knew he was my *hugacko*.

I run my fingernails up and down his back, Dom moans at the feeling of me clawing him. I'm not a wolf, so I can't bite him or claim him, but I can claw the shit out of him with my nails and mark him that way. Dom tears his lips from mine and begins to kiss his way down my neck, and slowly lick around the bruises that mark my breasts. He's replacing the feeling of another man's unwanted touch with his welcomed one. Once he's satisfied that he has thoroughly kissed the bruises and teeth marks, he sucks my nipple into his mouth and flicks the nub with his tongue. I cry out with sheer joy; this feeling he's eliciting from just licking and sucking my nipples is amazing. I have only ever had two good experiences with sex, and they were both with Dom. I want him to take me back to those good places and remind me of the pleasure I found in his arms.

Dom releases my nipple with a pop and then pays my other breast the same amount of attention, and it isn't long before I'm a withering mess beneath him, bucking my hips off the bed. Longing for some friction against my clit; he made me feel so good but then my clit was starting to throb from the tension. I needed him to touch me or fuck me right now!

She keeps thrusting her hips up at me. I know she wants me to focus on her pussy instead of her tits. I drag the moment out and finally release her nipple with a pop as she growls low. I smirk down at her and see frustration and lust in her gaze. Her eyes are glassy and her cheeks rosy, and she is so fucking turned on I can smell it. I can also feel the wet patch on the front of my boxers from when she was straddling my lap. The scent of her arousal is sending my wolf into a tailspin. I kiss between her beautiful perky tits and caress my way down to her pussy, peppering kisses over the bruises that mark her thighs. It takes everything to suppress my growl of rage. I hate that she has been hurt, I quickly push the dark thoughts out of my head, because right now Soph needs me to make sex an enjoyable thing for her and not something she should fear.

I settle myself between her thighs and stare down at her glistening pussy. I breathe in through my nose and release a satisfied hum, but her whimper snaps me from my ogling. I part her pussy with my fingers to expose her clit, and I can see so much wetness pooling between her folds. Leaning down, I flick my tongue across her clit, and she cries out.

"Dom, please." That's the only encouragement I need. I dive in and lap at her clit before I lick down to her opening and groan. Her wetness coats my tongue, and I growl in approval. My wolf is like a fucking cat, purring in the back of my mind. I return my attention to her clit and start feasting on her again. Just as I'm about to insert my finger inside her she stops me in my tracks.

"Stop."

I jump back so fast I stumble off the bed, and she giggles at me. She fucking *giggles*.

"What the fuck Soph?" She shimmies her naked ass all the way to the end of the bed and then drops to her knees. My eyes widen. Oh, fuck. This image right here, of her on her knees in front of me is going to be stored in my spank bank, not even gonna lie.

"Let's get one thing clear." I nod my head like an idiot. "I will never get on my knees when you demand it. It has to be my choice." I nod again like a bobblehead on a dashboard, too afraid she will stop. She reaches up and pulls my boxers down my legs and gasps. Her shocked eyes snap up to mine, and I grin.

"Let's hope our son takes after his dad, aye?" Sophia shudders and shakes her head.

"Don't ever, I mean *ever* mention our son's anatomy again, when I'm about to suck your cock, okay?" I shake my head and shudder. Yeah, that was fucked up to even think right now especially when his moth–.

"Fuuuuuuuucccccckkkkk." My thought is cut off the moment she wraps those fucking gorgeous lips around my cock.

Thank you, fate, for choosing this amazing creature as my mate!

Soph is sucking my cock like a fucking lollipop. She can't fit me all the way in, but that doesn't stop her from trying. Sucking sounds fill the room and fuck does it turn me on. She wraps her dainty hand around the base of my cock and pumps it while she sucks the head. I fist her hair in my hand and begin to fuck her face, and the sound of her gagging has my balls tightening. No way! I am not fucking coming in her mouth right now. I grip her head and pull back till she pops my dick out of her mouth. The sight of her on her knees, licking her lips and staring at my cock like she wants more, has me groaning.

"Get up and lay on the bed Soph." She looks up at me in shock.

"W-why?"

"Because I plan on coming inside you first. Then you can suck my cock later and I'll come down your throat and make sure you swallow every fucking last drop of my cum." She shivers at my words, but I can see by the way her pupils are blown wide that she isn't scared— she's horny as fuck. She jumps to her feet and lies on the bed, and I pull her legs to the end of the bed so half her ass is hanging over. I line my cock up with her entrance and meet her gaze.

"Are you sure babe?"

"Yes. Now please, for the love of Christ, ju–." I don't let her finish. I slam inside her, and we both cry out at the feeling. Fuck, her cunt is so tight it's gripping my cock like a glove. I don't move, letting her have a minute to get used to my size. When she nods her head and licks her bottom lip, I take that as my cue and begin to fuck her.

"Dom, oh my God." I'm gripping her hips and banging her in a steady rhythm, both of us gasping and moaning. After a minute or two, I feel her walls start to clench and I pick up the pace. She's about to come. I rub her clit with my thumb, hand splayed across her belly, and seconds later she is screaming my name. Feeling her pussy quiver around my dick has my wolf surging forward, and I know my eyes have changed when I see Sophia's gaze widen.

She doesn't say anything or shy away, instead, stunning me nearly still when she moans out, "Mark me when you come." *Holy fucking shifter babies.* I can't gain full control back; my wolf won't let me. I feel Soph start to tighten around me again and I know I'm two seconds from blowing inside of her. I lean down and suck her nipple into my mouth, and when she tilts her head to the side to offer me her neck, I don't hesitate, not this time. As my teeth lengthen, I tilt my head up and close my mouth between her neck and shoulder and bite. She screams out, not in pain but pleasure, and I come inside her with a growl more wolf than man.

CHAPTER 37
Sophia

The moment his teeth pierces my skin, stars explode in my vision, and I climax like I have never orgasmed before. As we both float down from our high, Dom's teeth are still embedded in my skin, and his cock is still inside me. The only sounds in the room are our heavy breathing. I forgot sex could be like this. That was fucking amazing! I hiss when Dom pulls his teeth out, and he laps at the mark with his tongue. He leans up on his elbows and growls his approval. When his gaze turns to me, a look of trepidation fills his gaze.

"What's wrong?" I ask.

"Soph, I just marked you."

"I know Dom, I told you to."

"You know what this means, right?" I smile up at him and bite my bottom lip. "I'm serious Soph."

"I know, I can feel how serious you are inside me." He groans and finally pulls his cock out. I sit up and lean back on my elbows. I can feel his gaze on me, but my eyes are stuck on his huge, wet cock. It fills me with pride to know that his dick is slick with my come. I wish he could go without washing my scent off, so all the bitches around would know that he is mine. Dom reaches over and uses his hand to lift my chin so my gaze will meet his.

"What's wrong little dove?"

"I want you to tattoo my name across your face or something." Dom chokes on air then starts spluttering.

"Excuse me?" he wheezes out, I grin up at him.

"Well, it's only fair, I have a mark on me, which means your scent will cover me at all times and let other male shifters know I'm mated. I think you should have a mark as well."

Dom starts to rub the back of his neck and is looking anywhere but at me; right, it's time for negotiations then. I drop to my knees and grip his still semi-hard cock in my hand. Dom hisses and glares down at me.

"I know what you're trying to do, you bloody vixen, and it–" I suck the head of his cock into my mouth and moan, the taste of him and me coating my tongue. It's such a heady and intoxicating flavor. I don't give him time to think. I grip the base of his cock and pump it while I suck and lick the tip of his cock. A moment later I taste his pre-cum and moan. I look up at Dom and find his gaze is glued to me, transfixed on the sight of his cock going in and out of my mouth. I may be on my knees, but I have never felt more powerful. This strong alpha male is at my mercy. Dom starts thrusting his hips and fisting my hair in his hand, holding my head still while he slams his cock in and out of my mouth. I have a shit gag reflex, and spit is dripping down my naked chest and I'm choking on his cock, but by the look in his eyes, he fucking loves the mess he is making of my face.

"Fucking hell Soph, that feels so good baby. You like that? You like sucking my cock?" I can't answer, so all I do is moan and attempt to nod my head. Then it hits me—I'm supposed to be using this as leverage! I smack his hand away that is tangled in my hair. He doesn't protest, but he does look wary. I keep up the pace to put him at ease, and a moment later his eyes start to roll back.

"Fuck, Soph, I'm so close." I release his cock with a pop and jump to my feet. He stands there in shock, mouth hanging open and dick hard as rock. I smile at him and pat his chest as I start to walk past. I'm almost out of reach when he grips my wrist and pulls me back. I shriek in surprise as I'm thrown down onto the bed. Dom wastes no time in crawling up my body and positioning himself between my legs. I smile sweetly up at him as he glares down at me.

"What the actual fuck was that Soph?" I run my fingers down his naked chest and lick my lips, which pulls a groan from Dom.

"See, the thing is I'm a jealous girl. You marked me, and I want my mark on you. Until you give me what I want, your cock will never get to explode inside my mouth." His shocked look turns to devious.

Oh no.

"So, your mouth is out of the question?" I swallow loudly and nod, the look in his eyes telling me I have just woken the beast. I have no time to prepare before he is slamming his hard cock inside me. I scream out as he continues to pound inside me.

"What about your pussy?"

"Fuck Dom, don't stop." The fucker stops moving, and I growl.

"It's not nice, is it?" I bare my teeth at him and snarl. Fucking bastard is using my own tactic against me. Then an idea hits me, and it's my turn to smile.

"If you don't make me come right now, I won't fuck you again till you get my name tattooed." Dom gasps and narrows his eyes, and I smirk triumphantly.

"Soph, that is fucking low! How dare you withhold the cookie from the cookie monster." I burst out laughing at his childishness, but my laughter dies in my throat when he begins to move inside me. Within minutes we both find our release. I have never felt so sated and loved. Lying here wrapped in Dom's arms feels like I may actually get my happily ever after.

Waking next to Sophia has to be one of the best moments of my life. Years ago, when I rejected her and she went missing, I thought I would never have this moment. I want to pinch myself just to make sure I'm not dream walking like Kai and Nico, but her soft snores confirm this is real. My dream Soph most certainly did not snore; I chuckle to myself.

She rolls over and smiles at me, and the relaxed look on her face and her just-fucked hair from last night has my cock stirring awake. After everything she has been through, she still allows me to be the one to give her pleasure and allowed me inside her. I'm not dense enough to think last night was easy for her, but I vowed to myself that I will always make her feel safe and wanted. She will never be shouted at or made to feel scared. I will spend the rest of my life loving my mate. I tilt my head to get a better view of her mark and smile proudly. Right there between her neck and shoulder is *my* mate mark. I have claimed Sophia Stone last night; she is my *ever after*.

"Why do you look like a proud peacock?"

I snort. "Don't ever put the word *pea* near *cock* again. As you know, my cock is definitely larger than a pea." It's her turn to snort and roll her eyes at my early morning antics.

"You're such a dick, you know that?" I roll until I'm resting on top of her, and she melts into the sheets. Her eyes hold so much love, and I have no fucking idea how I could have resisted the mate bond for so long.

"You're so beautiful." Her eyes widen at my admission. Why is she so shocked? She has to know how beautiful she is. "By the look on your face I assume you don't believe me?"

"It's not that, I just never expected something so sweet and tender to come from you."

"Well, don't go telling anyone now; I'll lose my street cred." We both break out into fits of laughter. Our laughter stops abruptly when my room door slams against the wall. I roll off Soph and quickly join her under the covers, I don't want anyone to see my ass or morning wood.

"Hah! How do you like it, fucker? Not cool when someone doesn't knock and walks right in when you're trying to get some, is it?" I smile wickedly. I'm about to watch Nico crash and burn.

"You do realize the person I'm trying to *get some* from is your sister, right?" Nico pales and snaps his gaze to my left to see his sister clutching the comforter in front of her. She turns and glares at me. "Babe, you do realize he can smell me all over you, right?"

Nico crosses his arms over his chest and stomps over to the window. "Fuck you, Dominic. You...you...asshole!" I laugh so hard I have tears coming down my face. Ryan follows him in the room, and when she turns to close the door, I can see she is fighting back a smile.

"Can you like give us five to get dressed?" Nico turns and scowls at his sister.

"You shouldn't fucking be undressed, So-So!"

"Dude, you do realize we have a kid together, right?"

"I'm fucking well aware, Dom."

"How do you think we made said kid?" I grin while Nico groans and looks up to the ceiling, muttering about being best friends with an asshole.

"Okay, Nico and I are going to give you two some time to get dressed and all that. We'll just meet you guys in the mess hall," Ryan says as she pulls Nico from the room.

Sophia and I take longer than expected. I was a gentleman and allowed her to lay in bed longer while I showered. As I was washing the shampoo out of my hair, the little vixen snuck in the shower and gave me the best fucking blowjob of my life. I'm not a selfish lover, so of course I had to return the favor, and forty-five minutes later we are finally sitting our asses down with plates filled with delicious food. I can feel Nico's glare burning a hole into the side of my face.

"Did you.... did you two?" Both Soph and I look to a dumb-struck Jackson. I smile proudly, and my blushing mate lowers her gaze back to her plate.

"Sure did." I answer proudly.

"What did they do?" Both Soph and I turn to Lucian, who is sitting next to Kai.

"We um...we thought that...maybe..." Kai saves Soph from her mumble fest.

"Your dad marked your mom. They are a fully mated couple now." Gasps ring out around the table, and Lucian's eyes widen to the size of my plate. A ball of nerves settles inside me. What if he isn't happy about Soph and me completing the mate bond? I really, *really* hope he is okay with this; I don't know what we will do if he isn't.

Ryan, Aurora, Kai, and Jax get up and congratulate us. I can see in Jackson's eyes he is envious that Soph and I have completed our bond, when he is yet to do the same with Aurora. Nico is glowering at us from his seat, and Lucian hasn't said a word.

"A-are you okay with this?" Soph asks Lucian. He doesn't reply straight away but the look on his face changes from shock to.... awe.

"Not in a million years did I think I would ever find my parents, let alone meet them. Finding you two and then knowing the situation, I never thought you would be together. The time in New York we spent together, I started to hope that *maybe* we could one day be a family. Finding this news out, fills me with so much happiness. I know we all have a long way to go —we still have a lot to learn about each other—but I'm willing to try if you two are?"

I look to Soph and see tears glistening in her eyes. I admit, I even feel choked up a bit. Sophia jumps to her feet and races around to Lucian for a hug. Not one to be left out, I do the same. It's so surreal to be standing here in this moment, holding my mate and my son. This right here in my arms is my fucking life, my world, *my everything*.

CHAPTER 39

A feeling of completeness settles over me. Standing here with Dom and Lucian is something I thought would never happen. Breaking apart, the three of us stand there with tears in our eyes. This moment means *everything* to me. Dom finally accepts me as his mate, and Lucian is okay with us being together. I didn't think Lucian would forgive me for keeping the truth from him for so long or even embrace the idea as Dom and I as his parents. In yet here we stand with him being overjoyed at the fact that he has his mother and father in his life. For the first time since Randall had taken me prisoner, my life feels like it's worth something.

"Okay, I think I might actually cry." All eyes turn to a glassy-eyed Ryan. I know she is happy for us. But most of all, I know she is happy for her best friend to have finally found his family. I know Ryan gave up a lot of time with my brother to be with Lucian. She never wanted him to feel like he was alone. I love my sister-in-law dearly for all that she has done for my son. She really is a selfless person. I turn to look at my brother to see if I can gauge his reaction, and he seems hesitant.

"Nico?" He meets my eyes, but all emotions are wiped from his face. Why?

"Don't tell me you're still hung up on Soph being my mate?" Nico shakes his head at Dom's question but still won't speak. Annoyed at my brother's lack of happiness for me, I snap.

"What the hell is wrong with you, Nico? Are you really that salty that I hid the truth of who Dom was to me from you?" Nico looked shocked as well as angry, and then his expression changes to sorrow. What the fuck?

"Nico, why the hell are you looking at us like that?" My brother closes his eyes and takes deep breaths. His shoulders are tense, and after observing for a moment I have a feeling that his mood isn't because of my mating with Dom.

"I don't like the idea of my best friend being mated to my sister, but that isn't my choice. I'm more concerned that, now that we all know who Lucian is, what if Randall is telling the truth?" Nico still won't lift his gaze from the table, and I can hear the uncertainty in his voice. I turn to Dom and see a range of emotions cross his features. His hands clench into fists at his sides, and he turns to Lucian with determination in his eyes.

"We teach you to shift, starting today. If that fat fuck is coming for you then we have to be ready. Can you access both your fae and witch magic?" Lucian pulls his gaze from his father to look at Ryan. They seem like they're having a silent conversation, and a moment later, after giving Ryan a nod, he turns back to Dom.

"I had no idea that I was anything but a fae, so I have never tried." Guilt struck me. Of course, he didn't know. He only just found out recently that I am his mother and Dom is his father. Dom places a comforting hand on Lucian's shoulder and smiles.

"Don't fret, we'll find out if you have access to all three." Dom then turns to Ryan. "Love, I'm gonna need you on hand to help out in case we push him too far." Ryan doesn't hesitate, jumping to her feet and linking her arm through Lucian's.

"You got it. There is no way I'm leaving his side till Randall is dealt with."

"The pack will help," said Jax.

"I can hang around a few more days as well." I turn and mouth a silent *thank you* to Kai.

"Just because he's my nephew, doesn't mean I automatically like him." Ryan turns and glares at Nico, who at least has the decency to look slightly sheepish. "I mean, sure, I'll stay and help. I'll just have to let Mav, Cyrus, and Larick know I will be away for a while...*again*."

We all leave the mess hall and make our way out back, where the old chapel once stood. It still had an eerie feeling about it, and I know Ryan hates coming to this side of the compound. Guilt still eats at her daily. She's doing better now. Dom leads the way and stops near the edge of the forest.

"Right, I need you to put aside the fact that we just learned who we are to each other." Lucian nods. "I know you think Tyler was a hard ass, but I'm worse. Unlike Ty, who didn't have any skin this game, I do. I will push you past your limits Lucian, because I won't let you fail. You will hate me for it, but trust me when I say you will thank me one day." Lucian and Dom stand there staring at each other for a moment, tension thick in the air.

"I don't mean to interrupt, but if he shifts, doesn't he need an alpha?" Aurora poses a good question.

"I'll do it." Jax says without hesitation, and Dom snaps his eyes to his friend and growls. Jax, being the alpha he is, rises to the challenge and growls back, his eyes turning to the color of his wolf's.

"If any anyone is marking *him* as their alpha, it will be me!"

"Then claim your pack Dominic. Right now, as you stand, you are not an alpha. Therefore, he will be under me."

"Fuck off Jax, keep your end of the deal and go to New York and sort that fucking pack out *then* I will take over and lead." So much anger laces Dom's tone. I think right here, in this moment, Dom finally makes the choice. He will become Alpha of the New York pack just so he can keep his son with him. I don't know whether to be proud or sad for him.

Before anyone can say anything, else Aurora begins to shake, her eyes turning white. Jackson looks so torn; he wants to hold her but knows if he does it could cause her harm. When she falls to her knees, Jax's arms shoot out to catch her, but Kai is the one to stop him from making contact with her. Jackson growls and shoves Kai.

"Jackson, don't! It could hurt her." Once the reality of Kai's words sink in, Jax stops and watches on helplessly as his mate shakes on her knees and there isn't a damn thing he can do to help comfort her. Maybe Jax should just claim her, at least then she won't have to go through this anymore.

CHAPTER 40

Dominic

I don't envy Jackson; I can see from the look in his chocolate brown eyes that he hates watching her have a vision. He told me it makes him feel so helpless that he can't hold her or even try to soothe her. A few weeks ago, a vision struck as Aurora was descending some stairs and she fell down. Jackson tried to catch her, but when his hand made contact, he said it was like being electrocuted.

Minutes later, Aurora finally stops shaking and flops forward onto her hands, panting, sweat dotting her brow. From the look in her eyes, that vision really took it out of her.

"Hey, you're okay baby. It's over now." Jackson drops down to the ground and gathers Aurora in his arms and holds her close to him. He rocks her back and forth like a baby, while stroking her hair. Jax is so patient and understanding. He and Kai are the better men out of the four of us. Both of them are noble and kind. Nico and I are assholes and crave control. Sometimes I wish I could be like Jax and Kai; maybe if I was more like them, I wouldn't have rejected Soph.

"Jax.... I.... bad."

"Shhhh, you're okay baby. I've got you. Deep breaths and

take your time. You tell us when you're ready." Nico opens his mouth to say something but quickly shuts it when Jax pins him with a death glare. Ryan and Sophia step forward to kneel down by Jax and Aurora. Ryan gently reaches out and strokes Aurora's head. Soph isn't one for cuddles and touching, so instead she just murmurs to Aurora that she was right here.

It's probably the worst time to notice how hot my mate looks today in a simple crop top and yoga pants, her black curls tied up in a messy bun on top of her head. I run my gaze over her once more and stop on her hip. I swear I saw a bit of ink right there on her side. How the fuck did I not notice that she had a tattoo? I will be inspecting that closely later tonight.

"Soph?" Aurora's voice is so low and timid that if I didn't have good hearing, I probably would have missed it.

"I'm right here."

"He's coming back for you. He thought outing who Lucian is to you would push you out. Lucian is *fine*. Stevie's power doesn't affect him. He just used that as an excuse to get you back–."

"Like fuck! She isn't going anywhere." All eyes turn to me, except Aurora's; her pale blue eyes are still glued to my mate. Fuck this. I grip Sophia's arm and haul her to her feet so I can tuck her into my side. I needed her to calm me, to tell me I'm not going to lose her. She wraps her arms around me and rests her head against my chest, and just the feeling of having her in my arms calms my wolf.

"Rora, can you finish what you were saying, please?" Clearly Soph still wants to hear the end of this vision, but I sure as shit don't. Don't get me wrong, I am beyond thankful that my son isn't in any danger. But the look in Aurora's eyes tells me that isn't where her vision ends.

"Soph.... Randall is amassing this army of rogues to get you back. I.... I saw it all Soph."

Aurora begins to sob in Jackson's arms, and Sophia stiffens in my embrace. "I am s-so sorry for w-what h-he did to –y-you." Sophia's breaths are coming in short fast pants, and she starts to tremble. I wrap both my arms around her and hold her tight; I try to convey without words that I'm here for her no matter what.

"Then we take him out, once and for all. I will not let him harm you again Sophia, I stand by my vow." I lift my gaze to Kai, his face a mask of anger. The hatred in his eyes isn't just for Randall—it's for himself. Kai blames himself for not being able to protect Sophia. I have to speak with him. Now that I know the reason why Kai never came to us, I understand why he kept quiet. I didn't like it, but I understood his reasons.

"What vow?" asks Lucian. Sophia untangles herself from my embrace and then clasps my hand in hers. She turns to look at Kai and gives him a stiff nod before focusing on Lucian.

"Kai doesn't need to uphold his vow; he has done enough." Soph turns to a sobbing Aurora and holds her head high. "Don't weep for me Aurora. What you saw doesn't define me. That woman you saw was beaten down and afraid, and I'm not those things anymore. All I ask, is that what you saw stays between you and me."

"Of course." Aurora chokes out between sobs. Nico marches around to us and stands directly in front of Soph, so many emotions playing across his face. He cups both her cheeks between his hands and strokes her face with his thumbs.

"I am so sorry, little sister. I don't need Aurora to explain it, I can see from your reaction what happened. I just want you to know, I will never let him touch you again." Tears begin to leak from Soph's eyes. I wanted to hold her close, but I know she needs this moment with her brother.

"What's done is done brother. I am not a *victim*; I am a *survivor*. Please don't treat me differently." Nico nods and pulls

Soph into an embrace. They stay there holding each other for so long, I swear I see a tear leak from Nico's eye. He tried for years to get her back. I searched the whole fucking world for her but could never find her. Kai told us years later, that she had been with Randall the whole time. Every time Nico tried to threaten Randall, he would hold the threat of killing Soph over our heads.

"I'll kill him!" Everyone turns to Lucian, whose eyes change to pure violet. Fuck, this kid really needed to shift.

"Lucian, you have to calm down. If you don't, you will shift." I turn to Soph and say, "I need to go back to New York, I need my dad to help with him."

"NO!" Aurora shouts. I swing my gaze back to her in shock. She quickly pulls out of Jackson's embrace and jumps to her feet, Jax scrambling to help her.

"Why not?" Aurora looks between me and Soph and then finally settles back on me.

"Because Louis wasn't alone in his bid to take Sophia." She turns to Jackson. "The New York pack needs to be stopped Jax, they are disgusting, vile and liars!" Aurora turns back to me, sorrow in her eyes. She moves toward me and grabs both my hands in hers. Tears anew leak from her pale blue eyes. I cock my head to the side, confused as fuck at her reaction, but not only that—Aurora is touching me! She never touches people if she doesn't have to; touching people brings on visions.

"Would you let me?"

"Huh?" I ask, confused. She takes a deep breath and steels her spine before meeting my gaze again.

"Will you allow me to see what no one else has?" Understanding finally dawns on me, and I stiffen and try to pull my hands back. She tightens her grip and won't let me go.

"Aurora, release him!"

"No Sophia, I need to see. Dom please, I didn't just see

Sophia in that vision—I saw you. If what I saw is correct, then your mother's killer lives." I feel my knees tremble like they are about to give out, and then I feel an arm around my waist then another around my shoulders. I look either side of me and see it's Lucian and Soph holding me up. I turn to my left to see Nico, Ryan, and Kai, they each give me a nod and a small smile, letting me know that they are here for me. Jax stands behind Aurora and nods.

"We are all here with you brother, you know you've always been family to me–to all of us. We will help you in any way we can Dom." I nod at Jax and swallow past the lump in my throat. Jax's words mean more than he will ever know.

"Okay, do it Aurora."

"I'm sorry if this causes you any discomfort. Try not to fight me." I don't do well in serious situations; my mouth tends to get away with me.

"Aww love, surely you're more comfortable with me than with the uptight alpha over there." She doesn't smile or react, just closes her eyes, and nothing happens for a while. Then out of nowhere, my head feels like it's going to explode.

"FUCK! STOOOOOPPPP!" I scream.

CHAPTER 41

Dom's scream snaps me out of my stupor, and I rip my arm away from him ready to pull him away from Aurora.

"Ryan, stop them!" Blue vines wrap around me and anchor my arms to my sides; I look to Lucian to see he's trapped as well. We both snap our gazes to Ryan, who holds both hands out toward us.

"Smurf, I don't want to hurt you by breaking these ropes, but I will if you don't let me go!" Lucian yells. He never yells at her like that. She flinches but recovers quickly.

"Luce, please listen to me, it will harm them both."

"How the hell do you know that Smurf?"

"Because she did it to me." Ryan chants something under her breath and then Lucian and I are floating toward her; I try to fight back but can't. What's the use of being able to access Dom's magic when I don't even know how to use it, except to open a portal?

"Let me go Ryan!" I grit out, and she recoils at my harsh tone. I will beat the shit out of her soon if she doesn't let me go to my *hugacko*. His screams are deafening, and he sounds like he's in so much pain. Dom needs me, and I can't even help him.

"If you don't release me now Ryan, I swear to God I will never fucking speak to you again. He fucking needs me you little bitch!"

"Sophia–,"

"Fuck off Nico, you would do the same! He fucking needs me." I turn to Lucian, and a look of understanding crosses his face, and he nods.

"I'm sorry Smurf." Lucian closes his eyes and begins to chant.

"Luce, no."

"*Fatalely cordeinga braka, fatalely cordeinga braka.*" I don't know if Lucian is strong enough to break Ryan's hold, but by the look on her face, he's putting up a good fight.

"Lucian stop, you're hurting her!"

"Then tell her to release us Nico, and he *will* stop." I snap.

"All of you fucking stop! He isn't in any physical pain; he's screaming because he is reliving the day his mother was killed. Sophia, Lucian, if either of you stop this now, he will never find out who really killed his mother. Aurora is Dominic's last hope, do not take that from him."

The fight flees my body at Kai's words, and I turn to see Lucian has stopped struggling as well. A few minutes later, when Dom's screams begin to quiet, the vines around us disappear. I thought Lucian and Ryan might hug it out and make up like always, but that doesn't happen. He moves to stand in front of her, and she looks up at him with so much regret in her eyes.

"I'm sorry, Luce–."

"Too far Smurf, way to fucking far. I would never have done that to you. I would have helped you protect your father, no matter the cost." Ryan hangs her head in shame, and Nico pulls Ryan behind him and glares at Lucian. I move to stand beside my son. I will not let my brother do anything to upset him.

"She was trying to help you!" Nico snaps.

"Yeah well, she didn't. All she did was piss me the fuck off!" Lucian's reply has me stumbling back a step. I'm angry too, but the way he's speaking is not okay.

"Lucian, maybe we–." He turns to me, and I stifle my gasp; his eyes are not his own. His wolf is close to the surface, that's why his angers out of control. He has to shift ASAP, or he is going to go nuts, and we'll all be on the receiving end of his anger. The only one who will be able to stop him is his best friend–Ryan. I have to try and defuse this situation; my anger won't help anyone right now. I tentatively step forward and clasp Lucian's hand in mine. He releases ⅄ a small growl, and I feel Jax step closer toward us; he must have sensed the change in Lucian as well. "You're okay, we're all okay. Dom is going to be okay."

"She kept me from him–from my dad." Lucian's voice is changing; he sounds more animal than man. I don't get a chance to answer.

"She did it to protect your dad pup. She didn't want him getting hurt, so she intervened to help you not hurt your father or my mate. Ryan only wanted to help you, not to anger you. You have to calm down and bring your wolf back inside of you; if you shift now, I will have no choice, but to make you submit to me. Your father doesn't want that and nor do I; you belong with him not stuck in my pack. Don't make me do it pup, please."

I can hear the pleading tone in Jackson's voice; he really doesn't want to do it, but he will if it means keeping everyone safe. Ryan steps out from behind my brother, and he grabs her arm, trying to stop her from approaching Lucian, but she wrenches her arm out of his grasp and blue light begins to cover her hands. Nico narrows his gaze at his wife.

"You really wanna do that little one?" The corner of her mouth lifts in a smirk.

"Don't tempt me big guy, he won't hurt me. I need you to

trust me Nico." I can see the struggle in Nico's eyes—he trusts Ryan, but he isn't sure whether or not he can trust Lucian. A moment passes before he nods his head, and Ryan moves to stand beside me and faces a trembling Lucian. He's struggling for control. I turn to see Dom and Aurora still in a trance-like state, gripping each other's hands.

"Luce, I'm sorry I overstepped. I never meant to hurt you, I was only trying to help buddy."

"You're always trying to help! I don't want your help Smurf." Ryan doesn't recoil or flinch at my son's harsh tone; she smiles and closes the distance between them. Lucian pulls his hand from my hold and his arm slaps against his side as he stands there staring down at Ryan.

"I will always try to help you Luce, I owe you my life—remember? Months ago, when I lost control at Lake William, you brought me back. When Ty bit me, you released my magic so I could defend myself. You're always helping me, and today I just wanted to return the favor. Don't hate me Luce, I can't live in a world where we are not best friends. I need you." All the tension flees Lucian's body: his trembling stops, and his eyes begin to return to their normal color, violet with a gray ring around the pupils. Lucian wraps his arms around Ryan, and she doesn't hesitate to return his embrace.

"I'm so sorry Smurf, I have no idea what the hell came over me. I didn't mean any of it, I swear."

"Shhhh, I know buddy. I think you may have to shift as soon as possible, your wolf is getting shitty about being caged up." Lucian nods into Ryan's neck. A loud gasp has all our attention turning toward Dom and Aurora; Dom rips his hands from Aurora's grasp and stumbles back a few steps. I race over to him and I am about to touch him when he jumps back and holds his hands up.

"Please little dove, I-I just need a minute." Hurt by his

actions, I nod my understanding and turn to face Aurora. She's as pale as a ghost, her lips taking on a blue hue. She's shivering, but it isn't even cold out. Jackson slowly walks toward her like he's approaching a wounded animal, scared she might flee. Aurora's gaze is darting around the clearing—what she is looking for, I have no idea. Jax raises his hands above his head, and Aurora looks at Jackson like he's her savior. When he's a few feet away, she ran to him and clung on to him like he was her last breath. Shocked, Jax stands there like a statue, but after the shock wears off, he finally returns her embrace. I see out of the corner of my eye Nico and Kai approach Dom, who is now sitting on the ground with his head clasped between his hands.

Seeing him like this, so destroyed and broken-hearted, hurt me. The look in his eyes when he told me he needed a minute will haunt me; he looks like a lost child. He doesn't look like the strong fae-shifter that I know and love. Nico and Kai kneel down in front of him, and Nico gently pry's Dom's hands from his face.

"We're here," is all Nico says. He and Kai drop onto their asses, and each places a hand on Dom's shoulders, letting him know without words that they have his back. When an arm wraps around my shoulders, I look up to see Lucian smiling down at me, I huddle in closer to his side. I feel a hand clasp mine and see it's Ryan, smiling shyly at me.

I release a loud exhale before saying, "I'm sorry for what I said, I had no right to say that to you–."

"Don't even sweat it sister. We're good, I should have listened and let go when you said."

I smile at my sister-in-law.

"Nah, you were right, I would have gone straight to him." We both smile at each other; Movement on the other side of us catches our attention. Jax leads a shivering Aurora toward Dom.

They stop a few feet away, and Aurora drops to her knees. Jax does the same.

"Dom I'm–" Dom cuts Aurora off, never lifting his head to meet her gaze.

"Did you find out?" Aurora looks to Jax, he nods and smiles at his mate. She takes a few deep breaths before finally answering Dom.

"It's more complicated than I thought." Dom's head slowly lifts until he locks gazes with the seer.

"Explain." Jax releases a low growl at Dom's harsh tone toward his mate, but Dom doesn't pay him any attention.

"Can we please go inside?"

"Why?" Dom snaps.

"Cut it the fuck out Dominic. I know you're hurt and pissed off, but don't take it out on her, all she did was try and help you." Dom turns his cold eyes to Jax; I have never seen Dom look so angry. He looks so cold and detached, like he just doesn't care anymore.

"Fuck. You. Jackson." Dom makes sure to pronounce each word slowly, so Jax doesn't miss it. Before this situation can escalate, I quickly pull away from Ryan and Lucian and stand between Dom and Aurora. Dom's gaze travels from my chucks all the way up my body to settle finally on my eyes. I don't say a word, just extend my hand toward him.

No one speaks. Right here, right now, is the moment where Dom shows he trusts me— or not. I'm scared shitless, my heart pumping a million miles an hour. What if he rejects me again? All those old doubts come crashing through my head and, not wanting to look like a fool any longer, I start to lower my hand. I am such an idiot for thinking I'm enough for Dominic Silver.

When I feel a hand grip mine, I lift my gaze to see it's Dom's. He climbs to his feet and looks down at me with so much grief and heartache. I can tell from how tense and corded his muscles are that he's not in a good space to hear what Aurora has to say yet. Without saying a word, I tug on Dom's hand and lead him back toward the compound.

"Do we follow?"

"Nah Luce, I think your mom and dad need a minute. Your dad needs to de-stress."

"Eww Smurf!"

"*Eww* is fucking right babe!" Ryan's laughter follows us all the way to the back door of the compound.

CHAPTER 42

I follow Soph as if I'm on autopilot. I don't take notice of where we're going. We enter a room, and she leads me to a bathroom, where she drops my hand and turns the faucets on to start filling the huge tub in the corner. She comes back and kneels down and starts to undo my shoes, then takes my socks off. Next to go are my jeans and my briefs, then my shirt. She doesn't pause; once I'm naked, she guides me to the tub. I step in and immediately slide down till the water covers my face. I try to scrub away the memories. I feel myself being pulled back under by my emotions.

Before I can spiral down the dark tunnel, small soft hands pry my hands from my face, and I push up out of the water and look up to see Soph stark naked and climbing into the tub with me. The water rises as she sits down on my lap facing me, and she turns the water off and then focuses back on me. She runs her hands down my face and through my hair. She starts to massage my scalp and my head tips back. When she shifts forward and lowers herself down again, I can feel her heat on my dick now. She moves her hands to my face and starts to trace my brow.

The movements of her hands on my body are calming me and starting to ease some of the tension from my body, so I close my eyes and enjoy this moment. I push all my feelings and thoughts aside and focus on Soph. Her hands travel down over my shoulders then my chest. She trails one hand down my abs, and the lower she gets the more I start to feel my cock awaken. She keeps running her hands all over me, and its sweet torture. I feel her lean forward and then I feel her lips against my neck. She darts her tongue out and licks me from my neck to my ear lobe and whispers, "I want you."

I groan. Fuck, I don't think there will ever be a minute of the day when I don't want Sophia. Before I can answer or even reach up to touch her, she pulls back. I snap my eyes open and watch as she stands and rests her ass on the edge of the tub. Watching the water cascade down her beautiful body has my dick standing up and slapping against my stomach. Her eyes dart to my hard cock, and she licks her lips. I watch as she balances on the edge of the tub and spreads her legs open, exposing her sweet, sweet pussy to me. My gaze travels up her body to her perky and full tits. Her nipples are pebbled and rock hard. I finally meet her gaze and see her pupils are blown wide. My mate wants to fuck!

I start to sit up, but she quickly uses her foot to push against my chest. I look up her, perplexed.

"You get to watch." Huh? Oh...*oh*. I settle back against the tub and watch as she starts to run her hands over her tits. She locks her gaze on mine as she tweaks one of her nipples and moans. I bite my lip to stop myself from groaning. She tweaks the other one and moans again., She continues to fondle that nipple while her other hand travels down her stomach, going lower and lower until it reaches her pussy. She runs her slender fingers through her folds and spreads them apart as she hums. She maintains eye contact with me as she inserts a finger inside herself. Her eyes slam shut as soon as she starts to pump that digit in and out. My cock is aching, and I want inside her now, but I'm enjoying the show too fucking much. She picks up the pace and then uses her other hand to circle her clit, her head falling back as she moans.

"Fuck, Dom, oh my God." Her breathing picks up, and I can tell she's close. I want her eyes on me as she comes apart. I want her to know that even though it isn't my hands on her or inside her, I am the one that grants her this pleasure. No other man will be able to see her do this except me.

"Eyes on me baby, I want you to look at me when you come." She lifts her head and locks her gaze on mine, her mouth forming a perfect O in a silent moan. Her cheeks are rosy, and her body taut with tension.

"Finger fuck yourself harder baby, and when you come, I want you to scream my fucking name." My words are her undoing—a second later she comes, screaming my name so fucking loud. I don't waste time or give her a chance to recover. I reach forward and pull her down to me. Her eyes are still glassy from her orgasm, and I can feel aftershocks wracking her body. I don't stop; once she's straddling my lap, I line my cock up with her opening and slam her little body down onto it. We both cry out at the feeling, having my dick buried so deep inside her feels like I'm on the greatest ecstasy trip of my life. Soph doesn't fuck around—she bounces up and down on my dick like a fucking pro. Water sloshes over the tub, and I don't give a fuck about the mess. All I can think about is Soph and how good she feels wrapped around my cock, her pussy clenching me. Her tits are bouncing up and down, and I lean forward and capture her nipple in my mouth. She cries out at the sensation and grips the hair on the back of my head so she can hold my face there. When the teasing touch of my mouth is too much, she releases my head, and I lean back watching as the most beautiful woman

I have ever seen ride my cock, her eyes lock onto mine. She leans forward and grips the back of the tub for more leverage, rolling her hips and grinding against me, my cock buried balls deep inside of her.

"Kiss me," she demands, and I capture her lips in a searing kiss, our tongues colliding as we explore each other. I grip her hips and slam her down on my cock, meeting her thrust for thrust. She tears her mouth from mine and looks down at me.

"I'm gonna come, fuck."

"Come all over my cock baby." She shatters apart a second later, then flops forward and rests her head in the crook of my neck. I wrap my arms around her and stand, and she twines her arms and legs around me. I climb out of the tub and rest her ass on the edge of the vanity.

"Give me everything you've got. Don't hold back Dom."

I don't waste time or deny her, my cock instantly hardens for round two, I pull back and slam into her, over and over. I grab the back of her hair and pull until her head falls back and she exposes her mate mark to me. Right as I'm about to come, I let my teeth extend and my wolf comes forward. I clamp my mouth on her shoulder and pierce her skin with my teeth, and she screams out her release, me tumbling over the edge a moment later, emptying my seed inside her.

Soph and I clean up and decide to have a shower rather than soak in the tub again. I mean, I wouldn't say no to round three, but I know Soph must be a bit sore. I allowed the beast inside of me to come out a little. She wanted me to let loose, and I did, and fuck, man, it was the best sex I have ever had in my life.

"Come on, the others will be waiting for us." Soph's voice pulls me from my thoughts, and I look over to see she has put on the pair of jeans she left here the other day and has used one of my plain white shirts, tying a knot in the front to show off a bit of skin. I growl at the sight. She looks at me in shock, her violet eyes wide. "What's wrong?"

"Do you have to knot the shirt?"

"Oh, I'll go change, sorry. I didn't mean to ruin your shirt." I move toward her and cup her face between my hands. She tries to pull away, but I won't let her. I know I upset her and embarrassed her, but that isn't the point I was trying to make. When she finally looks me in the eye, I smile at the miffed expression on her face.

"I don't give a shit about the shirt; I just hate that people get to see more of you than they need to." Seconds tick by, and I see the moment my words sink in. She deflates and wraps her arms around my waist, and I mimic her movement.

"Dom, I don't give a shit what anyone thinks about me or what they see. The only one who *really* gets to see me is you." I don't have words, so I lean down and capture her lips in a kiss. Before we end up going for round three, I pull back and smile down at my pouting mate.

"We have to go love." She reaches up with one hand and cups my cheek; so many emotions pass through her gaze, but the one that stands out the most is *love*.

"I've got your back no matter what. I will always be here for you Dom."

"I know little dove, and I don't know if I have ever said this before but thank you." She reels back, in shock at my words. "What?"

"Thank you for being you. Thank you for keeping our son

safe when I couldn't. Thank you for never giving up on life and never giving up on us. Thank you for loving me, Sophia. Without you I am nothing. I know it has taken me too many years to realize that, but I will spend the rest of my days making it up to you. I will make sure that you and Lucian are safe. I love you, Sophia." Tear's cascade down her face, and her hand trembles as she brings it up to cover her mouth. I didn't like the space between us, so I wrap my arms around her and pull her to me. We stand silently for a long time before she breaks it.

"I have been in love with you since I was a little girl. I just never thought I would ever be lucky enough to have you love me back. Let's deal with this Randall shit and then let's spend the rest of our lives together, getting to know our son." A thought struck me then.

"Soph?"

"Hmmm?"

"Do you want more kids?"

"For fuck's sake, let's go Dom."

"I'm serious."

"I know, that's why we're leaving to find the others. Just thinking about more kids is making me feel like your sperm is invading my eggs as we speak." I burst out laughing at the horrified look on her face.

CHAPTER 43

Not even gonna lie, Dom's question threw me. The last thing on my mind is kids. I already have a child that I barely know or even got to raise. Someday, sure, I would love to have more kids, but right now I needed to focus on the child I already have. Entering Jackson's office pulls me from my thoughts. Everyone is sitting on the couches. I see Alex, Chase, and Mya here. I like Ryan's cousins. They're good people. I pull my hand from Dom's and hug them saying hello to Mya. I'm not much of a hugger, but since being around this lot, it has kind of grown on me. Just as I pull back from Mya, a vision struck me.

Mya steps back and looks at me strangely. I snatch my gaze from her to look at Alex and Chase.

"Not a word," Mya grits out, and I nod my head, still lost for words.

"What's wrong Soph?" I turn to Chase, and I feel the blush start to coat my cheeks. I clear my throat twice and swallow, trying to control my nervous laughter.

"N nothing, just catching up with Mya." Chase doesn't look convinced, he looks from me to Mya and then reorganization shone in his eyes. I imitate the action of zipping my lips and throwing away the key. Dom, the ever-observant pest, notices the tension between me and the trio and grins.

"You do realize I will fuck the secret out of her, right?"

"Dominic! For fuck's sake, that's my sister!" Dom turns and grins cockily at my brother, who is a vibrant shade of red.

"You do know why we left you lot before, right? Soph had to help me *unwind*." Dom winks at me, and I groan. Fuck my life.

"Dude, no, just no. I never and I mean *never want* to hear that shit come out of your mouth again." Dom burst out into fits of laughter at Lucian's horrified expression, I cringe. Lucian really doesn't care to know that his parents just fucked.

"Eww Soph, you can do way better. I told you this before, warlocks are better company." Dom's laughter cuts off, and he storms over to me and wraps his arms around me until my back was flush against his chest. Then he yanks the collar of my shirt down to expose my mate mark to Chase, who gasps.

"Now I get why Nico finds you so fucking annoying. You look at her or even make a move on her that I don't like, and your cousin won't save you from me."

"Aww Chase, you poked the bear and now he's pissy." Chase breaks out into fits of laughter at Alex's taunt. I sigh. These boys are going to have fun winding Nico *and* Dom up now. They get a kick out of pissing my brother off, for some reason, and now it seems that Dom is on their radar.

"You two stop, leave Dom and Soph alone." I mouth a silent *thank you* to Ryan.

"Come on squirt, at least if we're picking on him, then Tink gets a break."

"Oh *Sabrina*, that is so thoughtful of you. Just because you're both kings of the Knox coven doesn't mean I won't beat your asses, now sit down and shut up!" Ryan elbows Nico in the stomach, and he groans then turns to glare at her.

"Those are my cousins you're speaking to, dick face." Nico looks at the cackling kings of the Knox coven.

"They started it!"

"And we're not in middle school anymore, so everyone grow the fuck up. Dom and Soph just fucked, cool. Nico and Ryan fucked in the clearing this morning as well." Ryan gasps and starts to turn red, while Nico stares at Kai.

"How the fuck do you know that?"

"Bro, it's the main running trail. You know I run every morning; if you don't want anyone to see your pasty white ass, don't fuck your wife on the main trail." The whole room erupts in laughter at my brother and sister-in-law's expense. I feel bad for them, but at the same time I'm thankful for the laughter that breaks the tension in the room. Everyone seems lighter and less tense, except for Aurora, who keeps glancing back at Dom. I grab Dom's hand and lead him over to the couches. He plonks down onto the cushion next to Kai then pulls me down onto his lap. I ignore my brother's groan and comment about needing to be sick.

"So.... can I ask why we're here?" Aurora tears her gaze from Dom to look at Alex.

"As the kings of the Knox coven, I need to ask you something. Faes cannot do what has to be done, and I don't think Ryan or Sophia have the recourse to do what I am about to ask." I look around the room and see everyone's faces scrunch up in confusion—well, everyone except for a somber-looking Jackson.

"Okay, Rora, what do you need?"

"I need to know if you or Alex can strip a wolf of their shifter abilities." Gasps echoes around the room then everyone begins talking and shouting over each other.

"Shut the fuck up!" Everyone quiets down at Jax's outburst. I can see from how tense and stiff he is that this isn't something he's okay with. "I don't agree with this, but Aurora thinks it might be the only way to stop Randall, to start stripping his army of their abilities, *if* we can."

"Jax is right; Randall has many moles in each race. My vision doesn't show me who they are, but there are many. A lot of people are not happy with how their leaders have chosen–."

"Chosen what Aurora?" Nico cut in.

"People are angry that you chose the woman who could kill your people and world. People are angry Jax chose to accept our mate bond when I am not a shifter. People are also angry that Dom called off his engagement to Sienna so he could be mated with a non-shifter."

"They can all get fucked and suck a fat dick for all I care," Dom tartly replies.

"So classy babe," I mutter.

"Oh God, I'm gonna be sick. They already have pet names." Chase, Alex, and Lucian broke out in laughter at Nico's dramatics. I roll my eyes and focus back on Aurora. Her face takes on a serious expression.

"Dom, may I speak freely?" I turn to look at Dom and find his gaze on me. I lift my hand and cup his cheek.

"I'm right here." A hand claps down on his shoulder, and we both look up to see Lucian smiling down at his father.

"I'm right here with you, as well." Dom places his hand on top of Lucian's and nods at his son, he leans in to peck me on my lips before turning to Aurora.

"We discuss this one time, then never again. I don't want pity or any apologies, got it?" A chorus of agreement rings out before Aurora continues.

"Dom, the men you...ended, were not your mother's killers." Dom stiffens beneath me. "They were part of it, but there are others.... many others involved–."

"How many?" Dom mumbles against my neck.

"Dom, I need you to under–" Dom pulls back and looks over

my shoulder at the seer, and I can tell from the way she tenses that Dom's eyes must have changed to his wolf's. Jax instinctively moves so he is half-blocking Aurora on her seat from Dom's gaze.

"How many?" Dom shouts. Aurora places a hand on Jax's shoulder, indicating that it's okay and to move aside so she can see Dom, and he does reluctantly.

"Pretty much most of the pack Dom. The only reason you could pick up on their scents is because they were the last to–."

"We get it!" I cut in before she can say the word that will cause Dom to lose control.

CHAPTER 44

Dominic

So much anger courses through my veins, anger like I have never felt before. For years my father has rubbed shoulders with men that raped and murdered the love of his life, my mother. We thought we dealt with them. How fucking wrong were we? Those cunts have been living and breathing air that my mother should have been. They robbed her of her life, the most gentle and kindest woman I have ever known. I will hunt them down and kill each and every one of those fuckers. They are living on borrowed time. I turn my gaze to Jackson, and the look in his eyes tells me he knows what I'm about to ask.

"With or without your permission Jax, they will pay with their lives."

"There has to be a trial Dominic—if you do this and they are innocent, I will have no choice but to force you to answer for it!"

"Fuck you, Jackson! They raped her and killed her like she was prey. I am not bound to you or any other alpha. I don't answer to you."

"You will answer to me when you become alpha of the New York pack." I smile wickedly at my brother.

"There won't be a pack when I'm done with them." Gasps echo around the room, and before Jax and I continue our verbal sparring match, Aurora speaks up.

"Dominic is right, the men involved have told their families and friends. That pack has hidden this secret, and they plan to overthrow Dom's dad very soon. Ian Silver pissed the pack off when he decided to make his half-breed son heir to the pack. To make matters worse, Dom mated with a half-breed and has a child with her. The pack wants to rise against you, as well Jax. A handful of members are innocent, mostly women, but the majority of the pack aligns themselves with Randall Cane. We have to get your father out of there now, Dominic!" I can hear the fear in Aurora's voice; those who are innocent I will spare, but if anyone knew about what happened to my mother and says nothing I will kill them.

"Allow him this vengeance Jackson. Dom and his father are better as allies instead of enemies. Once Ian learns of this, he will not be tamed—she may not have been his mate, but she was his." Kai has never spoken truer words, but my gaze is snatched by a glowing Ryan. Nico is trying to comfort her, but it's not working. Nico turns to look over my head at Lucian, and from the look in my best friend's eyes, I can tell it's hard for him to ask this.

"Help her, please." Lucian doesn't hesitate. He moves toward them and kneels down in front of Ryan. Reaching out, he tries to grab her hands, but she snatches them away, pushing past Lucian and moving to stand in front of Jax.

"If you don't let him do this, then I will do it for him. I promised you after what happened with Ty I would never interfere again, but this is different Jackson."

"Ryan, I can't–."

"Bullshit Jackson, I will surround you and your compound

in a dome of my making so Dom can do what he needs to do. You will not take this from him. I allowed you all to lock Lachlan and Victor away instead of killing those bastards after what they did to my mother. You will not do the same to Dominic!" I'm in awe of Ryan right now; I have never seen her so determined or angry since the day at Lake William. She looks fucking fierce. I turn to look at Nico, who is lounging on the couch. He doesn't have a care in the world; he knows his wife can hold her own.

"Jackson?" Jax tears his gaze from Ryan to look at his mate. "There's one more thing." Jax nods his head for her to continue. "If you get rid of the New York pack and take Randall out, the threat on your life will be gone, I don't know who the threat is, only that it will be eliminated if you all deal with this."

Jax sits there confused for a moment, and then out of nowhere, a huge smile graces his face. Quick as a snake, he leaps forward and grabs Aurora's face then smashes his lips against hers. The kiss lasts maybe five seconds, and then Jax is pulling away from his mate to jump to his feet and slinging an arm around Ryan's shoulders. Ryan now looks taken aback by his sudden change of mood.

"Right—Alex, Chase, Mya, you guys work on a spell, if there is one, to strip abilities. The rest of us will gear up to go to New York and deal with this, so Dom can have his vengeance."

"Why the sudden change of heart?" Chase asks, and Mya slaps Chase on the chest and looks at him like he's simple.

"If the threat on his life is taken out, Aurora will finally accept the mate bond."

"Oh my God," Ryan exclaims, who swings around and engulfs Jax in a hug and then moves to do the same to Aurora. I know Jax has his own reasons for doing this with me, but I'm happy that my brother will finally get his girl. Fuck knows he's waited long enough!

I have been trying to reach my dad for nearly three hours. His phone stopped ringing and now goes straight to voicemail. I start to get a sinking feeling that something is wrong. I ask Aurora if she has seen anything, she hasn't but will try to bring on a vision. Jax doesn't like that, but I'm desperate. We're just waiting for Kai, Nico, and Ryan to return with reinforcements. Kai is bringing some of his vamps and Nico and Ryan are bringing some of their army with us. We don't want to go in half-cocked and fuck things up. We all agreed that after we take out the pack, we'll go for Randall.

Everyone came to a unanimous vote that it's better to get rid of Randall sooner rather than later. The old fuck is becoming quite the pain in the ass. I requested that we hold him in the cells at Jax's. I want to torture the cunt for what he did to my son and my mate. I will make sure that he suffers as much as they did. Chase and Alex returned an hour ago and said that there isn't a spell to reverse shifter abilities, so therefore they will have to be locked up or put down. Jackson and I had agreed on terms: if they surrender, they will live in a cage. If they chose to fight us, they'll die, slowly.

"We have to be cautious when we go after Randall."

"Why, Soph?"

"He drank the blood of Jax's dad, Ryan's dad and Ryan's blood. I think that is the only reason the slimy bastard survived after Ryan's energy ball melted half his fucking face off." I smile at the thought of his face. The look on Sophia's face pulls me from my thoughts.

"What's wrong, little dove?"

"Randall what if he..." I close the distance between us, and embrace her.

"I won't ever let him hurt you again babe."

"It's not me I'm worried about Dom. Lucian hasn't shifted yet, and we're about to chase after the man who held him prisoner his whole life. We have to help our son shift, or he will lose control, and this time I don't know if Ryan can pull him back from the edge." Her words hit me right in the heart. If a shifter prolongs the change and keeps fighting, there's a high chance the wolf will turn rabid and not be able to shift back. We would lose him.

"After we get back from New York, we'll go out to the woods, and I'll get Dad to help us. He will be able to help Lucian like he helped me. I promise, little dove, I won't let anything happen to our son." Soph and I pull apart at the sound of Kai's voice. I didn't even know he was back yet.

"I never thought I'd see the day that you two would finally admit how you feel for each other. I mean, I hoped you both would, but seeing it is another thing. I'm so glad you two have each other. I'm also glad you pulled your head out of your ass and didn't let fear continue to rule your life brother." Soph walks over to Kai and wraps him in a hug. Kai is the most reserved out of the four of us; he is the quiet giant. Kai relaxes after the shock wears off, and kindly returns Soph's embrace.

Nico pretends he's over the fact that Kai entered Ryan's dreams and used his gifts against her, but he isn't. He still holds so much resentment toward our vampire brother. Kai has been dealt a rough hand; he was turned into a vamp against his will because he swore he would protect Ryan's grandmother, Nico's original intended bride, and then she died. Kai was locked into a blood oath with Randall for many years and is now finally free, but he still lives like he is on some sort of time frame. Sophia stands there looking up at the big giant of a man, and he looks down at her with so much love and devotion, like a brother looks at a sister. I know they have been through a lot together, and I know Kai will always look out for Soph, as she will him.

"I don't think I have ever told you, there are no words to express how much you mean to me, and everything you did, thank you Melakai. I wouldn't have got through those years if it wasn't for you." Kai sucks in a sharp breath at Sophia's admission. Everyone is looking at them. Kai may have the power to manipulate people's moods and emotions, but he was never able to express his own emotions very well. The dude is like a vault when it comes to his own feelings.

"You survived on your own So-So. You're stronger than you give yourself credit for. I will always watch over you and protect you as best I can. I am just sorry I couldn't do more for you back then." Kai lifts his gaze from my mate to look at me. "I'm sorry I didn't try harder brother. I swear on my life, if I had of known your son was alive, I would have fought tooth and nail to get him back to you. I'm sorry I failed you both." Kai hangs his head in shame. I approach the giant of a man and pull him in for a bro hug, which he returns. Lucian's voice has the three of us turning to him.

"If you had of known about me, I would never have found Smurf. Everyone ends up where they need to be, and now, I am where I need to be. Don't feel bad about my life; if I didn't endure what I went through I wouldn't be the person I am today."

"And what a fucking aaammmazing person you are! I am one lucky biarch to be able to call you my BFF." I turn to see Ryan and Nico walking through the office door. Ryan is smiling at my boy and pulls him in for a hug. Nico scowls at the two of them, which causes me to laugh.

"What's so fucking funny asshole?" he snaps.

"Dude, he's your fucking nephew, and you're jealous at the fact he's hugging his BFF/aunt."

"Fuck up Dominic." Kai, Soph, and I laugh at Nico's expense. That dick's jealousy knows no bounds.

We all moved outside to join the armies we are bringing with us. Dom opens two portals, one for Kai and the vamps, and the other for Jax and his shifters as well as Nico, Ryan, and their soldiers, each army given their destinations. So, they could cover each exit point. Chase, Alex, Mya, and Aurora would stay behind. The coven didn't want to be involved in this, and we don't blame them. Jax refused to allow Aurora to come. She doesn't like it but agrees none the less, to appease her mate.

"Are you both ready for this?" Dom asks Lucian and me. I clasp Dom's hand in one of mine and thread my other arm through Lucian's.

"Let's do this."

"I'm in," Lucian and I say in unison, and Dom opens a portal for the three of us to go through. It's time to end the New York pack once and for all. Then maybe, just *maybe*, my *hugacko* might be able to start healing from the tragic loss of his mother.

We emerge from the portal at the back of Dom's father's house. It's night here in New York. The lights in the house are on, as well as the back porch light. I take a step forward and I am halted by Dom yanking me back. I turn to glare at him and ask what's his problem but stop short when I see the look on his face.

"What is it?" Neither Lucian nor Dom answer me, they both keep scenting the air.

"Can you smell that?"

"Y-yeah, I can. What is that?" I'm getting pissed that they aren't including me in this conversation; I can't smell shit.

"It's blood." I snap my gaze back to the house, dread pooling low in my belly. Dom starts to move toward the house, and I quickly pull my phone from my pocket and send a message on our group chat for the others to meet us at Mr. Silver's house. Once we climb the stairs, an eerie silence surrounds us. There is no crickets chirping in the trees. The silence is almost deafening in its completeness. I'm straining to hear any nearby conversations or even cars. Something is going on here, and I don't like it.

A portal opening behind us draws our attention. Kai, Jax, Nico, and Ryan step through. Dom motions for them to join us and remain quiet; we move toward the back door, which is ajar. No sound is coming out of the house, and I start to worry for Mr. Silver. This house is never quiet. Dom takes a few deep breaths and then before anyone can say or do anything, he pushes the door open and steps inside. We follow him in, but as we round the corner to the living room, I nearly slam into Dom's back. I peek around him and gasp. There is so much blood it covers the floors and walls.

"What the fuck happened here?" Jax whispers and I turn to see Kai making his way upstairs. Dom is still standing in the same place; he hasn't moved an inch. Ryan moves toward Lucian and holds his hand, offering her silent support. I move around Dom and stand directly in front of him. His gaze is on the walls behind me. I place my hand on his chest to get his attention. He looks down at me, and I see so much sorrow in his eyes.

"It's his blood, it's all his blood." The anguish in Dom's voice guts me.

"You guys are going to want to see this." Everyone follows Kai up the stairs, Kai stops in front of the closed door and looks at me, then Ryan. "I must warn you, it's not pretty." Ryan and I don't hesitate to nod our heads; we have been through some tough shit so I know we'll be fine. Kai doesn't look so convinced. He opens the door and steps inside, the guys all follow behind. Ryan and I are the last to enter the room.

"Oh my God!" Ryan breaths, I don't even know what words to use to describe the sight in front of me, or how to describe what I'm feeling. I have never in my life seen something so sick and horrifying. Dom wraps his arm around my waist and pulls me against him. Sitting on the bed is the lifeless body of a woman who could have been my sister. She wore a crop top and jeans with chucks, and on closer inspection I can see she even has a flannel shirt tied around her waist. This woman is wearing the same type of outfit I wear most days, and she even has long black curls, though her eyes are green unlike mine. This poor woman paid a price for my freedom; there is no doubt in my mind that she was killed by Randall Cane so he could send me a message.

"Did you search her?" I ask Kai.

"Are you for real Soph? You want her ID so you can call her

family? She's human. We can't even return her body." I turn my head and scowl at my dumbass brother.

"I'm not fucking asking you; I'm asking Kai." Kai moves toward me and pulls out an envelope from his back pocket. It has specks of blood all over it. My name is written in bold letters on the front.

"She had it clutched in her hand."

"What the hell is that, Melakai?" Jax asks.

"A letter addressed to So-So. I believe it's from Randall." I didn't need to open it to know for sure; I just knew it was him. He used to do sick shit like this all the time, but he never killed anyone to get my attention.

I tear the flap open on the envelope and pull the letter out, reading it aloud so everyone can hear.

Hello my darling treasure,

Oh, how I have missed you!

It's time to come home now treasure, I am tired of these playthings. I want my real dolly back so I can play with her.

I will continue to leave bodies behind until you come to your senses.

I have given you more than enough time to make your point, and now I am over waiting. If I see you with that mongrel dog again, or if he has defiled you in any way, I will kill him.

Come back to me and I will end this war. I have no issues with your brother or his wife now.

I just want my treasure, and then all will be forgiven.

You have 48 hours, if you are not back here by then, I will come for you, and I will make sure to hurt the ones you love, starting with that bastard kid of yours and the dog.

. . .

Your love,
    R.C

I feel bile rise in my throat. I push away from Dom and run to the bathroom, I drop to my knees in front of the toilet just in time to empty the contents from my stomach. A dead woman who looks like me is not the reason for making me sick, it's the thought of going back to Randall. What the hell is wrong with me?

"Soph are you okay?" I look up to see my sister-in-law in the doorway. I nod my head and quickly stand so I can rinse my mouth. I splash cold water on my face and slap my cheeks a couple of times to shake myself from my thoughts.

CHAPTER 46

Nico, Jax, Kai, Lucian and I remain in the bedroom with the corpse while Ryan goes to check on Soph.

"We have to get rid of the body and then find out where the hell the pack is." Nico's right, we can't leave a body here in my dad's house. Fuck, my dad.

"I need to find my dad!" I can see by the looks on my brothers' faces that they think the worst, but I know in my gut that my dad wasn't dead. I would have felt it, right?

"I'll help you find Poppy." I give Lucian a stiff nod, and my three brothers exchange a look between themselves. Finally, Kai speaks.

"Where do we even begin?" I have an idea, and I just hope I'm right. I never thought he would need it, but I always left it open just in case the pack ever tried to turn on him. I guess I was right; it's not Randall's scent that covers the house, it's the pack members. The pack did this and left the body for us to find.

"We have to go to the cabin where my dad took Ryan."

"Dom, there is no way he could hop a plane with that amount of blood loss."

"I left a portal open here for him," I grit out. I want to slap Jackson for reminding me of the blood loss.

"Let's go, were running out of time." I turn to the doorway to see Sophia and Ryan standing there. Soph looks pale and shaken, but she's putting on a brave face. I have to find a way to reassure her that I will keep her safe, but words fail me. I hate to admit it, but Randall is more resourceful than we thought if he managed to get to my dad. My dad is one tough son of a bitch, and for Randall to find a way to get near him means he has more allies than we do at the moment.

What if he can get to Soph or Lucian?

I will do everything in my power to make sure that doesn't happen. I can't let Sophia go through that hell again. I know she told me what happened, but I also know she gave me the watered-down version just to appease me. Lucian had lived in a cold, dark cell his whole life, all because I'm his father. Randall hated him because he was a reminder of what Soph and I had shared. So much is running through my mind, my emotions are out of control. If I don't stop and breathe for a minute, I'll lose control and shift. I have to get out of this room. All I can smell is my father's blood and a rotting corpse.

"I've just linked Lucas, and he and the rest of the pack will scout the area for anyone left behind. They will also deal with the body. Nico, is there anyway Maverick or Larick can stay behind to bring my pack home?"

"Yeah Jax, I'll leave a few men here and send the rest back."

"Can you open a portal for my guys as well? I'll leave a few here to help with the clean- up and scouting, but the rest can return to the mansion in case Randall decides he wants to try a mutiny." Kai has a valid point; that's a real possibility.

After Nico, Kai, and Jax organized their men, we all made our way to the Eastern side of the pack lands. I hid the portal in a small cave so no one would be able to find it. At first leaving this portal opened took a toll on my magic, but after years went by, I just got used to it and learned to build my power around it. If we get there and the portal is closed, that means someone has used it, but if it's still open, then that means my dad didn't go through it. Trepidation courses through my body the closer we get. I hope and pray that my dad was able to get out and use the portal. I know it seems like a lot of blood loss, but shifters heal fast, as long as it isn't a fatal wound. A phone ringing breaks the silence of our group.

"What's wrong love?" It's Jax who gets the call. "Slow down love, hang on—I'll put you on speaker." Jax pulls the phone away from his ear and puts it on speaker so we can all hear. "Okay, you're on speaker now."

"Randall has the moon stones, he sent a few of them to your father's pack members Dom. That's why there is so much blood; your father isn't able to heal." I growl low in my throat. "Alex, Mya, and Chase have returned to the coven to speak with David. We have to find a way to see if we can destroy them, as far as I know David Knox is the only one who has experience with them—"

"No, my gramps is the one who told my uncle about them. You guys go to the cabin to see if Dom's dad is there, and Nico and I will go to Yukon and speak to my grandparents."

Having a seer on our side is pretty freaking awesome. Aurora having that vision about the moonstones explains a lot. Ryan and Nico portaled to her grandparents while the rest of us go to the cave. As soon as we break through the dense trees the cave comes into view, I quickened my pace, and as soon as I poke my head through the opening of the cave, its complete darkness.

"YES!"

"What is it?" I spin around and clasp Sophia's face between my hands and kiss her.

"Eww, that is fucking gross." I quickly pull away from Soph and grin at my boy.

"You'll get used to it."

"I really hope I don't have to. No one needs to see that PDA." I chuckle at Lucian's disgusted expression.

"Come on, I'll open a portal to the cabin. We will have to trek through the forest to get there."

"Why Dom?"

"Dad warded the cabin so no magic user can penetrate it or find its location." Kai nods, and I turn to open a portal, I stop when Soph places her hand on my chest.

"I'll open the portal, I spent a lot of time there as a child, and I know a place closer that we can get through." Dumbfounded and in shock that Soph knows my family cabin better than I do, I just nod. She raises her hands and begins to chant.

"*Portaly openinga cabruna muntina, portaly openinga cabruna muntina.*" A portal appears in front of us, and Sophia is the first to go through, then Lucian. The look on Jax and Kai's faces has me pausing and turning to them.

"What?"

"Since when can Sophia open a portal Dom?" I reach around and rub the back of my neck.

"Yeah, she can siphon my power, apparently. We have no idea how she does it, but she figured it out when she came to Jackson's compound." Both my brothers stand there with their mouths hanging open. I chuckle at their dumb-looking faces and go through the portal.

Sophia's not wrong—we exit the portal a couple minutes from the cabin. How she knew about the blind spot in the wards I have no fucking idea. I'm not about to question her either, when I see lights on in the cabin. My heart rate picks up. I scent the air and get a whiff of pine, mildew, antiseptic, blood and...Dad. I take off running toward the cabin, and burst through the door, my dad shakily climbing to his feet, ready to fight if need be. I stand there and stare at the man that has always been my hero.

He's shirtless but has bandages wrapped all around his torso, blood is seeping through the gauze. He looks so pale and weak. I have never seen my dad like this. I always thought he was invincible. This is the first time in my life that I might actually lose my hero.

At the sound of the others bounding up the porch steps, I quickly head over to the old boy. I know he's in pain, but fuck it. I wrap my arms around him and pull him to me. He lets out a small hiss but doesn't hesitate to return my embrace.

"I'm so fucking glad you're okay," Dad scowls at me.

"Watch your language, I'm not dead yet." He bites in his deadpan voice.

"That's not funny Dad."

"I'm sorry Dom." I reel back in shock at his apology; what the hell is he sorry for?

"Why are you sorry?"

"I know you must have been worried." Before I can answer, Lucian pushes his way past me, and dives in for a hug. Dad looks at me over Lucian's shoulder, a moment passes and the shock bleeds away to comfort and love. The surprise on his face is overwhelming that his grandson cares so much about him. Once Lucian steps back, Soph, Jax, and Kai join in on the hugs.

"As cozy as this place is, I think we should make our way back to my compound sir, so the Doc can take a look at your wounds."

"Thank you Jackson, now that I'm away from those flipping stones, I've started to finally heal. It was touch and go for a minute there." A loud growl sounds in the tiny cabin. I turn to Jax and find his gaze locked on...Lucian. Shit, I have to get my dad back pronto, the quicker he heals the quicker we can help Lucian shift. Soph moves closer to Lucian and interlocks her fingers with his. The contact seems to ease some of the anger from his body.

"We will kill them all for what they did to you Poppy." Dad shudders at the nickname but politely nods his head; he knows Lucian isn't in the right state of mind to argue about what he calls him.

"Let's get out of here. I need the doc, shower and then sleep. Tomorrow, we start getting you ready to shift. Your wolf is too close to the surface, and the more you put it off, the harder it will be to phase back." Lucian gulps loudly then nods his head quickly. I know this is a shock for him; he will be scared to shift, but if he doesn't then it will make things ten times worse when his wolf breaks its cage and takes over.

CHAPTER 47

Sophia

After Mr. Silver's examination with the doctor, Dom and I escort him to his room. His wounds are now healing, but I can tell from the strain in his face that he is still in a fair amount of pain. Once Dom is satisfied that his father is comfy and tucked in, we bid him goodnight and make our way back to Dom's room. As we enter the room, I step back in shock to find my bags from Dom's dad's house are all here. I look to Dom, waiting for him to explain, and he shrugs his shoulders and says, "We're mated Soph. You sleep where I sleep." I have no smartass reply to that. My heart swells at the thoughtfulness of this man; Me being me though, I have to keep him on his toes.

"What if I don't want to share a bed with you?" Dom whirls around so fast he nearly loses his footing, and the look on his face makes me want to burst out laughing. He looks like he's seen a ghost.

"The fuck does that mean you don't wanna sleep with me?" I take a couple of deep breaths to stop myself from smiling and making sure to keep my face blank.

"Well, I would like some space. This is all new to me and very overwhelming; I feel like I'm losing myself in you." Dom's face changes—the shock is quickly replaced by anger. His eyes switch to the color of his wolf. I wanted to run now; I've pushed him too far. I turn to hightail it out of the room, but his words stop me.

"You run, I chase, *mate*." I spin back to face him, and he stalks toward me, a little more beast than man. His muscles strain against his shirt, and as my eyes travel downward, my attention snaps to the bulge in his jeans. Dom likes it when I play hard to get... good to know.

He stops directly in front of me, and I crane my neck back so I can look into his eyes. A small smirk ghosts across his lips. "Are you playing games with me *mate?*"

I shudder at the raw huskiness in his voice—the heat radiating off his body and the possessive look on his face is turning me the fuck on.

"I-I was.... I mean..." Dom places his index finger against my lips, shushing me, slowly leaning down till his lips are against my ear.

"I planned to fuck the night away and *lose myself in you.* But since you want some space, I'll give it to you and go take a cold shower instead." I gasp. Those words from his sinful lips causes liquid to gather between my thighs. I hear him inhale as he pulls back and looks down at me. He can smell how turned on I am, and the smile on his face tells me he plans to toy with me.

"I would help relieve that ache between your fucking luscious thighs babe, buuuutttt I would hate for you to lose yourself in *me.*" The bastard grins as I stand here gaping at him. He spins on his heels and peels his shirt off, making sure to stop at the bathroom door dropping his jeans. I groan at the sight of his nakedness. He peers over his shoulder and winks at me before saying, "Thought I'd go commando, so you had easier access." My mouth waters at the sight of his hard cock. I try to stand tall and not give in as he disappears into the bathroom. I hear the water running and think of how hot he would look with the water cascading down his masterpiece of a body. My pussy begins to throb, fuck! Is my pride really worth it? Do I really want to win that much?

Fuck this!

I strip quickly and stride toward the shower stark naked, and my pussy fucking *flutters—* yes, I mean *flutters*—at the sight in front of me, Dom is hunched over with one hand against the wall, water cascading down his body while his other hand pumps his thick, hard cock. A gush of wetness pools between my thighs, and Dom snaps his gaze to me. I see his nostrils flare, and I know he can smell how wet I am. I can't drag this out any longer. I open the glass panel and step in. Dom doesn't stop stroking his cock as he turns to face me. My tongue darts out to moisten my lips. This sight will be filed away for a lonely night, because *fuck*. Dom has never looked so fucking hot.

"You gonna keep looking at it or get on your knees like a good girl and suck it." As much as I hate being told to kneel, when he says it, I want to obey him. Not because I have to, but because I *want* to. I drop to my knees and push his hand away and wrap my own around the base of his cock and start to pump him slowly. He hisses and then throws his head back. I lean forward and dart my tongue out to taste him, humming as soon as the taste of his pre cum hits my tongue. People say cocks don't taste good, but let me tell you, Dominic Silver's cock tastes fucking divine!

I wrap my lips around his cock and take him as deep as I can, but he's too large so I use my hand to pump the base of him while I suck the rest of him into my greedy mouth. Hearing his moans and pleas spurs me on. I attempt to take all of him in my mouth but my gag reflex just won't allow it. I know it turns him on to hear me choking on his cock, He grips the back of my hair and starts to fuck my face. I clench my legs together to try stop the ache between my legs, but it doesn't work. I need to touch myself. When I move my hand to rub my clit, his words stop me.

"Don't you fucking dare! I had to watch you do that already, and I'm too far gone to watch it again. When you come it will be on my cock, not by your own hand." I moan around the mouthful of cock; his dirty words just cause more liquid to gush out of me. I want his cock inside me now. If I have to wait any longer, I just might fucking cry. The ache between my legs is so intense, my clit is that swollen it would only take a couple of flicks and I'll be crying out my release. Minutes later, Dom grips my hair and pulls hard enough for me to release his dick with a popping sound. I look at him and see he is smiling down at me; I must look like shit. With the amount of times I've choked on his cock, I can feel spit running down my chin and through my cleavage, but the look on his face tells me he doesn't give a fuck. He releases my hair and helps me to my feet, and then he spins me around so my back is to him.

"Place both your hands on the wall and bend over." I do as he says. "Good girl, now lift this leg." I lift my right leg, which he grips and hoists it higher. "Fuck, your pussy looks so good baby." I blush; he may think it's pretty, but I still think they look like oysters. Dom doesn't warn me, he just buries himself so deep that I swear I can feel him hitting my collarbone.

He slams into me over and over again, and I can feel my orgasm right there on the horizon, but it's still out of reach. I feel his cock swelling inside me and know he's close. I need to fucking come, but I can't!

"Dom–"

"I know, I got you babe." He snakes his hand around and begins to rub my clit, and seconds later, we're both crying out our release. Dom screams my name like I'm the answer to his prayers. Feeling him inside me and knowing that I am the one who brings him so much pleasure fills me with pride. I find it so amazing that I, Sophia Stone, can give this God of a man so much pleasure. The more I am around him and the more time I spend with him, the harder and faster I am falling in love. I have never given anyone this type of power over me; I swore I would never let a man have power over me after what I endured from Randall. I just hope that with the amount of power I have freely given to Dom, that he doesn't burn me with it.

CHAPTER 48

Dominic

After a good night's sleep we quickly dress. I'm eager to check on my dad to worry about a shower. Soph, being the amazing woman that she is, decides the same. Dad has recovered well, and nearly back to full health. Dad, Soph, and I grab some breakfast from the mess hall and meet up with the others out the back. Jax, Kai, Lucian, and Aurora stand there to one side. I'm in shock to see Nico and Ryan emerging from the woods. They look like shit: Nico's eyes are bloodshot from lack of sleep and Ryan looks like she's barely able to stand from exhaustion. I feel so bad for them; they must have spent the night talking to her grandparents and just got back now. The closer we get to the group, I notice Jax, Lucian, and Kai's faces scrunching up. It doesn't hit me what that look means until Nico snaps his gaze toward me and glares. I break out into laughter and clap Nico on the shoulder, but he slaps my hand away like it's riddled with germs. The three girls look confused. My dad, being the gentleman that he is, hasn't said anything this morning when Soph and I checked on him.

Lucian whispers, "Is that smell because—."

"Yes!" Nico snaps, and I turn toward Lucian and shrug.

"How do you think you were conceived?" Lucian shudders and scrunches his eyes closed while shaking his head.

"What the hell is going on?" Sophia demands. I turn to my mate and smile sheepishly.

"Maybe next time we shouldn't skip the shower, aye?" Soph cocks her head to the side, confused as fuck.

"Oh, *oh!*" I turn to see Nico whispering in Ryan's ear, a devilish smile spread across her face. She points to me and says, "Huh, now the shoes on the other foot!" I smile and shake my head, but my attention is drawn back to Soph when she groans and places her hands on her hips. I turn and rest my hands on her shoulders, kneeling down slightly so we're eye to eye.

"Don't be mad babe, they're just fucking prudes. Nico's salty cause he didn't get laid, Jax is always uptight 'cause he has blue balls, and Kai.... well, Kai is always a broody bastard."

My head whips forward when some asshole slaps the back of it, and I turn to see who the fuck it is and to my shock it's Aurora! The tiny woman stands there with her hands on her hips, glaring up at me. I rub the back of my head.

"You know, for a pocket-size woman, you pack quite the slap." She narrows her eyes at me; clearly she isn't in a laughing mood.

"You can be such a...such a..."

"Charmer?" I say, and the frown leaves her face as she smiles wide.

"You can be such a fucktard! That was so rude. Jackson's balls are fine, thank you very much."

As soon as the words come out of her mouth, Aurora's eyes round to the size of plates and a blush coats her pale cheeks. I turn to see Jax staring at her with his mouth hanging open. I look between them for a while and then the penny drops—no fucking way!

"How do *you* know that his balls are fine love?" Jackson's

growl doesn't deter me; I have to know what the hell happened between them. Aurora swore she wouldn't mate with him until the threat on his life was taken care of.

"Well...It's just–" Jax cut in to save Aurora from floundering.

"That's none of your fucking business! We ain't telling you shit, you're the biggest gossip here." I feign shock and clamp a hand over my heart, jutting my bottom lip out in a pout.

"Soph, Jackson hurt my feelings!"

"Oh, grow the fuck up Dominic, you're being a little dick." I hear Dad groan; he appalls all this swearing. I turn to Nico and smile, the smug look drops from his face— he knows I'm about to say something that he's gonna hate hearing.

"Your *sister* can vouch that my dick is anything but little." I turn to Soph to see her smiling at her brother. "Tell him I'm not little babe." I can see the laughter in her eyes; she's enjoying how uncomfortable this conversation is making her overbearing brother.

"I swear to God, if you answer that Sophia, mate or hugacko or whatever the fuck he is to you, I will still beat his face. Dominic, you asshole, keep your fucking dick away from my sister." I don't get a chance to answer; Lucian beats me to it.

"Keep your dick away from my best friend, and then he'll stop doing the wild thing with my mom." Silence.

Dead. Fucking. Silence.

Kai breaks the silence when he snort laughs, Jax and dad follow suit, then we're all laughing. Lucian gets his quick wit from me, that's for damn sure. The laughter helps us all relax, but I won't be deterred. After the laughter dies down, I focus back on Aurora, who refuses to meet my gaze. I look to Jax and there's a warning in his eyes not to push it. I know this is hard for the seer, so I want to make the situation easier for her. I reach out and lift her chin till her gaze meets mine, full of guilt and shame. I smile sadly at her. I understand her situation more than she knows.

"Don't hide from it love, I know it's hard. I fought it for nearly eighteen years, and I'm lucky enough that she even gives me the time of day. Jackson is a big boy and a strong as fuck alpha, but he also has a heart. He is trying so hard to be patient with you–" Jax tries to cut in, but Aurora raises her hand to silence him.

"From the moment he learned the truth of who you are to him, he has devoted all his time and effort to make you happy. He may not tell you, but he has been trying to find the threat on his life for months so you would finally let him in. Don't keep pushing him away love, it will not only hurt him...but you as well." Aurora pushes my hand away and hugs me. I stand there stunned for a moment. Sophia smiles and nods her head encouragingly, and I wrap my arms around the seer and return her embrace. I'm a bit standoffish to touch her after last time, so when she moves away from me, I release the breath I was holding. Aurora walks over to Jackson and stops in front of him.

"We should talk." Jax nods his head, clearly at a loss for words. She grips Jackson's hand and pulls him toward the back of the building, and just before they open the door, Aurora turns back and shouts my name.

"Yeah?" I yell back.

"I know what his balls look like because I have seen them every night for the past two weeks." I choke on air. How the fuck did I not know this? How did I miss the signs? A hand landing on my shoulder pulls me from my thoughts.

"Believe it or not, sometimes there are things that you don't know." I glare at Kai. He always found so much happiness in my shortcomings. I shrug his hand off and go to Soph, who opens her arms and cradles my head against her shoulder. I hear Nico moaning behind me but ignore him. I was gonna grope Soph's ass just to piss him off, but thought better of that when I remember Lucian is present.

"Is he always like this?"

"Like what?" my dad replies.

"An overgrown baby?" I pull out of Soph's embrace and spin around to glare at my smirking son.

"Thank you, Karma," I hear my dad whisper gleefully, and turn my glare on him.

"Boy, for years I wanted you to get a taste of your own medicine, and finally my prayers have been answered."

Lucian laughs.

"You won't be laughing for long, shithead, now get ready to shift." All traces of laughter die from Lucian's face. When a look of fear passes his eyes, I feel like shit, and Soph shoulder-checks me on her way to him. Yeah, I deserve that.

"You will be fine, I promise. Your dad and grandfather won't let anything bad happen to you." Lucian swallows loudly then nods. It is time.

It's still strange referring to myself and Dom as mom and dad to Lucian. I think it will take some time getting used to that. Lucian still doesn't call us mom and dad to our faces, but I have heard him refer to us as that to other people. It fills my heart with joy when I hear him say *mom*; he may not say it to me directly, but hearing that word out of his mouth makes me feel light as air.

"Okay, it will be easier if you strip down to your boxers. That way your wolf won't have to shred your clothes." Lucian nods his head robotically at Dom, his muscles tense and worry lines are creasing his face. I have never seen a wolf shift for the first time, let alone the wolf being my son. Nerves wrack my body, but I trust Dom and his dad to keep him safe. I know Dom will do whatever it takes to make sure this process is as painless as possible. An arm wraps around my shoulders, and I look up to see Kai smiling down at me.

"He'll be fine So-So, Dom's got this under control." Kai's words fill me with a renewed sense of hope.

"Lucian is part fae, warlock, and shifter. Does that mean *he* is the strongest supe?" I turn to Ryan; I know she isn't asking because she worries someone will be stronger than her. She's asking out of curiosity.

"Nah little one, from what I can tell, Luce can only access his fae and shifter side, same as Do–his dad." Hearing my brother, of all people, refer to Dom as Lucian's father, causes tears to gather in my eyes. Nico turns to me and smiles; I know that took a lot for him to say. He doesn't like the idea of his little sister being with his best friend, but he knows he doesn't have a say, Dom and I have a child together, and he is my *hugacko* and I am his mate.

"You need to center yourself. Close your eyes and feel deep inside of you. Can you feel your wolf?" Mr. Silver asks Luce.

"I-I think so."

"What does it feel like?"

"Like it wants to be free, it wants out. He's anxious and worried."

"That's good. Pull on the tether that binds you to your wolf. Allow your wolf control." Mr. Silver is so calm and in control; a quick glance at Dom tells me he's stressing. I want to go to him and tell him Lucian will be okay, but I can't get my feet to move.

"Arggghh!" Lucian hunches forward and drops to his knees. He then pitches forward and quickly puts his hands out to break his fall. Lucian screams out again as I see his shoulder pop. Then his elbow breaks, and he screams again. Dom takes a step toward Lucian when Mr. Silver cuts him off.

"Leave him be son, he has to go through this." Dom grabs chunks of his hair and starts to pull as Lucian cries out again, his other shoulder pops. Tear's flow down my face as I watch my son writhe in agony. Kai's grip tightens holding me in place.

"Dad, please, I can't watch him suffer like this."

"You must, Dominic!"

"Dad, he's hurting!" Dom shouts.

"Think as an alpha, not as his father!" Dom stills then

stands taller, his dad's words finally registering. "Go to him as his alpha, as a guide, but not as his father Dom." Dom nods his head and moves past his father. Lucian is curled in a fetal position on the ground. Movement to my right catches my eye, and it's Nico holding Ryan back. She's trying to go to Lucian. Tear's stain her cheeks just like mine. Dom kneels down near Lucian's head and strokes his hair.

"Don't fight it son, let your wolf come. Allow him control and then the pain will stop."

"It hurts so much." I can hear the pain in Lucian's voice, and my heart aches.

"I know, let go now son."

"I can't!" Lucian screams, and Dom looks up at me and mouths, *forgive me*. His eyes change from violet to pure gray, his wolf now in control. He turns back to Lucian, and rises up, and looks down at our son.

"Let go now!" Lucian's screams die off, and his bones pop so fast I can't keep up. He's silent, no screams of pain coming. I try to move toward him, but Kai holds me back. Dom turns his head and growls, black hairs dotting his arms. Holy fuck, Dom's about to shift.

"Release her now Melakai." Kai releases me and moves back raising his hands at Mr. Silver's command. Once Kai is a fair distance away, Dom turns his attention back to Lucian. White fur dots his body and Dom begins to strip his clothes off. I look for Dom's father and see him standing next to me.

"Why is Dom shifting?" Sad green eyes stare down at me.

"Dom needs to make him submit; I don't know whether my son has told you or not, but by him doing this for Lucian, he is becoming the one thing he *never* wanted to be." A gasp from my other side snags my attention—it's Nico.

"Holy fuck, he's really doing it. What will happen between him and Jax?"

"The seer's departure with the alpha isn't random son. Jax and Dom will have to learn to work together, or they can never be near each other."

"No offense, Mr. Silver, but can someone please explain to me what the hell is going on?" Ryan takes the words right out of my mouth.

"In order for Lucian not to be locked to Jackson's pack, he has to have another alpha to claim him. I refused, so Dominic has no choice but to step up and claim his son as his pack, or Lucian will be a pack less rogue. Dom's wolf will never allow Jackson to claim his pup; this is the only way."

"So Dom and Luce will be a pack of two?" Ryan is on a roll and clearly reading my mind somehow.

"Yes love, something like that." My attention is drawn back to my mate and our son when snarls erupt. Dom has now shifted into his massive black wolf, a sight to see. Pure black with gray eyes, he's triple the size of a normal wolf. I look to Lucian to see his hands and feet are now paws. His body had taken on the shape of a wolf, and then my eyes land on his face, I see he is now all wolf. He is Dominic's complete opposite: Lucian is pure white with violet eyes.

They were both huge; Dom is half a size bigger than his son, but Lucian still wasn't small like you would think a young pup would be. Dom begins to circle the shaky young wolf, who can't get his balance. He has no idea how to move on four legs, and I want to help him. It's up to Dom to teach our son.

Lucian tries to follow Dom's movements but keeps stumbling, and Dom begins to growl.

"What's happening?" I ask.

"Dom is giving Lucian the chance to submit willingly." I sense a *but* coming. "If Lucian doesn't willingly submit, Dom will force him to."

"How?"

"Fight love. If Dominic doesn't gain the upper hand and become Lucian's alpha, then it will mean that Jackson will have to step in and claim him. He will be bound to Jackson's pack and have to remain here." I understand now why Dom didn't want that; he didn't want Jackson to have any say over our son's life. I hope and cross my fingers that Lucian submits willingly. Dom approaches Lucian, snarling and growling low in his throat, and my heart sinks when Lucian's haunches raise and he begins to growl back. Dom doesn't pause—he keeps advancing on Lucian, his growls intensifying when they are nearly nose to nose. Dom stretches his head higher and growls loudly. Lucian tried to growl back but couldn't match his father's volume. Tense minutes pass as Dom snaps his jaws at Lucian, and I start to worry that this is going to end badly. Finally, Lucian surprises me—he lowers his head, then bows to Dom. Dom circles him while he remains in that position and suddenly lunges toward the submitting white wolf.

I can't let her screams affect me; I clamp my jaws around his hind leg. He lets out a loud howl and then begins to whimper. I release his leg when a sensation I can't even begin to explain spreads throughout my body; it feels like my mind is being invaded, and then I hear a voice.

What the hell?

Lucian?

Dad? My heart swells at the word dad.

You can hear me?

Yeah, when you bit me, a strange feeling overtook me then I felt you in my head.

It worked!

What worked?

The alpha bond, I wasn't sure if it would work, but I'm glad it did.

Lucian spins around and growls at me.

You didn't know if it would work or not?

I try not to react at the anger in his tone.

Your grandfather told me it would work. I couldn't let you be claimed by Jax.

Why not?

Because you're my son Lucian, if anyone is going to make you submit and be your alpha, it was always going to be me. I will teach you everything that my dad taught me. I will fuck this up Lucian, I'm not perfect, but I will try my fucking hardest to be the best dad I can be for you.

How do I shift back?

My heart deflates at his blatant brush off. I explain to him what to do, minutes later we're standing in front of each other, butt naked and on two legs.

"This moment turned out differently in my head," Lucian says as he chuckles, and I cock my head to the side. "I wanted to shift back so I could give you a hug and tell you that I would like that, but I kind of don't feel like touching *dong* to *dong*, if you get my drift." I break out into a fit of laughter, he fucking *for sure gets* his humor from me.

Soph makes her way over to us, and I smile at her and open my arms for a cuddle, but I am in fucking shock when she slaps me clean across the face! Gasp's ring out from the guys, as I cup my cheek and glare down at her.

"The fuck was that for Sophia?" I grit out. She places her hands on her hips and narrows her eyes at me.

"The next time you fucking bite my son I will cut your fucking dick off and make you eat it!" I reel back in shock and quickly cover my dick.

"I had to do it!"

"What the hell for, Dom?"

"To form the fucking alpha link, you crazy minx." It takes her a minute to figure out what I mean, I see the moment it finally clicks. Her eyes round and a blush begins to coat her cheeks. Still butt hurt that she hit me, I move past her to join Lucian and start getting dressed. Once I finish, I walk with Lucian to join the others. Ryan immediately wraps my boy in a hug when we get close. I smile at them. I love the bond that they share, and I'm glad Lucian has Ryan. Sophia comes over and joins us, and I chose to be the mature one, so I ignore her. I feel her gaze on me but don't acknowledge her. I'm fucking pissed that she doesn't trust me and thought I would seriously attack my son!

"You did good Luce, I am so freaking proud of you!" Lucian beams down at Ryan, and it's probably just me, but I'm sure I saw him puff out his chest a little.

"Thanks Smurf."

Everyone retreated inside to the mess hall, Lucian and I both needed food after shifting. We burn through a shit load of calories every time we shift. After eating our body weight in food, we all head to Jax's office. Once inside, Ryan's phone rings, and she excuses herself and leaves the office. Jax and Aurora are both freshly showered, and I grin from ear to ear.

"Not a fucking word Dominic." I wave my hands around and feign hurt.

"Why do you always assume I'm going to say something?" Jax cocks one brow at me and gives the *are you for real* look. "Okay, point taken." Me being me, I can't *not* poke fun at him.

"I would have thought a good roll in the hay might have loosened you up a little." Kai shakes his head, Nico groans, Dad and Lucian ignore me. I refuse to look toward Sophia, but Jax is on his feet and coming at me. He pauses a few feet from me and drops into a fighting stance. I stand there and stare at him, confused.

"Why do you smell like an alpha Dom? My wolf doesn't like it." Oh Shit! I look to my dad for guidance, and he moves around the couch and comes to stand beside me.

"He claimed Lucian and made his own pack. By doing so he has appeased his wolf and will now no longer need to uphold his vow to become alpha of the New York pack." Now I turn to my dad with my mouth hanging open. *I never fucking knew that.*

"Why the hell didn't you fucking tell me?" Dad scowls at me.

"Watch your bloody language boy! I didn't tell you because I didn't want it to be a factor in your decision. I wanted you to choose it for you and your son, not because it got you out of leading the pack you hate most!" Well, when he says it like that, it makes sense. Jackson's growls pulls our attention back to him, and I sigh.

"I am getting really fucking tired of everyone growling, snapping, shouting and hitting me. Can't we all just get along?"

"You start half the fucking trouble!" I turn to give Kai a piece of my mind, but stop short when the office door opens and Ryan walks in. Ryan looks around the room and notices Jax's position. Nico fills her in on what's happening.

"That's gonna have to wait Jax, can you hold off on your wolfy drama? My uncle and cousins need to speak with us in regards to the moonstones." Aurora is on her feet and in front of Jackson in seconds. She whispers something in his ear, which makes him pull back and relax. Thank fuck.

"Do you want me to open a portal for them?"

"Yes please." Nico turns and opens a portal at his wife's request, and a couple of minutes later, Chase, Alex, David, and Mya step through. Everyone greets the newcomers and then we all settle on the couches. Sophia sits on the couch opposite me—

I still won't look at her. The silence in the room is deafening. I hate awkward silence and bite my tongue to stop myself from blurting out some stupid shit.

"I vote that we put Sophia in a time out!" Yeah, that didn't work out so well.

"The fuck?" Soph snaps at me, and being the grown ass man that I am, I ignore her and look around the room, hoping someone will back me up. Instead, I find half the room trying to mask their bloody smiles. The new arrivals seem perplexed.

"Stop pouting Dom, you're mated to her, so get used to it!"

"Fuck you Nico, she hit me," I growl out.

"Dominic, stop cussing!" I turn to glare at my dad.

"Suck it old man, you didn't protect me! You stood by and let the little Tasmanian devil slap me."

"That, my boy, is called Karma!" I growl at the old fool.

"I thought you hurt him." I turn back to Sophia to see her seething with anger, and I move so I'm standing in front of her. Not one to be intimidated, she rises to her feet, and we're chest to chest—well, her head to my chest. I see Nico move to intervene but is stopped by Ryan.

"Next time fucking ask before you start throwing hands." Soph throws her arms out wide and yells.

"How was I supposed to know?"

"You didn't bloody well ask, did ya?"

"You hit me all the time!" Growl's break out around the room, and I quickly turn to scan their faces and see all the guys, including Lucian, wearing looks of anger.

"Rephrase that shit now before a fight breaks out." I snap at my mate. Her eyes dart around the room then settles back on me.

"It's true though, you slap my ass nearly every time I walk past you!" I smile devilishly down at her, and her eyes narrow.

"Your ass pretty much has a sign on it that reads *slap me*

Dom, how am I supposed to ignore that?" Soph groans and plops down into the couch.

"The next time you lay a hand on my sister I will fucking break your face!" I turn to a seething Nico and grin.

"Your sister loves it when I slap her ass, she's just salty because I called her out on being a bit of a psycho today." A slap lands on the back of my head, turning around I find it's Soph. I pull my lip back and snarl at her, and Chase makes a move to grab her and pull her away from me. I face him and growl loudly in warning.

"You lay one fucking finger on *my mate* I will rip your fucking arm off little Knox." Chase drops his arm but doesn't step back. I focus back on my handsy mate. "That is the second time you have hit me today, you vicious little crow. Do it again and I promise I will take your punishment out on your body." Soph blanches, and I hear murmurs around the room but ignore them.

"The fuck does that mean?" I don't turn to face the brooding king of the fae, instead I smile down at his sister. The look in my eyes has her standing up straight.

"That I won't let my little mate enjoy her orgasm for a long, *long* time."

"Oh, for the love of God, please stop. I have been a wolf for an hour and now that my senses are heightened, I cannot deal with the scent you are both putting out." Sophia blushes at Lucian's admission. I, on the other hand preen like a proud peacock. One point to Dom, zero to Sophia.

CHAPTER 51

After Dom returns to his seat, I drop down into mine and refuse to make eye contact with anyone. Maybe I was out of line, hitting him not once but *twice*. I really thought he hurt Lucian, and the second time he deserved it because he was being an ass! I can tell from how relaxed and smug he looks that he feels pretty proud of himself for winning that little squabble. I hope he doesn't mean it he wouldn't really not let me orgasm, right?

"I don't have a lot of time, so if you don't mind can we get on with this, please?" David Knox's voice pulls me from my inner turmoil. I have to get my head in the game. According to Randall, we have forty-eight hours, and we are already nearly down a day, so we have to focus.

"Please, enlighten us David, on your knowledge of the moonstones." Gone is Dom's joking old man, he changes to the leader of the shifter council now.

"Okay, after the day of Ryan's wedding, the moonstones were returned to the coven. Stevie had no use for them after capturing Ryan; they didn't diminish her power, so she was happy to give them up. We took all thirteen stones back and buried them atop Knox Mountain. I checked this morning and all thirteen remain there. I have no idea how Randall acquired more stones, as far as my father and I were aware, there were only ever thirteen stones in existence." What the fuck? How the hell did Randall get more?

"So does that mean someone made more?" David turns to face his niece.

"That is the only explanation, but in order for that to happen, someone has to be bloody strong, I mean like have the same amount of power as you, strong." Gasps ring out around the room. Ryan is the strongest supe ever. So who the hell else is able to make such a weapon?

"If Smurf didn't do it, then who did?" David turns to face Lucian, a solemn look on his face. The look in his eyes sets me on edge.

"My sons tell me that you were held captive with Ryan?" Lucian nods. "Did they ever draw blood from you?" Lucian scratches his head and closes his eyes, trying to remember.

"When I was younger, they did, it stopped when I was around fourteen years old." David hangs his head and releases a long exhale before turning back to Ryan.

"Your blood is strong enough to grant vamps the ability to walk in the daylight. But your blood isn't strong enough on its own; I believe Randall kept Lucian prisoner for a reason." Dom and I are on our feet in an instant, the others follow.

"If you know something about my son and why he was held, I suggest you don't keep us waiting." Dom sounds more animal than man, his eyes flickering to gray. I move beside him and interlock my fingers with his, trying to calm him. A second passes before he tightens his grip on my hand.

"In order to create moonstones my father told me you need the blood of four races, Fae, wolf, witch and vampire–."

"Lucian and I aren't vampires so our blood wouldn't have

worked." David smiles sadly at Ryan before he turns his gaze to Kai and says, "But he is." Kai's eyes round in shock.

"I didn't do shit!" Kai snaps.

"I know that, Kai; in order for the stones to be made, those whose blood was used have to be linked but unaware. I believe Randall has been trying to make the stones for years to try and overthrow the council. He would never have been able to make them with ordinary blood."

"What do you mean Dad?" Alex asks.

"Melakai is the first fae to ever be turned into a vampire; his blood is special. Lucian is the first trifecta: fae, warlock, and wolf. Ryan is the first ever fae and witch mix. Aside from Dominic, Ryan is the only one who is able to access both sides of her magic, or so we thought until we found Lucian."

"So what you're saying is because they are the first of their kinds, their blood is able to make the stones?" I ask David, he nods.

"Why doesn't Randall use mine or Sophia's, then?"

"Because Dom, Sophia can only access one side of her power. Plus, when would Randall ever have had the chance to draw blood from you?" The man has a point there—the fae magic I use isn't my own, it's Dom's. My blood would never have been any good to him.

"Holy fuck!" Kai whispers, but the force of his words is almost like he shouts it.

"What's wrong Kai?" Mya asks, but Kai doesn't meet her gaze. He looks from Lucian to Dom and then finally settles his gaze on me.

"That's why he took him So-So. He kept him prisoner so he could have access to his blood at all times." I dug my nails into Dom's hand, but he doesn't pull away.

"That means he's been planning this for years; Randall isn't that smart." Dom says.

"He may not be smart, but he is cunning." Kai's got that right.

"Wait a second, so Randall knew Dom was Lucian's father?" Dom gave my hand a gentle squeeze, offering me his silent support. I turn and address my overbearing brother.

"He didn't know at first, I hid it from him."

"Who the hell's kid did he think it was then?"

"I told him I had a one-night stand." Nico scrunches his face up in disgust; it wasn't my best lie, but it was the one I had told.

"How did he find out who Dom is to Lucian?" I straighten and look my brother in the eye.

"When he came to take the baby, I screamed and yelled and told him that I lied. I knew who the father was, and he would kill him when he found out. He started laughing until I told him that the father was Dom."

"What happened after that?" I look to Kai, and he answers for me.

"He brought back a dead baby's body and told her that the baby died." Gasp's ring out again around the room, and my brother looks at me with so much sadness. I have to change the subject ASAP.

"So, what do we do now? How do we destroy the moonstones?" David's face takes on a somber look, that look sends dread pooling in my belly.

"*If* we are right, and I mean it is a big *if*, we will need Kai, Lucian, and Ryan's blood to perform a spell."

"That sounds easy enough," comments Ryan, but the look on Mya, Chase, Alex, and David's faces tells me that this spell isn't as simple as we think.

"A spell this big comes with a price dear." Ryan, Lucian, and Kai exchange a look among themselves before Lucian asks.

"What price?"

"We don't know; one of you will pay the price for it."

"Well, that doesn't sound very appealing." I agree with Jackson.

"When you say *price*, do you mean like we die or—?" I can hear a bit of fear in Lucian's tone. I can't let him do this.

"I mean, it could be you might lose your hair, or magic, or a chance to have a child of your own. I really don't know, and even if we do it, I can still be wrong. This is a huge gamble for you three to take." We sit here for hours talking about the spell and trying to form a plan, I come up with the best plan, but Dom, Nico, and Kai don't like it. Dom is so mad that he won't look at me or even answer me when I speak. I know he's only angry because he worried for my safety, but this is the only way to get Randall out in the open and try to get the upper hand. If we wait the forty-eight hours, then it will be on his terms, not ours.

By the time we finish forming a plan, it's late, and everyone makes their way to the mess hall, but I'm not hungry so I chose to retire to my–our—room and wait for Dom to get back so we can talk.

CHAPTER 52

Dominic

I push the food around my plate, my appetite long gone. I only followed the others here because I don't want to be alone with Sophia. I would say some dumb shit and hurt her. She came up with a good plan, I admit, but the fucking plan puts her in harm's way. I know Nico is with me and so is Kai...I think. They both agree to help come up with a different plan, but we keep coming up short. None of our ideas will work, but I won't give up hope.

"Stop pouting and go to her and try and fix this Dom." I look up and meet Ryan's gaze. She truly is beautiful. Long brown hair, strange green eyes, but most of all, her personality makes her beautiful. Nico totally doesn't deserve her.

"And how do you propose I fix this love? She won't listen to me."

"Try Dom. Don't give up on her; she has been through enough." I slam my hand down on the table and scowl at Ryan; she has no fucking right. Nico jumps to his feet, but I choose to ignore him.

"You don't think I fucking know that? She has been through more shit than any of us can ever relate to. I am trying to keep the mother of my fucking child safe and yet all you lot have done is agree to her stupid fucking plan!" Ryan lowers her gaze, and guilt weighs on me. I meet Nico's eyes and I can see he's torn.

"So, what now, you agree? I should just let her go through with this?"

"You don't fucking own my sister Dominic!" I'm on my feet now, my magic surging inside of me, yellow ribbons swirling around my hands and arms. Nico let his magic unfurl, emitting purple light. The others scoot back from the table to get out of the firing range. Lucian stays close by me, as Ryan does by Nico.

"She is my mate!"

"You fucking rejected her!" I release a long and loud growl. I'm tired of hearing that same line over and fucking over.

"I did it to keep her fucking safe."

"You're a fucking coward! Because of you my sister was taken from me!" I snap, like proper snap. I launch a yellow energy ball at Nico so fast he doesn't have time to react, and I erect a dome around him and me to keep the others out. Ryan can probably break it, but it's worth a try. Nico is back on his feet and charging at me. He launches purple energy balls at me, and I keep flicking them away, but one manages to clip me on the shoulder and it fucking hurt! I block the pain out and focus on fucking my best friend up. He needs to learn his fucking place.

"She is mine, she always has been!" I yell as I throw ball after ball at Nico; he retaliates, and a few of mine manage to knock him down. The last ball we throw at each other has us both on our asses. We sit there, staring at each other, panting and sweating. My body fucking aches, my shirt and jeans are torn and singed from the energy balls. Tense minutes pass as we sit here glaring at each other.

"Do you love her?" I don't miss a beat.

"More than my own life."

"Why then Dom, why did you hide it from me?" I can hear the hurt lacing his tone, and it's about time I was honest with my best friend.

"Because you were right, I was a coward. I was scared that loving her would cause her more harm than good. I never told you because I was afraid of what you would think."

"Dominic, you're my brother, my best friend. You piss me off more than anyone, but I will never not be supportive of my sister ending up with you. I know you like I know myself; I know you can keep her safe."

"Then why the fuck are you being an ass?"

"Because I'm hurt you hid it from me you dick! I said I was okay with you two being together, but that doesn't mean I want to know about you boning my fucking sister!" I laugh, and a second later Nico joins me. I climb to my feet and make my way over to him, extending my hand to him. He looks at it for a moment and then finally accepts my help up.

"I'm sorry I lied to you." locking eyes with his so he can see the seriousness in my eyes.

"And I'm sorry for this." Nico's fist connects with my cheek. I stumble back a few steps and rub the side of my face. I turn and glare at the smirking fucking bastard.

"The fuck was that for, you fuck face?" He grins and brushes invisible lint from his shoulder as he says.

"For sleeping with my sister and not telling me about it. Also, for knocking her up, you fucktard."

"I didn't fucking know she was pregnant!"

"Use protection, you dumbass."

"You should be fucking thanking me!" Nico's brows lower in confusion.

"Why the fuck would I thank you for knocking my sister up?" It's my turn to smirk and brush my shoulder off.

"Because thanks to my magical swimmers, your wife has a shield." Nico opens his mouth to reply then shuts it. I laugh at his expense, and he's muttering under his breath about killing me in my sleep. One point to Dom and zero to the asshole king.

I leave the mess hall after ensuring everyone that I'm okay, wanting to shower and change. Lucian insists on accompanying me back, and how can I say no to him? Plus, I want to talk to him anyway to make sure he's cool with doing this spell. One of the three of them will pay a price. The catch is, we have no idea which one of them it will be. As we approach my room, I take a few deep breaths and brace myself for the argument that I know is coming. Soph is as stubborn as her brother; she won't let this go without a fight. I open the door and I'm stunned to see the lights are out. I dart my eyes toward to the bed and see that Soph is fast asleep. I sigh, I won't be able to sleep with how things are between us. I turn to Lucian and see him staring at his mother's sleeping form, a range of emotions flitting across his face before it finally settles on determination.

"No matter what it costs me, I won't let her do this. I'll pay any price ten times over just to ensure she remains safe." I stand there gaping at my son, watching how mature and wise he seems in this moment. I slap him on the shoulder and squeeze.

"I won't ask you to pay any price. If I could trade places with you, I would. I will protect you and her with my life. I will never let any harm come to you or your mother if I can help it Lucian." I wrap my arms around him and pull him to me for a hug. At first, he's a bit stiff and unsure, but after a minute he relaxes and then returns my embrace. This is a moment I will never forget for the rest of my life. I'm holding my only child in my arms and fuck, it feels good. The more I'm ~~was~~ around Lucian the more my emotions and feelings are growing toward him. I'm already protective over him. Lucian pulls out of my embrace and smiles before saying goodnight and that he will see us in the morning. I agreed that Soph and I would wait here for him; he wants to speak to her before we meet with the others tomorrow. Sighing, I strip off my ruined clothing and head to the bathroom to grab a quick shower. I know sleep will elude me; my mind is running away with me with all the things that could go wrong with Soph's plan.

CHAPTER 53

I wake the next morning feeling like I haven't slept. I tossed and turned all night I roll over and find Dom's side of the bed empty, and when I slipped my hands under the covers, it was cold. I don't think he even came to bed last night. Sighing, I sit up and startled when I see him sitting at the end of the bed, staring at me. His eyes are bloodshot, and black rings are forming under his eyes. I don't think he slept a wink last night. Hating this tension between us, I decide to make the first move and try to smooth things over before we go ahead with my plan today. I crawl down to him and straddle his lap, and he sits there with no movement. I grab his hands and place them on my waist and cup both his cheeks, I lift his head until his tired violet eyes meet my own. Dom's eyes show you everything he's feeling, and right now I can see he's scared, not for himself but for me.

"Don't do this little dove, please." He's pleading for me to listen, but I can't not this time. I want to end this so that we can finally be free of Randall. I don't want to continue to live while looking over my shoulder—what life is that? I'm not the only one; we've all been hunting him since the battle at Lake William. My brother has doubled the guards on Lachlan and

Victor to make sure Randall doesn't try to break them out of their human prison. Our lives have been so focused on tracking Randall that we have all forgotten what a normal life is like. I don't want that anymore. I want to live and enjoy life with my friends, my family, my son, and the love of my life. I have to do this. I want Randall gone so I can start to work on myself and heal. I still struggle some days—memories assault me randomly—so when this is finally over, I will meet with the healer Nina has been seeing to try to help myself move past my trauma.

"I can't keep living like this Dom, I don't want this threat hanging over us any longer. I love you Dominic Silver, and I would do anything for you and our son, but please don't ask me not to do this. I have to do this so I can keep you and Lucian safe. He won't stop Dom. We have to stop him now." Dom's eyes slam shut and he exhales loudly, his shoulders hunch. I hold my breath as I wait for him to reply, his hands tighten around my waist. I lean forward and rest my forehead against his.

"I can't lose you little dove. I can't live in a world where you don't exist." Tears gather in my eyes. I can hear the sincerity in his voice. I know he's scared, but so am I.

"You won't lose me! I'm scared to live in a world where Randall is free. I have to finish this Dom. I love you for wanting to protect me, but I'm a big girl, and I need you to trust me." Our eyes lock, conveying what we can't, the fear of finally getting to be together and just to be torn apart. Dom closes his eyes.

"I do trust you little dove, I just don't like this plan. I don't want you to use yourself as bait, we can find another wa–."

"No, we don't have the time for another plan. This is the best one we have and the only one that will take him by surprise." Dom doesn't get a chance to reply— a knock sounds at the door. Dom sighs but doesn't release me, he shouts for whoever it is to come in. When the door opens, and I turn to see who it is, I leap off Dom's lap like it's on fire. The asshole just sits there and grins while I turn a shade of red. I avert my gaze, so I don't have to look Lucian in the eyes; I'm beyond embarrassed to be caught in such a compromising position by my own *son*.

"Okay, so, three things: One, eww. Two, don't ever say come in when she is sitting on your lap, that is something I never want to see." Dom chuckles. Thanks to his wolfy senses, he *knew* it was Lucian knocking on the door. Lucian turns to stare at me with a somber look on his face, and I tense in anticipation.

"Three, you have the best plan there is–" Dom growls. "–*But* it isn't the safest. *If* we go through with this spell to nullify the moonstones, then that leaves him vulnerable. I agree to this plan *only* if Smurf and I accompany you–."

"No!" Dom snaps as he launches to his feet.

"Smurf and I are the strongest supes here! We can take him. If you, Nico, and everyone follow us, she will never get close enough to draw his blood." I cock my head to the side, confused.

"Then who will do the spell, if David isn't with me?" Lucian squares his shoulders, a look of determination in his eyes.

"Me and Smurf."

"You can't access your warlock side, can you?" Dom sounds taken back by Lucian's declaration, and I must admit, I am too.

"No one knows this—Smurf has been helping, as you both know." Dom and I nod. "I can't access the elements, but I do have the power to cast spells."

"All fae can," Dom replies, but Luce shakes his head.

"I can cast spells from nature. I can manipulate the elements, but I can't call them to me like a witch or warlock. Trust me, I can do this." Lucian and Dom are locked in an intense stare off. Dom growls and starts to pace the open space between me and Lucian, tugging on the roots of his hair.

"What am I supposed to do then, huh?"

"Dom—" I try to reassure him, but he cuts me off when he stops and stares down at me, the look of anguish on his face nearly bringing me to my knees. Since Dom found out Lucian is his son, his whole demeanor has changed. He isn't as cheeky or carefree as he once was. He isn't always cracking jokes and goofing off with the guys. He's grown up so much and in such a short time he is now a mated wolf, an alpha, a father, and my *hugacko*. I am so proud of the change he has made to try and prove himself worthy of me and Lucian, but what he hasn't realized yet, is that he never has to change, he is perfect the way he is.

"How am I supposed to stay behind while my mate and my son are out there in danger? I can't stay back; my wolf won't let me Sophia. Every time I hear that cunt's name, my wolf tries to gain control and hunt him. The thought of you or Lucian being near the man that hurt you both has me on the verge of losing control and saying fuck it, I'll hunt him myself." My body deflates; I can understand how he feels, but it doesn't change anything.

"I'll keep her safe. I swear on my life no harm will come to her." Dom turns to face Lucian, and to Lucian's credit, he doesn't shy away as Dom approaches him.

"You shouldn't have to, that's my job." Lucian's eyes soften.

"I know, but let me take this on, just this time. No one will think less of you, *we* won't think less of you. We know you care and want to protect the both of us, *old man*." Dom reels back and clutches his chest like he is fatally wounded, and I chuckle at his silly antic. Lucian's eyes fill with silent laughter.

"You *nearly* had me, but then you went and ruined the moment by calling me *old*! I am not fucking old; I am in my bloody prime kid. Old is your grandfather, that dude is damn well ancient as fuck." The three of us laugh, and the laughter helps lighten the mood and ease tensions. I know Dom won't let this go, and I really don't want to go behind his back. I look at Lucian, a silent conversation transpiring between us. So much determination and fierce loyalty shone in his eyes, and pride swells in my chest. I am beyond blessed to have both these amazing men in my life. Lucian is such a sweet and kind soul, and loyal to a fault. He reminds me so much of Dom: they both love fiercely and wholeheartedly, and never do anything by halves.

After changing and grabbing breakfast, the three of us met with the others out by the old chapel ruins. It's nice to gather in different surroundings instead of Jackson's office for once. Everyone stands around, stiff and alert, the tension thick in the air. A feeling of love and gratefulness suffused me. These people aren't just my friends—they are my family. Blood doesn't make you family, loyalty does.

"My uncle is preparing to do the spell; all we need is a drop of Randall's blood and then we can complete the spell." Anxiety churns inside me. I know I'm the only one that can get close enough to him for what we need.

"How is she supposed to do that babe?"

"Simple Nico, Soph will ask him for his blood to help heal her wound." Nico looks at Ryan like she's out of her mind.

"What wound?" he says as he looks over me, trying to find my injury.

"I'll cut my hand or something. Randall hates damaged goods. If he sees me with a mark or anything, he will want to remedy it straight away, so his *treasure* isn't damaged." All eyes turn to me, and Aurora's eyes are the worst to look at. She knows the truth–the whole truth. I tear my gaze from hers, so I don't get pulled down into the black abyss of my memories. No good will come of my spiraling down that dark hole right now. Randall took years of my life from me and I won't allow that filthy pig to occupy anymore of my time!

"The hell you will cut yourself, are you out of your fucking mind?" I stare at Dom for a moment, how the hell else does he think I will get his blood? Just walk up with a knife and stab him? I snort at the thought. "What the hell is that look in your eyes for, little dove?"

"How did you think I was going to get his blood? Just ask him for it?" Dom looked around at the others and then after a moment he rested his gaze back on me and shrugged his shoulders.

"Well, yeah, I kind of thought you would." I roll my eyes at him. So much for growing up.

"We stick with the plan. Ryan, Lucian, and I will go." I turn to Ryan before anyone can protest. "You're sure you can do this spell? We will only get one chance at this." Ryan doesn't hesitate for a second.

"Yes."

Dom remains quiet and stoic the rest of the conversation. Ryan, Lucian, and Kai follow David inside to start the spell and give their blood. I make sure to stay out of my own head and keep present; I engage in the conversations around me, because if I don't I know I'll spiral and old fears will win out.

"Are you sure about this Soph?"

"Yes, Aurora, I'm sure."

"I haven't had a vision to tell me how this will end. I have been trying to bring one on but due to...circumstances... my visions aren't coming as regular as they once did." I can hear the guilt in her voice; Jackson may not have marked her yet, but with Aurora falling in love with him and doing everything but completing the bond, her visions are already starting to leave her. I clasp her smaller hand in mine and squeeze.

"Aurora, do not feel guilty about loving Jackson. Your visions help us, but they are not the reason we love you and care about you. With or without visions Aurora, you are still a huge part of this group of misfits." Aurora smiles; her eyes glassy with unshed tears. I know she was more worried that if her visions were gone, we might not want her around. My gift of seeing people's love lives comes in handy sometimes.

"Do you...do you think Jax will–you know?" She speaks quietly so the others can't hear.

"Aurora, Jackson would love you no matter what. You are his fate, his soulmate. No one can live without their soul. Let him claim you and live your life. Don't waste the time you have together because of what ifs. You may not have seen it, but I have—he will love you till the end of his days." I've seen their happily ever after. Aurora just needs to take the final leap and let Jax mark her.

I trail behind Soph, who says she needs to change before meeting up with Luce and Ryan. I voiced my disgruntlement over the fact that Soph needed to *show more* in order to make Randall more compliant. I slam the door shut behind us as we enter our room, and I'm breathing fast and hard. Sophia ignores me and walks straight toward the closet, returning moments later with a long, red silk dress that I have never seen before. My blood pressure skyrockets. She shouldn't be wearing that for him, she should be wearing that for *me!* I sound like a jealous asshole, but I don't give a fuck—I am jealous, and I am an asshole. I've never denied that.

Soph makes quick work of stripping off her clothes off and standing there in her black lace bra and panties, she looks fucking good. My dick doesn't register that now is not the time to be hard, as the sight of her always has my cock standing at attention. I can't help it. Her presence always stirs something primal inside me that just wants me to claim her every time she is near. She pulls the dress off the hanger and when I growl, she raises a brow at me in question.

"One, your tits will be spilling out of that and two, the slit in the side ensures you won't be wearing fucking panties!" She ignores me and places the dress back on the bed and unclasps her bra, letting her full breasts become visible. My mouth waters at the sight. Sophia Stone is a goddess in her own right, with curves in all the right places and full, kissable lips. Standing here right now, in this moment, it hits me. She isn't just my mate. I don't just love her; I am *in love* with her.

I stalk over to her and spin her around so her back is to the bed and her naked chest is pressed up against my shirt. I can feel her nipples start to pebble, and when her arousal hits my nose, I release a pleased growl. I love that my mere touch or presence has this effect on her. I want her to *need me.* Reaching up, I rub her cheek, and when I start to caress her face, her eyes close on their own accord. A content sigh escapes her beautiful lips. My eyes travel down her body and then stop at her hip. I drop to my knees and gently peel her panties off. She doesn't protest. I turn her slightly and see Roman numerals tattooed on her side. I dart my gaze back to hers and find her staring down at me.

"They're dates," she whispers.

"For what?" There are three lines, not big at all, and can be hidden by the elastic of her panties.

"Lucian's birthday, the day I knew I was in love with you, and...the day you and Lucian found out the truth about who you are to each other." I drop back onto my haunches and just stare at the three dates that mark her perfect body. I have no idea when she found the time to get the tattoo, but my heart swells.

"Why Soph?" My voice is barely above a whisper.

"Because the day I had Lucian was the best day and worst day of my life, as you know. The date I fell in love with you, because I knew it would always be you Dom, it always *has* been you. You just needed sometime to figure that out for yourself. The last date, well, because the two greatest loves of my life were finally together, and I never thought I would ever see that day." I am man enough to admit that tears gather in my eyes as she speaks. I don't deserve her—after all the shit I have put her through, she stands here before me with a date I don't even remember tattooed on her. Guilt settles inside me. I nearly destroyed her, and here I am claiming to be the right and best man for her. I'm a piece of shit and don't deserve the time of day she gives me.

"Why do you look like someone stole your puppy?"

I don't have the balls to meet her gaze. "Because I don't deserve you Sophia. You deserve someone who would never have rejected you and been there to protect you. I'm not that guy; I'm the guy that pushed you away, and then when you come back, I barge my way into your life and don't give you a choice because I'm a selfish motherfucker." Soph pushes me back until I'm sitting on my ass with my legs stretched out in front of me. She doesn't give me time to recover, just straddles my lap and clasps my face between her hands. The look in her eyes is scary as fuck and has my balls shrinking.

"You don't get to do that. *We* can't keep doing this to each other. We have to let the past go and never dwell on it again. I love you Dom, flaws and all. What happened before doesn't matter. If we didn't go through that, we wouldn't be where we are or who we are today. We have a son who needs us. He doesn't need to see us struggle to get over old wounds, he needs to see us united and strong."

I have no words, so I do the only thing I can think of to show her how I feel—I kiss her. Soph pulls away before the kiss becomes more, and I pout up at her which causes her to chuckle. She climbs off me and stands, offering me her hand. I sit there and just stare at her. Fuck, she is perfection.

"Take my hand and get off your ass Dommy." I glare at her, and my look causes her to clamp her mouth shut so she doesn't laugh. I push her hand away and climb to my feet, crossing my arms over my chest.

"I told you to *never* call me that."

"You call my brother *Nicky boy*."

I smirk. "That's different, your brother's a dick."

Soph lets out a snort. "And you're not?" I close the small sliver of space between us and grip her luscious ass in my hands and squeeze, and she lets out a gasp.

"You love my dick though." Her lips are parted, and her breathing starts to pick up. Her scent starts to cloud the room in arousal and fuck I wa—. The knock at the door cuts off my train of thought.

"Soph?" Shit, it's Ryan.

"Give me a sec, I'm just changing." Soph pushes me away and quickly grabs the red dress and starts to slide it over her head. Once the dress is on and she finishes pulling her tits into the cup things properly, I scowl at the fucking piece of material. It's a halter top, which causes her tits to be pushed together, and either side of the dress has the *longest* slit I have ever seen—it runs up past her thighs and stops at her hip. She's not wearing a bra or panties, and if a fucking strong gust of wind comes, the dress will move out of place and my snack-box will be revealed to the fucking world!

"Dom, stop." I rip my eyes from her bare feet to face her. The look in her eyes is nearly my undoing—she's petrified.

"How am I supposed to let you go little dove?" Her eyes soften.

"Don't ever let me go Dominic. I just need to leave for a moment, but I'll never go completely." Soph moves around me and opens the door. On the other side is Nico, Jax, Ryan, Kai, and Lucian. Kai, Jax, and Nico step inside but I pay them no mind; my attention is focused on Sophia. I see her and Ryan exchange a strange look as Soph crosses the threshold to stand by Lucian and Ryan–then it hits me.

"What have you done babe?" Jax, Kai, and Nico turn to me, confused, but my gaze is still focused on the three people that just fucked me over.

"Look after my heart Dom, it's always been yours."

"The fuck?" Nico snaps as Soph turns and walks away.

"I'm sorry big guy."

"Ryan, what the fuck?" Nico starts to move toward the door, and once he tries to pass through, he's sent sailing back from the magic blocking the door. I knew it.

"When did you three plan this?" I ask my traitor of a son; he looks like shit, and I see guilt and shame warring in his eyes.

"It doesn't matter, I'll protect the both–"

"Drop the spell, Lucian." Nico cuts Lucian off.

"I can't. Smurf cast the spell to prove to you she is able to complete the blood binding when she has Randall's blood." Lucian's gaze turns back to me. "I'm sorry for deceiving you, but if you knew that your dad would ruin a great plan and therefore put your mother and best friend's life in danger, would you not do what I have just done?" I don't hesitate.

"Touché, just remember that this spell will fade and when it does, you better run–fast. If any harm comes to her Lucian, I'll be coming for your best friend."

"The fuck you will."

"Fuck up, Nico. Go, Lucian." He turns to follow the girls out, but my next words stop him. "If there was ever a moment to be a proud father, now is it. What you're doing for your mother and what you're risking for her, makes you an amazing son. Don't you dare fucking die, Lucian."

He doesn't turn around when he answers. "I won't Dad. I'll bring Mom back safe. I swear."

CHAPTER 55

Sophia

I shouldn't have lingered around the corner, but I did. Hearing Lucian call us mom and dad squeezes my heart like a hug. Ryan senses something is off with me. She clasps my hand in hers and smiles at me, and I return her gesture. Once Lucian rounds the corner, followed by Nico and Dom's roars, the three of us exit the compound. Chase, Alex, Mya, Aurora, David, and Mr. Silver meet us out back. Mr. Silver looks agitated; he knows once his son breaks out of that room there is going to be hell to pay. I hate having to go behind his back and ask Ryan for help, but I know he will never let me go through with this. Ryan already had the forethought to devise a plan of her own to lock my brother up, as he is the same—he would never let her go on her own.

"You know he's gonna go apeshit right?" I smile sadly up at Mr. Silver.

"I know, but this is the only way I can think of to keep him safe." Ian Silver is a beast of a man, he may look rough and scary on the outside, but on the inside, he is the kindest, sweetest man you will ever meet. He rests his big hand on my shoulder and looks me directly in the eyes.

"You, Sophia, are the daughter I never had. You make sure you and my grandson come back to me–to Dom. I will not allow him to go through what I went through; if this plan goes sideways, I will intervene." I nod my head. I know this is hard for him, and I respect him so much more now. He's still helping us, even though he knows his son is spelled inside a room against his will.

"Okay, Kai sent a messenger to Randall. I have no idea how Kai knows where he is hiding, but apparently Randall will be here in twenty, so you should all get a move on. Ryan, have you got everything?" Ryan nods her head at her uncle, and we bid the gang goodbye; they're all going to get in their positions. This plan better work!

Lucian, Ryan, and I head toward the clearing on the northern side of the property. We break through the forest and walk toward the center of clearing, as anxiety churns inside me. Doubts start to creep in. What if I fail? What if I can't get close enough?

"Are you sure about this?" I look at my sister-in-law and then to my son; I am so thankful to have them with me.

"No, but I have to do this." Lucian surprises me when he steps forward and engulfs me in a hug. I return his embrace and rest my cheek against his shoulder.

"I won't let him hurt you again Mom." My vision becomes blurry as tears fill my eyes— he called me *mom*! My heart swells with joy. I pull back and look up at my baby. He is everything to me, half Dom and half me. Our love made this amazing young man. Reaching up, I cup his cheek and he nuzzles into my hand. His eyes lock with mine and I see so much innocence. It guts me to know these eyes have seen so much hurt and pain. I will spend my life trying to make sure he never sees any of that again.

"I know, I just need you to promise me one thing?"

"Name it."

"If shit goes south, you get out–" He starts to shake his head, but I push on before he can speak. "He won't kill me Lucian, but he will kill you."

"That won't be happening. I swear Sophia, I will not let him harm you or Lucian. I'm here to help you, but to also seek vengeance for my sister. I just need a drop of his blood Soph. Once all four mix together, it will mute the stones' magic until I destroy them. After that, Lucian and I will hold the army back while the others come and take Randall." I nod my head. I see anger and bloodlust swirling in her strange eyes. Ryan has waited a long time to seek vengeance for Stevie Knox. If Randall hadn't planted the seed of doubt in Stevie's head, maybe Ryan would have had more time to help her sister. Thanks to Randall's interference, Ryan will never know the answer to that question.

Standing here between Lucian and Ryan, I feel so exposed in this scrap of material. Everything is on display. Is it sick that I know this dress will have Randall eating out of the palm of my hand? When we hear footsteps approaching from the other side of the clearing, a feeling of dread washes over me, and I school my face into an emotionless mask. We have gone over what needs to be said and done, but it doesn't change the fact that I'm still wary of being sliced with a knife that Ryan has stashed in the back of her jeans. I look to either side of me and see both have placed a mask of indifference across their faces. Minutes tick by as the sound of footfalls draw nearer, and then figures break through the dense brush of trees on the other side. A random thought crosses my mind. If I die on this beautiful sunny day, I would only have two regrets: one, I didn't get nearly enough time with my son, and two, I didn't get more time with Dom. If me dying today means Dom and Lucian get to be free and not look over their shoulders forever, I'll be happy with that. I know Dom still wants the New York pack to pay for their sins against his mother, and if all goes well today then he'll get his vengeance.

The group of supes are drawing closer; Randall always loves to make a show. He brought his whole fucking army to this *meeting*. I scan the crowd, and over the heads of the beefy muscles of the vamps that are in front, I see the top of the short plump bastard's head. He is such a fucking coward; he hides in the middle of his army instead of leading them. My hand has a mind of its own as it begins to rub my hip where my tattoo sits. Those dates mean everything to me, so it feels right to have them marked on me for life.

The crowd of supes stop a good distance away, and so much hate and anger shines in their soulless eyes. I have no idea how he managed to get so many different types of supes on his side; were they all really that pissy that Nico, Dom, and Jax have mated or married outside of their races? Love is love, no matter what race, gender or color. People are allowed to love whoever the fuck they want. The heart wants what the heart wants, right?

One of the beefed-up vamps toward the middle of the front line pulls his upper lip back in a sneer then spits on the ground in front of him.

"Mixed breed mutts," he sneers. Too nervous to speak, I just cut him a dirty look. Randall pushes his way through his wall of muscle to stand in front, now that it's safe. Just seeing him face to face transports me back to the darkest moments of my life. This man ruined me. He tried to break my soul and spirit, and he did, for a while there. Once Kai managed to set me free, a new sense of worth and strength came over me. I'm not that weak half-breed anymore; I may not be able to access my fae side, but I sure as fuck can siphon my *hugacko's* magic.

Randall's mouth begins to lift into a gleeful smile; he likes what he sees. When his gaze swings to either side of me, his smile falters slightly. We may not have an army with us, but I do have two of the strongest supes in existence with me, so I'm pretty happy with the statistics. Randall runs a hand through his greasy blond hair, his dull blue eyes darting around the clearing like he's waiting for the rest of our squad to appear. He's nervous.

"No one's coming," Ryan says loud enough for him to hear, and his gaze locks on hers. A satisfied smirk graces his thin lips.

"My, my, Miss Knox I must say I am surprised that your overbearing husband has allowed you off your leash."

"Yeah, well, I'm surprised you haven't been killed yet!" Ryan snaps back through clenched teeth. Her anger only causes Randall to smile wider.

"Oh, my dear, I am a *very* resourceful man, am I not *treasure?*" The pet name sends a shiver down my spine. I fucking hate being called that.

"This trade is between us; you don't speak to her!" Ryan snaps.

"You are outnumbered and outmanned dear, you will do good to watch your fucking tone! I am the KING!"

"King of what, exactly?" asked Lucian, and Randall turns to stare at my son, a disgusted look plastered over his ruddy face.

"I should have killed you when you were born." I gasp at the cruel words, but Lucian doesn't falter.

"That still doesn't answer my question."

"I am the king of all supernatural's, as you can see, you abomination!" I flinch at his harsh tone and cruel words. I have a part to play, and I can't come to Lucian's defense or risk fucking this whole thing up.

"Actually, my Uncle Nico is king of the fae. My Uncle Jax is head alpha, and if I recall, my other uncle, Kai, is king of the vamps." Randall's face turns a shade of red from anger.

"But your deadbeat *father* is still a nobody." Randall spits the word father at Lucian like it's the most horrible word to ever leave his mouth.

"My dad may be a lot of things, but a deadbeat sure as fuck isn't one of them. My dad is one of the strongest supernatural's alive, and he will kill you, given the chance." Randall's gaze swings back to me, apprehension clear in his eyes. Lucian's defense of Dom, although touching, was not helping us. He has to keep up the charade or he will tip Randall off.

"So, you're not here to trade?" Randall quirks a brow at me.

"I said my dad isn't a deadbeat, I never said anything about *her*." I know he doesn't mean it and has to say these things, but it still doesn't stop the sting of his words.

"So, you don't care for my *treasure*?"

"Not one damn iota, she kept me from my father. If he had known the truth, then I would never have lived in a cage at your fucking mansion. I would have been freed; my father would have come for me." Everything Lucian says may be part of this plan, but it doesn't make it any less true. If Dom knew I was pregnant, he would have come for me, he wouldn't have cared about starting a war. I hang my head in shame.

"Did you hear that *treasure*? All those years of heartbreak and disobedience for nothing; I told you the bastard wasn't worth it." I don't react or lift my head, just stand there and wallow in my own shame.

"I'm over this. I have shit to do, so let's get on with this." Ryan's tone takes on a harsh edge, and I am proud of the actress she is being. She even has me fooled.

"What do you propose, Miss Knox?"

"It's Mrs. Stone. I want you gone, and in exchange for you to fuck off, we'll give you Sophia." Randall looks between the three of us. I can see he isn't convinced. So now it's up to me to sell this bullshit. I step forward and then turn my back to Randall. What I'm about to do next I know will seal the deal. If I do this, he will know it isn't a trap and we didn't set him up. I drop to my knees and stare up at Lucian and Ryan; Ryan quickly masks the look of shock on her face. I hear the sharp intake of breath from behind and just know it's Randall. I never willingly sunk to my knees for him, I always fought, yet here I am kneeling before my sister-in-law and son.

"Don't do this, don't send me back there. I promise I won't take Nico or Dom's time away from either of you. I'll disappear and never return." Lucian refuses to meet my gaze, but Ryan makes sure to wear a mask of annoyance.

"Do we have a deal?" Lucian asks Randall.

"I'm assuming that your husband has no idea you're trading his sister, since he is not here?"

"That's none of your concern Cane, now do we have a deal or not?" He doesn't hesitate.

"Yes." I jump to my feet and try to push past Ryan and

Lucian, and like a viper, Ryan struck out and a blade is at my throat before I can even push past.

"NO!" Randall shouts, and I look to Ryan and see uncertainty in her eyes. *Do it* I mouth to her, and she reaches around and grips my hair then spins me, so I now face Randall, the knife still at my throat. Fear enters Randall's eyes, and the back of my knees are kicked, and I fall to the ground. My hair is pulled back, and I scream out in pain as the knife digs into my throat and I feel blood trickle down my chest.

"Don't fucking hurt her!"

"Soon as she stops struggling, I'll stop. Now come claim her or I kill her right here." Randall moves toward us flanked by two of his goons; my neck being cut isn't part of the plan, but by the look of horror on his face, cutting my neck is a great idea. Ryan tugs on my hair till I am standing. I breathe a little bit easier now that she isn't pressing the knife in so hard. I take a few deep breaths, knowing he will be here within seconds to claim his *treasure.*

CHAPTER 56

Dominic

"We have to get out of here!" Nico and I have been trying to break through Ryan's barrier since those traitorous shits locked us in here. Needless to say, since we're still stuck in here that none of our attempts have worked. Nico is still pacing and ripping at his hair. Kai is standing, staring out the window without a care in the fucking world. Jax sits on the end of my unmade bed, cupping his hands over his face. I'm about to lose my shit and shift soon, if I can't find a way out. They fucking left us behind. I'm so fucking mad at them, all three of them. How the hell could they have done this to us? I can feel through my mate bond that Sophia is still alive and breathing, which brings me some form of relief, but that's about as good as it gets. Lucian went behind my back to help his mother and best friend. Part of me is proud as fuck of him for doing what he thinks is right but another part of me wants to beat the shit out of the idiot!

"I am going to punish her for this!"

"Calm down Nico, getting shitty isn't going to change our situation. We're fucking stuck in here for God knows how long." Jax may be right, but hearing him sound so blasé about our predicament still pisses me off.

"Trust them." It's the first fucking words Kai has spoken since we got our asses trapped in here. Something isn't sitting right with me—why the hell is he so calm? I know for a fact he still harbors feelings for Ryan, and I know he loves Soph like a sister. So why the hell isn't he over here trying to find a way out like Nico and I?

"Why do you seem so unbothered by this?" Nico asks the giant blond vamp, and Kai releases a long sigh before he turns to face us.

"Because Ryan and Lucian are very, *very* powerful, and Sophia is no novice either. They need us to trust them to play this out, we would never allow them to do this."

"The fuck do you know about any of this Melakai?" His gray-blues dart to me.

"I helped them lure Randall here to do what needed to be done." As soon as the words finish leaving his mouth, Nico strides across the room and clocks Kai straight across the jaw. He tries to hit him again, but Jackson is lightning fast and catches his arm before he can hit Kai again.

"You fucking traitor!" Kai's unfazed look changes to anger, and he begins to vibrate with rage.

"Fuck you! I have done everything you have ever asked of me Nico, I have never betrayed you. And yet you still don't trust me. I gave up everything for you. I am what I am now because of you, and never once have you thought about my side of things. All you think about is yourself and what you have lost. You're a selfish son of a bitch." Kai turns angry eyes to me. "And you, Dominic Silver, are just as bad. I did what I could for Sophia. I tried to help her every fucking day. I was the one who set her free, not you or Nico—me. You pull back from our friendship because you're jealous that I formed a bond with your mate. Both of you are assholes, and once this shit with Randall is done...so are we." Kai's words have me staggering back a step. What the fuck have we done to our brother? My gaze cuts to Nico to see the same look of shock and fear on his own. Kai has never spoken to us like that. Worst of all, I can hear the truth in his words. One look at Jackson tells me he scented the air and confirms Kai is telling the truth by nodding. To make it worse, it hits me then that Jackson is in on this too. He knew we would be locked in this room. Are Nico and I that bad?

"Boys." We all turn toward the open door and see my father and David Knox standing there. "I told the girls I would give them as much time as I could to get it done, but something doesn't feel right." I move toward the door and glare at my dad through the barrier.

"You and I will be speaking about your double-crossing ways after I find my mate and son and deal with them." I growl at my father, he nods his head and says, "Noted, now let's get you guys out of here."

"Sir, Ryan spelled us in here."

"That's why I have David with me Jackson, he has one of the moonstones from the coven." My eyes double in size. I never thought I would be glad to hear that someone had a moonstone. David pulls out the small stone and wraps his hand around it, and in the next second I feel a whoosh of air and the barrier is gone.

"Where are they?" Nico snaps.

"The clearing on the northern side; the scouts we sent after the three of them say he has come with his whole army. Nico, son, if you go in there guns blazing and don't think things through, he will kill them. You need to be smart about this, boys, you won't get another chance like this again." I pull my gaze from my father and look to my three brothers, all of them wearing different looks of worry.

"We need to portal in as close as we can before the moonstones cancel our magic. Once we get there, we will be defenseless. No wolves, no magic, and no vamp speed or healing. We have to wait until Ryan does the spell to nullify the stones, then we join the fight and take the old fucker out." Each of my brothers nod their heads, and David leaves with the moonstone so we can open a portal. Dad lets us know as we open a portal that scouts and teams from every race are waiting in the forest. They came in after Randall got there so he wouldn't sense them when he arrived. That's bloody good to know.

As soon as we exit the portal in the forest, I see an army of supes hiding. Wolves, vamps, witches, warlocks and fae. The four of us march over to the group near the front. Shocked looks greet us as we join them.

"I knew he would let him out," says Chase. Aurora, Mya, Alex, Larick, Cyrus, Maverick, and some of Kai's vamps are in this group. Kai nods his head to his three men and they all back away. Aurora moves toward Jackson and hugs him.

"I did as you asked, they're all here."

"Thanks love." Fucking Jackson got Aurora to lead his wolves here while he was locked in the room with us. The smug fuck turns and shrugs his shoulders at me, I glare back.

"Cyrus, why the hell are you three, and half our army here?" Nico whisper shouts, and the color drains from Cyrus's face. He looks to Mav and then to Larick before looking back at his king.

"The queen ordered us to sire, we were only doing as she

commanded." I can tell Nico wants to rip him a new one but doesn't.

"The next time your bloody queen ask's you to go to fucking war you make sure I know about it first, got it?" All three of them nod their heads.

"So, what's the plan?" I ask the group, and Mya's gaze swings to me. I see apprehension in her gaze.

"Randall is coming to claim Sophia now, and when Ryan gets his blood and completes the spell, we attack." I push away from the group and move as far as I dare to try and see my mate, I can't see clearly but I can hear well enough. Dread pools in my belly as I see three figures approaching Lucian, Sophia, and Ryan. I strain, trying to listen in to their conversation. When this is over, I swear Sophia will be on her fucking knees for the next month taking her punishment in the form of sucking my fucking dick!

"Remove the knife from her throat." I know that voice, it's Randall's. I look to my side to see the rest of the gang has moved forward with me.

"Not until I have your word." That's Ryan.

"My word on what, Miss Knox?"

"I fucking told you already Randall, it's Mrs. Stone. Keep fucking with me, and I kill the pain in the ass where she stands and tell my husband you did it."

"You touch her or harm her and my army will take you out." Ryan laughs at Randall.

"You're funny, I would like to see your army try."

"Are you forgetting we have the moonstones dear?"

"We forget nothing," Lucian says.

"Fine, you have my word, I take my *treasure* and leave." Once the words leave Randall's mouth, a scream rends the air, and I move forward but am pulled back and locked in a bear hug. I turn my head to see its Kai. I glare at the giant bastard.

"You fucking cut her, you bitch!"

"That was a warning, she tries to come back here or go anywhere near my husband, I will kill her." Ryan sounds so cold and detached, and I look over to see Nico tense. He has to know Ryan is full of shit and only saying this so they can get what they want from Randall.

"If it bothers you so much, give her your blood. She deserves so much worse than that anyway." It's my turn to flinch. Lucian sounds angry and cold, and the way he speaks about Sophia, like she is nothing or means nothing to him, has ice filling my veins.

"You really are stupid boy, your father is nothing. He is a nobody. Why you chose him over my *treasure* is beyond me. Here *treasure,* drink this." Silence descends for a few seconds. I hear material rip and then Randall speaks again. "Wipe your mouth and fix yourself, you're a sight, and I will not have you looking like that as I announce you to my army as my future bride."

I feel a growl rise up my throat, and my wolf is thrashing against its cage—wait, my wolf? Ryan must be doing the spell; I shouldn't be able to feel my wolf now that I am closer to the clearing. Hope flares to life inside me, we might actually do this. Before this day is over, I am going to kill that son of a bitch for what he has done, for the horrible deeds he has done to not only my mate or my son but to my friends and brothers. We all want a piece of him, and today is the day we get our pound of flesh from the wannabe vampire king.

"What are you doing?" I hear the panic in Randall's voice, and our group exchanges worried glances. Is he on to Ryan?

"She's casting a spell to make sure you are never able to step on these lands again."

"How?"

"Your blood on the cloth, it's enough to link you to the spell. You don't mind, do you? I mean, you did give your word that if we handed over the woman who birthed me, you would disappear." There's a long pause before Randall answers Lucian.

"I gave my word we would never return, I never said anything about not taking you all out now." That double crossing son of a bitch!

CHAPTER 57

Sophia

Dread, fear, guilt and anger.

All those feelings were warring inside me as I stand in the middle of Randall's two goons, each of them has a hold of my arm. I can feel a slight tingle inside me—my magic is coming back! A look of rage crosses Lucian's face. Ryan still has her eyes closed and the cloth napkin clutched between her hands, silently chanting the spell to link Randall's blood with hers, Kai's, and Lucian's. Randall didn't see as I passed the cloth to Ryan that she had the small vial of blood enclosed in her palm. I saw her tip it, so all four of their bloods were now on the napkin. Randall's greed and power-hungry ways blind him to the sleight of hand directly in front of him. His arrogance will be his own undoing; today is the day he will die and we'll all be free of this tyrant.

"You lying son of a bitch!" Lucian snaps. I swear I hear a growl come from the trees behind Ryan and Luce, but the sound is gone so fast I swear I imagined it. I thought this plan would work, but I overestimated what I meant to Randall. My stupidity has put my son and sister-in-law in danger.

"Let them go and I'll do whatev– "I don't get to finish what I was saying, Randall spins around and back hands me across the face, I would have fallen to the ground if it wasn't for the grip the two goons have on me. After the shock wears off, I straighten and see looks of indifference on both Lucian and Ryan's faces, but their eyes give them away. Burning hatred shines in the depths of their strange eyes.

"You don't speak unless I say so; I see I have my work cut out for me again. Oh, my *treasure*, I will enjoy re-breaking you."

"Lay one fucking hand on her again and I'll burn you alive, you fucking cunt!" I snap my gaze to the side of Lucian and see Dom, Nico, Kai, Jax, Chase, Alex, and Mya striding toward us. Dominic looks lethal, his face a mask of pure rage. I can feel the power oozing off their group as they approach. Randall steps back closer toward me and his goons catch my attention. I look to Ryan and see sweat dotting her brow. Before I have a chance to panic. A sly smirk graces her lips and I feel my magic surge to life.

"Your presence means nothing; you are a few ants in the way of my army." The others come to stand with Lucian and Ryan. Nico steps slightly in front of Ryan to shield her, and Dom stands side by side with our son. Lucian drops his mask, and he looks just as lethal and fucked off as his father. I hear Randall's sharp intake of breath as he looks to Lucian and Ryan.

"You really think I would willingly hand my mother over to you?" Randall jumps back and smacks into me when Lucian's hands start to glow yellow.

"The fuck?" comes from the beefed-up goon on my right.

"H-how are you doing that?"

"Magic." Dom says, and I roll my eyes internally at his silly answer. "You see that woman behind you belongs to *me*. She is mine! I would never let her leave with you; the fact that you think my son and Ryan would hand over my heart is fucking pathetic. Sophia will be leaving here with me!" Tears gather in my eyes at Dom's declaration. I don't even care that he speaks about me like an object. He's right, I do belong to him in every way possible! I will say I swooned when he called me his heart.

"Yeah, you and what army mutt? This bitch is leaving with us!" says left beefy guy. Dom's left eye twitches, and he begins to shake. I dart my gaze to my brother to see he has his magic out to play as well.

"Call my sister a bitch again, you juiced-up fucker, and I'll cut your fucking balls off, feel me?" A chuckle escapes me, my brother and I think alike. My chuckle is cut off when I'm backhanded across the face, *again*. This time I drop to the ground. The beefed-up goons drop their grip on my arms. I don't know which one hit me but whoever did just started the battle. My eyesight is blurry and unfocused thanks to the hit I have just taken. My arm is gripped, and I'm yanked to my feet. Still disoriented I don't bother to try and focus my sight to see who has grabbed me, my feet stumbling as I'm tugged along.

"Hurry the fuck up!" That voice sends shivers down my spine and dread pooling inside me. I try to yank free, but thanks to my dazed state, I'm a fumbling mess.

"SOPHIA!" I try harder to pull out of Randall's hold and I manage to wrench my arm free but stumble back and fall to my ass. My eyesight thankfully is now starting to clear, and I look up to see Randall coming toward me. I call on my magic but can't concentrate properly due to the fear wracking my body. We're in the middle of the field among the battling races. I look either side of me and can't see any of my friends—I'm on my own.

"You're mine *treasure*, this is all for you. You belong to me!" I start to scoot back along the ground, shaking my head up at him, tears falling freely. My hand manages to land on something, and I take the risk and peek down and see it's a small dagger. I quickly grip it and hold it out in front of me. Randall pauses his movements directly above me and smiles down at me, the star of all my nightmares. I would rather die than ever be back in his cage.

"You can't kill me, I'm too strong now." He's right, he may be a coward and a vile pig, but even I can feel the increase of power radiating off him. I do the only thing I can think of—I turn the knife on myself and hold it to my throat, and his eyes double in size.

"Don't do anything rash and stupid now."

"I would rather die than be your pet." Randall lunges for me, and everything around me stops and begins to move in slow motion. I close my eyes and behind each lid I can see Dom and Lucian's faces. I whisper my love for them as I'm about to run the blade across my throat and inflict the one wound vampire blood can't heal. I feel the first drop of blood and then my hand is yanked away.

No!

CHAPTER 58

Dominic

The battle is raging on around me, and I try to find Lucian and managed to spot his silver and black hair toward the middle, closer to where Sophia was dragged. Everything happens so suddenly—as we took out the goons that held her, three portals opened and Randall's army started to come at us, and our army came running from the trees to help fight. Jax linked the rest of the pack and the soldiers at the compound to come help fight. I blast the little witch in front of me and run toward my son to help him. He stands there battling two warlocks; spell after spell is thrown at him, but he manages to keep a shield over himself to block their attacks. As I near, I see a vamp coming at me from my right, and as I readied an energy ball, he is tackled to the ground by none other than Melakai. Kai looks up at me as he struggles to subdue the juiced-up vamp.

"Go now, she has a knife and is going to kill herself!" Fear overtakes me—not my little dove. I can't lose her; I won't survive it. I call on my wolf and shift instantly, I shake out my coat and take off like the ground is on fire. I near Lucian and jump through the air to take out one of the warlocks; I see a look of surprise on his face before my jaws clamp around his throat and rip out his flesh. I turn to the side to see Lucian uses my distraction to take out the other warlock.

She needs us.

I know but I can't see her Dad! I can hear the panic in Lucian's voice even through the mind link.

Follow me, I can scent her.

We take off. I follow her floral and honey scent toward the middle of the field and then skid to a stop. Randall is standing over her, and as my gaze drops to the ground, my blood turns to ice. She has a dagger to her own throat.

"I love you." I hear her whisper as Randall lunges for her. I take off, and eight feet away from them, I launch into the air and tackle Randall to the ground. I underestimated him. Using my own momentum against me, as we hit the ground, he throws me over his head, so I land away from him and not on top of him so I could have ripped his fucking throat out! I bounce back and climb to my feet, teeth bared and growls ripping out of me. The gutless pig darts his eyes around, no doubt trying to find his minions to help.

He has the blood of Jackson's father, Ryan's father and Ryan and Lucian's blood running through his veins. I can sense the increase of power inside him, why isn't he using it against us? While Randall is looking around, I quickly search to make sure Soph is okay, and when my eyes lock on her and find her being cradled against Lucian I release a relieved breath. She's alive. My moment of distraction cost me though—six of Randall's groupies are surrounding him. Whatever he is feeding these guys, I want some.

They all look like they're on steroids or something; they are bigger than the average shifter and vamp. I feel a ripple in the air, look around and see shimmering magic; one of the six guys is a fae and he just erected a dome with me trapped inside with them. I don't like my odds, but I'm no fucking pussy. I won't go down without a fight; my daddy raised me better than that.

The six of them form a line in front of their *king*. I rise to the full height of my wolf and bare my teeth while letting out a deep and menacing growl. I may be outnumbered, but I will fight till the death; I have too much to live for now. I move around, trying to circle them. My hackles raise as I look at the six roided-up assholes. Each of them have a smug look on their ugly as fuck faces. I start pacing back and forth down my end of the dome, knowing a moving target is harder to catch than a still one. I know I can take three of them out in my wolf form, but indecision wars inside me. If I shift back, I have access to my magic and can attempt to take all of them on, or I stay in wolf form and use my jaws.

I'm strong in both forms, but right now I'm just not sure which form to choose. One of the goons takes a step forward, his lips pull back in a snarl. I see his fangs lengthening. He makes a move toward me, and I stop my pacing, waiting for the right opportunity to strike. The opportunity presents itself faster than what I could have imagined, when he charges toward me with his arms extended in front of him. I crouch down on my front legs, waiting to pounce on him as soon as he's close enough. A second passes, and when he's within reach, I pounce. I don't fuck around—I go for the kill shot. My jaws latch on to the soft skin between his shoulder and neck and as I pull back, blood spurts from his neck.

As I land on all fours, he drops with a loud thud. I look to the others and see a look of horror cross Randall's face. The next two step forward, both of them wear a look of glee. They think they have me cornered. They think they have a chance to take me down. I crouch low on my front legs, waiting for them to attack, trying to anticipate their next move. They move as one toward me, and I try to keep track of their movements, but I'm failing. They're bloody quick. As one of them attacks, I lose sight of the other. I try to go for the kill shot again, hoping it will be easy as the last. But that's the funny thing about hope, it never works how you think it will.

I miss the kill shot. He wraps his arms around my middle and squeezes, and I howl in pain. I think he just cracked some of my ribs. The other juiced up beefcake comes toward us, and he clamps his hands around my head, trying to pull. These fuckers are trying to rip my head from my body!

I'm man enough to admit that fear is coursing through me at this present moment. I feel my muscles begin to stretch as one pulls my head and the other pulls my body back in the other direction. I feel the only way to get out of this is to shift back, so I do just that. I shift back into my human form, hoping that my magic will be able to get me out of this sticky situation. The grip that the beefcake has around my middle begins to loosen and I suck in a long pull of air and then try to get my magic to wrap around me and blast these bastards away.

I feel my magic start to course through my veins, and heat begins to warm my body. I relish in the feeling. I call enough magic forward to blast these bastards away, but just as I bring my magic to the forefront and push outward, my magic is cut off. I lift my gaze and notice the magic user standing next to Randall has a smirk plastered across his ugly face. The fucker just cut off my magic somehow. I struggle against the two guys holding me, trying to break free. I continue to try and call on my magic. The grip around my middle tightens, and I feel the crushing of my ribs and cry out. I'm sure that one side of my body is pretty much fucked. The dick face trying to pull my head from my body starts to pull harder. What the hell am I going to do?

Just as I start to resign myself to my fate, I hear a loud whooshing noise and the shimmering of the dome surrounding us evaporates. Someone just shattered the dome, and I have a pretty good idea who it is. Yet again she has saved my fucking life.

"Get your fucking hands off him now!" Ryan shouts, running toward us, arms extended, blue light covering her body. It's more like blue flames. She looks like a force to be reckoned with. I see Nico and Kai running beside her, both of them have a murderous look on their faces. I don't think I've ever been so happy to see these three running toward me.

"Fucking kill that bitch now!" Randall shouts, and I can hear the fear in his voice.

"I'll give you two seconds to get your fucking hands off him now or I kill all of you. I only want Randall Cane. You have my word—if you release Dominic, none of you will be harmed. You will be released." The two fuckers trying to tear me limb from limb pause their movement and look each other in the eye, debating whether or not to take Ryan up on her offer or listen to their so-called King.

"Why the fuck are you just standing there? Kill him now and then kill her and those two!"

"Shut the fuck up Randall. You are not leaving here alive today," Nico snarls back at Randall.

"I have an army behind me. You don't stand a chance of winning today, King," Randall grinds out through clenched teeth. He has no fucking idea who he is up against. The two fuckers that tried to tear me apart drop me to the ground. I groan at the pain in my ribs. Kai makes his way toward me, lifts his wrist toward his lips and tears the flesh using his fangs. He places his wrist against my mouth and tells me to drink. As much as I detest drinking blood, I need it to heal and be able to help the others win this war against Randall fucking Cane. Instead of heading toward Randall, the two guys raise their hands in the air and begin to back away from us. Randall snaps his gaze towards them and narrows his eyes.

"You dare to leave when your King needs you?"

"We followed you because we thought the cause that you were fighting for was just, but now we can see that this is for selfish gain, not for the better of the races. You are no King, Randall." The big fucker turns toward Ryan and the guys. "We chose to fight alongside Randall for the betterment of our races. We don't agree with how our races have been treated and how we are segregated into different factions. We were led to believe that Randall felt the same way and wanted to make a change. After what we witnessed here today, we see all Randall wanted from us was just an army at his back so he can take an unwilling woman to his bed. On behalf of my brother Luca and I, we apologize for any involvement in today's actions."

"I give you my word that no harm will come to you. You and your brother may take your leave. If you wish to return to these lands, if you wish to become a part of the new way, things will be dealt with. You are welcome to stay, no race will be made to feel they are unwelcome. My husband Nico and I are trying to make these changes. Kai is trying to make these changes as well on behalf of the vampires, and so is Jax with the wolves. My cousins are the kings of the Knox Coven, and they too are trying to make a change. My husband is a fae. His best friends are a vampire, a wolf and a half breed. We're not like Randall. We do not judge others on their race. Love is love."

The two brothers exchange a look of confusion. I don't know where these guys have been or what they have been through, but even the other three guys standing by Randall seem confused. Clearly Randall has fed them some bullshit about the races not being able to be mixed. I push Kai's hand away from my mouth, and I can already feel my bones rejoining. It's painful but it beats standing here gasping for air. I stand, placing my hands over my junk. Nobody has to see little Dom swinging in the wind.

"My name is Dominic Silver, and I am half fae and half wolf. My mate is a mixed breed as well. She is half fae and half witch. We have a son together, and Lucian Is part fae, part warlock and part wolf. I don't know what Randall has led you to believe, but we don't discriminate against races here. We embrace everyone, like Ryan just said. My brothers and I are all from different races, but we don't care. If you are good to us, we're good to you. We are not against Randall because of his race. We are against Randall because of the lives that he took— he took my mate and held her against her will for seventeen years. She gave birth to my son while she was with Randall, and that son of a bitch took my son from her and told her that he was dead. My mate and I just recently found out that our son didn't die. He was still alive. He was kept as a blood bank for Randall just so that he can keep using his blood to help fuel his own strength. And yet here he stands now, with the blood of an Alpha and the blood of the original King of the Knox coven running through his veins. Yet he cowers behind you three like your lives mean nothing. Is that the type of King you want leading you?"

"Don't listen to that mutt. He will say anything just so that he won't die." I don't know if Randall has more to say or not, but his speech is cut off when Ryan releases her magic and it wraps around Randall like blue flames. He is lifted from the ground, and I can tell from here he is already shaking in fear. What a little bitch. Ryan lifts Randall high into the air, so all those in the clearing can see. The battle and the sounds of grunts and groans begin to die off around us. Everyone stops to stare at the show. Ryan uses her own magic to propel her up. She levitates next to Randall, her gaze darting around the clearing to look at all those here. Her eyes take on a sad cast when they land on the bodies of those who have lost their lives today.

"My name is Ryan Stone. I am the Queen of Farrarie, and I am the prophesized hybrid. This piece of shit next to me is full of lies. He has deceived you! My friends and I did not come here today for a battle. We came here to try and end this. You have my word and the words of my friends, if you stop this battle, you will all be set free. No one else has to die here today."

Randall tries to open his mouth to speak but Ryan lashes out with her hand and magic burst from her, knocking Randall the fuck out. Ryan looks down at me, sadness welling in her eyes, and I motion for her to pull me up. Kai takes his coat off and hands it to me, and I wrap it around myself, as best as I could, but my ass is still hanging out and going to be on display. Those fuckers should think themselves lucky to see this ass. Once the jacket is secure, I nod to Ryan, and she lifts me into the air opposite her. She knows what I want. I can't let this go, not after what they did. Looking down at the crowd surrounding us, I see Lucian clutching Sophia to him.

"Ryan's right. You can all go free—except the New York pack that is led by my father. You all know why I want you. I know the truth now. You will all come to me and submit to the human lie detector Jackson. If any of you fail any questions or a show in any way that you were involved with the murder of my mother, my father's chosen mate, you will die." Gasps and murmurs break out around the clearing. Turning my head side to side, I can see a few of the New York pack members. I glare at the bastards. How dare they be able to breathe and live when they took my mother from me!

"Why the fuck should we listen to you?" My eyes land on the fucker who spoke. I recognize him from my father's pack. He's one of the louder ones. He was never shy to be vocal about how he feels about me and my mixed heritage.

"Because if you don't listen to him, you smart little fuck, you will have the whole of the Alaskan wolf pack on you. You will have the entirety of the Vampire clan on you, as well as the fae army. Is that enough of a reason, or no?" I grin down at Nico. He sounds like a true fucking King, and I am so proud of my brother and thankful to have him on my side. I know shit has been rocky with us since it came out that Soph is my mate, but Nico and I will work it out, we aren't the type to hold grudges or stay mad at each other for too long.

 Sophia

Strong arms wrap around me and lift me from the ground. I feel so weak, so vulnerable. I'm ashamed of my actions today and how I let the fear inside of me overcome my senses. I was prepared to end my life today just so I didn't have to return to the misery that was my life before. I can tell from the scent overwhelming me that I'm in Dom's arms. He clutches me close to his chest and I rest my head against him. I don't know where we're going or what the hell happened with the battle. Everything was a blur to me.

After Lucian pulled the blade from my hand and stopped me from ending my life, I closed my eyes, not wanting to see anything, not wanting to see the death that surrounded us. The loss of innocent lives, all because Randall thought that he was in love with me. Visions have plagued me for years. Everyone thinks that it is a gift to be able to see everyone else's love life. Well, let me tell you, it's a fucking curse. For years I have been able to see through Randall's eyes—the way he views me, his thoughts, his feelings. It made me sick.

Sometimes before things even happen, I would be able to see what Randall had planned for me that evening, and what he would subject my body to. In a way I was thankful, as it helped me mentally prepare and detach myself from my feelings so that the pain wouldn't be so fierce. I could transport my mind somewhere else to a happy place and try and block out the torture that he was subjecting me to.

"I got you little dove, it's over now." Dom's words don't bring me the comfort that I thought they would. I thought knowing that this is over I would feel differently. But I just feel hollow, empty like a shell. I push those dark emotions down that are trying to rise to the surface. I would deal with those later on my own. I don't want to crumble and cry while Dom is holding me.

"Lucian?" I ask.

"He stayed back with Ryan and the guys. They're bringing Randall and the New York pack back to the cells. The next few days are going to be long, Soph, but this will all be over soon, I promise you me and our boy will go somewhere and get to know each other without a threat hanging over our heads when this is dealt with. I'm so sorry. I failed you today Sophia. I should have been there. I tried so hard to get to you, I have never felt fear like I felt today." Guilt ate away at me. None of this is Dominic's fault, I thought I was doing the right thing by locking him and the guys in the room. Instead, all I did was cause pain to everyone. There was a whoosh of wind, and I turn to see Dom has opened a portal. I don't question him; I just rest my head against him and close my eyes as we enter the portal. A few seconds later we exited and we're back at the compound. This place is becoming a lot like home. Poor Jackson.

Dom leads us back to our room. He doesn't stop as he enters, just walks us both to the shower. This wasn't like the last time we shared the shower together—this time it's different it's as if we we're both trying to scrub away the memories and wash away the pain of the day. There is still so much that we have to discuss, but I just don't have the energy to relive the pain, fear or trauma of today. I know Dom is still royally pissed at me; I can tell by the look in his beautiful violet eyes that there is still so much anger simmering below the surface.

I deserve his anger. I shouldn't have gone behind his back like I did, but it was the only way I could think of to keep the man that I am unconditionally in love with safe. I would rather have his anger directed toward me than not have him with me at all. Once we get out of the shower and dry ourselves, we change silently. I avoid looking at him as much possible.

I chose to go with comfy clothes: sweats, an oversized T-shirt, and a hoodie. I make my way toward the bed and climb under the covers. Dom sits at the end of the bed with his back toward me. His muscles are tight and tense, his shoulders slightly hunched.

"You were brave today, you know?" I reel back in shock. That is not what I expected to come out of his mouth, that's for damn sure.

"I don't know what you saw or heard today, but what I did is far from brave Dom." Dom turns on his side and looks me in the eye. I can see so many different emotions swirling in those beautiful expressive eyes. I don't want him to see me as damaged or broken. I want him to see me as strong, beautiful, and independent. Even though I don't feel like those things right now, I want him to know that I can be those things again.

"You saw the real me today, Dom, and I never wanted you to see me as that person. I always wanted you to see me the way that you've always seen me: strong-willed, brave, independent. I was none of those things today, and I am so sorry that you and our son got to see me at one of my lowest points today."

Sob's wrack my body as Dom crawls up the bed and gathers me in his arms. I sob against his chest. I know his shirt will be wet from the tears, but no matter what I do or how I try to hold them back, they just continue to fall. I don't know how long

Dom holds me in his arms while I break. I have never broken down like this before in my life. After everything that transpired today, so many old feelings, fears, concerns, and worries comes crashing down. Today I thought I was about to lose everything that I had worked so hard for. I thought I would lose a chance to get to know my son and spend more time with my *hugacko*. I don't know if I was crying for what I could have lost today or crying for the girl that was taken against her will all those years ago. Almost like crying for the girl that thought for years that her baby had died? Or was I just crying for me? Dom doesn't say a word as he sits there and holds me.

"Do you wanna know what I realized today?" I don't know how much time passes before he speaks.

"What did you learn today my love?" I hear Dom's sharp intake of breath at my pet name for him. There is no other name fitting aside from *my love* because it's true, Dom really is *my love*.

"That I couldn't live in a world where you don't exist Sophia. You are everything to me. I don't wanna go another day in this world without you by my side. I can't do this thing called life without you. I don't know how I've done it for so many years before, but I don't wanna do it again. Soph, you are and always have been the better half of me, and I want to spend the rest of my life with you. I'm not gonna lie—I will probably piss you off every single day, and you will hate every minute of being with me, but that won't stop me from trying to make you the happiest woman alive and trying to keep a smile on your face till the end of my days. We have a beautiful son together Soph, and don't get me wrong, I want more, but I want them with you.

"Would you make me the happiest man on Earth, Sophia Stone, and marry me and become Sophia Silver?" I didn't think there was any way I could have more tears left, but lo and behold, I was wrong. Tear's leak from my eyes as I pull away to stare into Dom's eyes. I see fear in his eyes. It isn't because he's scared, it's because he was worried that I would say no. I cup his face between my hands and run my thumbs up and down his cheekbones. I smile softly at the man that is everything to me.

"I will probably spend the rest of our lives pissing you off and keeping you on your toes and going against you and defying you at every turn. If you can put up with me and all my fucked-up problems, then I would love nothing more than to become your wife Dom. Spending the rest of my life with you has always felt like a fairy tale. I never thought I would get the chance to ever hold you in my arms or kiss you or ever join my body to yours again. It's always been you, Dominic. It will never be another. There is no other choice for me in this world aside from you." Dom doesn't say anything. He leans forward and captures my lips in a heated kiss, a kiss that promises me he will love me forever, flaws and all. This kiss promises that Dom will never think that of me. He will help me overcome these fears. He will love me till the end of my days, warts and all.

Two days have passed since the battle. I don't even really know if you could call it a battle. I'd call it more of a slaughter of innocence. If I'm honest with you, many had lost their lives that day for such an unnecessary cause. Nico had told us that Randall and the New York pack had been locked in their cells at Jacksons. I was shocked to learn that thirty-six pack members are in those small cells below with Randall. It's so hard to believe that so many of them were involved in the death of Dom's mother.

Today is the day that we are all going to deal with the pack and with Randall.

The army that had come with Randall was given a choice to have their freedom or to join one of the factions. Most of them had chosen to join, but others who did not have the belief that change could be done fled. It hurts to know that so many of our kind out there didn't feel that the leaders of these races were doing right by them. I know it weighs heavy on my brother, Jax, and Kai. I believe the three of them are fair rulers.

Dom left our bed early this morning to meet with his father to discuss what they will do. Dom doesn't want me to come with them. I will not be left behind. I would stand by my mate, and I would watch as the assholes who dared hurt an innocent woman—and in the process break the heart of my hugacko— were punished. A knock at my bedroom door pulls me from my thoughts. I told whoever it is to come in, and the door opens to reveal Ryan and Aurora standing on the other side with Lucian. I smile at them and wave them on in.

"What are you guys doing here?"

"And here I was thinking that my mother would be happy to see me." I can hear laughter in Lucian's voice. Lucian now calls Dom and I Mom and Dad to our faces. It's probably gonna take us a long time to get used to, but every time hearing that three-letter word out of my son's mouth brings joy to my heart and has me bursting with pride. Lucian will accompany us today as well, to dole out the judgment against the pack and Randall. I honestly don't know if I'm ready to face Randall yet, but I know if I don't do this, I'll regret it.

"You know I'm always happy to see you. I just thought that you guys would be getting ready to go to the cells with the others." Each of them smile sadly.

"We know this is hard for you and we don't want you walking over by yourself." Gratitude swells inside me; I'm so lucky to have these guys in my life. I honestly don't know if I would have gotten through these months of being free of Randall without each and every one of them. I grab Aurora's hand and give it a squeeze as I thank her for her kind words and thoughtfulness.

"You guys are the best, I am so thankful to have all of you guys, honestly." I turn to Ryan. "I know this is just as hard for you as it is for me. Thank you for saving Dom's life again Ry, I hope this doesn't become a habit." We all chuckle, and after a moment I turn to face my beautiful son and rub his cheek, his brows furrow in confusion.

"Thank you."

"Huh?" I smile at the dumbfounded look on his handsome face.

"Thank you for being you and for being so forgiving. I am so sorry for what you nearly witnessed me do the other day–" Lucian tries to speak but I shush him; I need to get this out. "I have a lot of demons that I need to work through, and I just want you to know that your father and I have reached out to Ryan's mother, and she has agreed to help me and coach me on some of the healing tactics she has learned." Lucian's eyes begin to mist, and he knocks my hand away and engulfs me in a breath stealing hug. I melt in his embrace; I don't think I will ever get used to the feeling of being in my son's arms.

"I am proud of you; after what you have been through, you are more than entitled to feel the way you feel. I know this journey will be hard for you, but just know that dad and I will be with you every step of the way." Not wanting to cry, I pull back and smile at my boy. I know he means every word he says. Just knowing Lucian and Dom support and believe in me gives me the strength I need to work through my demons.

CHAPTER 60

With everything that has been going on, Soph and I decided to keep the news of us getting married to ourselves until we get a chance to tell Lucian first. Soph doesn't want to tell him now while we are all under a lot of stress, I want to deal with the prisoners quickly and then move on. Soph is trying her best to remain in high spirits, but ever since I told her that Randall is being held in the cells here on the compound, she has retreated so far inside herself that I'm scared she won't be able to come back. My dad's voice pulls me from my thoughts; looking at him now, I see how much stress he is under — bags are present under his eyes, his hair is a mess, and I think he is still wearing the same clothes as yesterday. This is hard for my dad to deal with, he stayed as the alpha of the pack that killed his chosen mate. He has been blaming himself for days, and I know today will be ten times harder for him than it will be for me.

"No matter what Pops, I'm here with you every step of the way. After today we can let her rest, we can let Mom be in peace now." Sad, tormented eyes land on me; guilt has been eating at my dad. This strong and caring man has been a shell of himself since we brought the pack and Randall here. Each of the thirty-six will go before us and Jax, and he will determine if they are lying. Having a human lie detector for a best friend has its perks, not gonna lie.

"I stayed Dominic; I broke bread with these people! Those bastards killed and...and–."

"Shhhh dad, I know...I know old man, but blaming yourself won't change anything." I pull the bear of a man into a hug. I have never and I mean *never* seen my father break apart like he is now, his sobs shattering the quiet of the room. His tears soak my shirt, and he's gripping me so tight I swear I will bruise. His tears aren't just for himself and the guilt eating at him, they're for my mother. For everything she went through and endured at the hands of the people my dad spent so many years leading and protecting. I grind my teeth together to keep from cursing, and renewed anger flows through me. Those fuckers will pay for what they did to my mom and what they are now putting my father through.

After dad finally gathered himself and I managed to convince him to shower and change, we made our way to the back of the compound to meet the others. Trepidation settles inside me; I don't relish the idea of killing a woman, but I won't spare them if they were a part of my mother's death. We exit the back door and immediately frigid air assaults us. Alaskan weather is so unpredictable—hot one day and snowing the next. Dad and I walk sluggishly toward the others; this side of the compound is so gloomy, the sun is blocked out from the large trees, it's an eerie feeling on this side. As we approach the old metal shack, I see the others waiting there for us.

Nico, Jax, Kai, Aurora, Ryan, Soph and Lucian. Because we have chosen not to let the elder council in on what we are about to do today, Chase, Alex, and Mya stayed away so they wouldn't be accomplices. I don't know honestly if we would be punished for this, but at the moment I just don't give a fuck. We stop a couple of feet in front of the others; my eyes go straight to Sophia. She has her arms wrapped around her middle. Her bright violet eyes are dull today, and her beautiful black hair doesn't seem as shiny either. I dart my gaze to Lucian in question, but he nods his head and gives me a reassuring smile.

"Just so we're clear, if shit goes wrong, we're all going down for this." Before I can answer Jackson, my dad does.

"We understand son, if you or any of you kids do not wish to be a part of this, we understand." No one moves, everyone meets my dad's gaze with a look that says *we are with you till the end*. As Nico turns to open the door, he is stopped by Aurora's words.

"No one will come after us."

"How do you know love?" I ask, and the seer smiles proudly.

"Because the council doesn't want to fuck up and go after another high-ranking member like they did Ryan and lose. Plus, it helps when you have the leader of the shifter council and the alpha king as well as two other kings and a queen in on this." Now it's my turn to smile widely; I'm glad to know that none of my friend's will be punished for my revenge.

Nico opens the door to the shack, everyone but Soph, Lucian, dad and I enter. The shack is a tiny, rickety looking building. It's so small inside that we might not all fit, but it's just a cover though. Once inside, the shack doubles as an elevator, it will only work for Kai, Jax, Nico, me, and two of Jax's most trusted men.

Once the elevator returns, the rest of us enter, and I clasp Sophia's hand in mine and pull her against my side. I want to know if she's okay.

"Are you sure you want to do this little dove?" My dad and Lucian's eyes dart to Sophia; she keeps her head down as she answers.

"No. But I need to do this, if I don't, I'll never know if I'll be able to move forward. I need to face my fear and let that bastard know he won't take up any space in my mind or rule my fears any longer." Her gaze lifts to mine, and I can see tears gathering. I drop her hand and wrap my arms around her as the door opens to reveal the cell floor.

"I'll be with you every step of the way babe."

"As will I, my dear."

"Me too Mom." I smile at my dad and son and mouth a silent *thank you*.

We exit the elevator and immediately my senses go haywire. I can scent so many wolves—and fear. I can taste their fear on my tongue and relish in the feeling of it. All the cells are full; the bars are made of iron and down here the concrete is so thick that you're cut off from nature—magic isn't accessible down here. Thanks to Ryan, who put a bubble of sorts around us so that we can still access our magic, it means we don't have to move the prisoners above ground for Jax to determine if they lie or not. Ryan is the only supe who is able to use magic down here. I tow Soph by her hand down the corridor and pass the full cells until we round the corner where the others wait in front of Randall's cell. I feel Soph stiffen, but she doesn't stop walking, and I am so fucking proud of her for how brave she is being.

"How are we doing this?" I ask the group.

"One by one. It's gonna take a while so may as well have a seat on the floor." Everyone remains standing. "Okay, well, Kai and Nico will bring the wolves out one at a time, I'll ask them a range of questions and then we'll decide their fate from there. Once they're done, we move onto Randall." I look to Dad to see him nodding, so I do the same. Jax cuts his gaze to me. "We have to talk after this brother." Jax's tone leaves no room for argument, so I nod my understanding. I hope it isn't bad news.

CHAPTER 61

Aurora, Ryan, Lucian, and I all have our backs against the wall as we watch Kai and Nico drag a struggling, middle-aged man to Jax, Mr. Silver, and Dom. The man has dried blood caked to the side of his head, his clothes torn and his feet bare. His eyes are so dark they almost look black, his mouth twists into a snarl and hard lines grooving his face. This guy gives me the creeps. Once in front of the three guys, Nico kicks the back of his legs and the man drops to his knees.

"The fuck is the meaning of this Ian?" the man snaps.

"You will address your alpha so informally?" The man turns his head to Jax and some of the color drains from his face; plainly he just realized who is standing beside Ian Silver.

"Forgive me Alpha, I didn't know you were here." The man bows his head slightly to Jax, and Dom shakes his head and mumbles something under his breath that I can't make out. Lucian chuckles beside me, so I turn to him and ask what's so funny.

"Dad just called the guy a drop nuts." I bring my hand up to cover my mouth so it will muffle my laughter, and Dom turns and winks at me. Being down here in the cell block is strange;

fear was strangling me while we were up top but now that we're down here, fear has given way to resolution. When we leave here, I won't be looking over my shoulder every day, I will actually be free. I won't live in fear that he will come for my son or for me.

"Dude, you're gonna die." The man whips his head up and looks to Dom, the submissive look in his eyes that was there a moment ago has been replaced with loathing and hatred. I want to cut the fucker's eyes out for looking at my man like he's nothing.

"Fucking hell Dominic, seriously?" Nico snaps, and Dom shrugs his shoulders unapologetically.

"I'm going to ask you some questions, and I want you to answer them truthfully. If you lie, I will know."

"Why should I answer?"

Dom smiles cruelly. "Because you're fucking worthless life depends on it!"

"I want a fair trial, with the council present. No, I demand a trial!" This dumbass has no idea who he is dealing with. Kai chuckles and then placed his hand on the man's shoulder. He must have squeezed him, because the man flinches and turns to face Kai.

"You have four members of the council here, and you also have the leader of the shifter council as well. I'd say your demands have been met, *mutt*."

"Did you have anything to do with Monica Silver's death?" Jax asks, and the man's eyes dart around wildly. Wolves are standing behind him, peering through the bars, but none of them say a word. The silence stretches for so long I fear the man won't answer.

"I want your assurance first." Dom lets loose a growl but stops when his father places a hand on his shoulder.

"Your wife and son will be spared Thomas, *if* they had

nothing to do with my wife's death." The man swallows loudly and nods his head.

"Tabitha and Evan had nothing to with it."

"But you did, didn't you Thomas?" Jax asks, the man nods his head and drops his gaze. "I need the words, Thomas."

"Yes!"

"Truth. As Alpha of all wolves, I, Jackson Marshall, sentence you to death." Insults are hurled at us from the not so silent wolves now. Out of nowhere, Dom releases a growl so loud I have to cover my ears, and I watch as yellow swirls begin to dance all over his body. The shouts and cursing cuts off when the wolves eye Dom.

"You will all be judged, and if you had nothing to do with it, then you have nothing to fear. But if any of you so much as knew or helped in any way with my mother's death, you will die as well!" Dom ran his eyes over the wolves, each of them drop their gaze after a moment. I'm amazed that Jax and Dom can be in the same room, now that Dom is an alpha, but apparently being mated to me is a big factor for Jax not wanting to kill Dom which I was actually happy about because that would have sucked if they couldn't be near each other.

After a couple of hours, we are now down to the last four wolves, who all happen to be females. I don't pity any of them. If they could be as cold and heartless as the others, they deserve their fate. So far, all thirty-two—yes thirty fucking two men—have been found guilty. I think Dom and even Mr. Silver are in shock to discover that thirty-two men were involved in the murder of Monica. To say I am disgusted is an understatement. Randall still hasn't made a sound from his cell down the hall or even moves from his bed; he knows what is coming next.

The first woman is brought out and she doesn't put up a struggle. She is plain, with brown hair, brown eyes, and a slender figure. She drops to her knees in front of Jax, Dom, and Mr. Silver but doesn't meet their gazes.

"I must say, I am in shock to see you here Mary." The woman still doesn't lift her head or acknowledge that Mr. Silver spoke.

"You know how this works. Were you involved in any way with Monica Silver's murder?" She doesn't hesitate.

"Yes," she says so quietly that Jax cocks his head to the side and studies the woman like she is a science experience.

"What's wrong?" Dom asks Jax.

"It's the truth, but it's not."

"What does that mean Jackson?"

"Just give me a second Dom."

Jax turns his gaze back to the woman Mary and asks, "What are you not telling us?" She still doesn't lift her gaze.

"I never aided in her assault or murder," she says.

"You tried to stop it, didn't you?" Jax questions, and the woman snaps her eyes up to Jax and it's then I see she has tears flowing down her cheeks.

"Of course, I did! She wasn't the only woman who endured that. She was the lucky one."

"How the fuck was my mother lucky exactly?" Dom shouts. She flinches at his tone but meets his gaze, "Because she got to die while the rest of us still live in hell every fucking day!" Gasps ring out. What the hell is this woman saying?

"Mary, I need you to elaborate dear." She swings angry eyes to Ian.

"Why? You're our alpha and never gave a fuck before. All you and your son ever cared about was your wife, not the pack. We have been suffering for years, and you still didn't notice. None of the woman in the pack had anything to do with your wife's death. We fucking loved her too!" the woman shouts, and I turn to look at the three women in the cell and notice them huddling in a corner. A man moves toward them, and I notice the smallest out of the three start to tremble.

"Get the girls out of there now, Nico!" I shout, and my brother and Kai turn to see the three scared women in the corner and quickly jump into action. I have no doubt in my mind that the man was going to hurt those three women, and I am so sick of men treating women like shit! Nico opens the cage and uses his magic to propel them from the cell. They quickly rush toward Mary, who is now a sobbing mess on her knees. They wrap their arms around her and whisper words of comfort, and the sight in front of me nearly breaks me.

"How the fuck did I miss this?" Mr. Silver wonders aloud, devastation on his face.

"Your wife found out what was going on and tried to help. Not only was she hated for offering her help to the women in the pack, but also for being a non-shifter."

"Shut your fucking mouth, Mary!" One of the wolves' shouts from inside the cell, and I turn to glare at the greasy-looking pig.

"What the fuck are you going to do if she doesn't, you spineless cunt?" I yell at the dog of a man. For some reason I feel so fiercely protective of these women.

"Fuck you *mutt*–" The man doesn't get to finish—two yellow energy balls whizz past my head and hit the man in the face and chest. His eyes widen and he screams out in pain as he drops to his knees, his eyes are wide with terror. Not wanting to see any more, I turn to see both Lucian and Dom with their arms extended. They both threw the balls to defend my honor. Not wanting to be distracted by my swelling heart, I approach the girls and kneel down in front of them. The three girls shy away and hide slightly behind Mary. She lifts her tired brown eyes to me, and I feel so much guilt for judging her and thinking her plain.

"My name is Sophia Stone. I'm Dom's mate." The three women share a look, but Mary just smiles sadly. "I want to help you ladies, if you'll let me?" Mary's eyes narrow suspiciously.

"Why would you want to help *us?*" I take a deep breath and count to three in my head before answering.

"Because I have been where you ladies are–." Mary growls low in her throat but stops immediately when Dom growls back and Lucian steps forward to stand behind me.

"How the hell has the princess of Farrarie been where we have?" She sounds so angry.

"I was taken prisoner for seventeen years by Randall Cane. I gave birth to our son there, and he was taken from me. I was told he had died, but the whole time my son was locked in a jail cell beneath me. I was beaten and raped over and over, treated like a doll, just used and put away." All four of the women stare at me in shock, but I stared steadily back, refusing to see the pity in the eyes of my friends and family. I won't live in shame anymore for what happened to me. I feel a hand land on my shoulder then another on my other side, and I look up to see Dom and Lucian smiling down at me proudly.

"I'm s-sorry...I didn't know, I just assumed–" I cut Mary off.

"That I lived the life of a pampered princess? Spoiled by my brother and loved by all? My father hated the sight of me, as did my mother; the only one that has ever loved me since birth is my brother. My life is not a fairy-tale, and if what you say is true, I would love to help you in any way I can, as well as the rest of the women in your pack."

"I-is Brady d-dead?" asks one of the women who is hiding behind Mary.

It's Lucian who answers. "Yes. No man will ever harm any of you again, I swear it." Four sets of eyes lift to look over my shoulder and stare at my son. "He would have died anyway for what he did to my grandmother. My father is the future alpha of your pack, and I am now part of his pack, and I pledge myself to your safety." I can barely contain my pride at the man my son was becoming.

"We will all make sure you are safe, I swear it." I turn and smile at Ryan. Aurora is by her side with a fierce look on her face. The girls will help as well, to make sure these women get the help they need.

"Mary, could you please explain more? I know this is hard for you, and I am so sorry. I just need to know why this happened to my wife...please." I can hear the raw heartbreak in Mr. Silver's voice, and it's painful to hear. Mary swallows loudly and nods her head.

"Monica had been helping us in secret; we begged her not to tell you out of fear. We didn't think the men would do anything to her, being that she was your mate. We were made to say such horrible things to her in public. We hated it, but Monica assured us that she held no hard feelings against us for it. The night she died, she was helping me and Tamara. Wendall had gone off the deep end and attacked me, beating me so bad he broke my eye socket. Tamara came to help, but Wendall turned on her as well. Monica somehow heard the commotion from your house and came to help and then...then...he went off on her, and then the rest of the pack turned up and we tried—we begged and pleaded. We told them we went to her so they would direct their rage on us, and not her, but Monica lied. She told them she hated us and never helped us... She did that to protect us!" Mary broke out in gut-wrenching sobs, and I wrapped my arms around her and cradled her frail form against me.

After Soph calmed Mary down, Jax asked the women if they had anything to do with mom's death, they said no, and they were telling the truth. I can see Dad is struggling with his feelings and wants to break down, so I asked him to escort the women up top and look after them until we were finished. He agreed, but only because we agreed not to execute the shifters without him. We all make our way down the corridor to Randall's cell. He doesn't stir when we approach him or even roll over in his bed. Nico inserts the key and slides the door open, yet Randall remains still and silent.

"You either get your ass up or I drag you out of that bed!" Kai growls, and after a few tense moments, Randall moves. He is as stiff as a board as he rolls over, his face covered in bruises, his eyes sunken in and ringed in dark circles. His blond hair appears brown from the dirt and blood coating it. I have no idea where the bruises had come from or the blood for that matter, it looks like he's lost weight. How the fuck is that possible after only two days?

"You look like shit," Lucian comments. Randall tries to glare at my boy, but his facial features barely move. What the actual fuck is going on?

"Why do you look like utter shit?" Nico asks, but it isn't Randall that answers, it's Kai.

"Because he's decomposing. You see, when you drink such powerful blood, like that of a king, an alpha, a trifecta, or the strongest supe in the world, you must maintain that blood supply. Going without that blood means he is dying slowly." Kai sounds positively gleeful.

"You bastard! That's why you kept my son! He was your blood bank to maintain your strength!" I look at Soph in shock, and my eyes swing back to Kai, who is nodding his head. That fucking greedy prick kept my son in a cell because he wanted his blood. Randall looks to Soph and tries to smile but only ends up grimacing. He looks like the gate keeper from *Goosebumps*.

"*Treasure*, help me." Sophia scowls and moves to enter the cell, but Kai blocks her path. Soph places her hands on her hips and looks up to the giant vamp.

"Let me through Kai."

"I won't allow him to hurt you again So-So." The tension in Soph's shoulders loosens, she lifts her delicate hand and places it on Kai's chest.

"He won't hurt me again Kai. I need to do this." They stare at each other for a moment before Kai steps aside. Soph walks inside the cell and stops a foot away from Randall. I follow her in. I want to be close in case this fucker tries anything on my girl. Soph takes a deep breath and squares her shoulders.

"I will never think about you again after this moment. I will forget you ever existed. I'm sure the same cannot be said for you. I'm sure you will think about me daily as you wither away and die. You tried to break me, but you didn't succeed. I hope you rot in hell!" Randall stumbles and drops down on his concrete slab bed, looking up at Soph in shock. Soph turns and clasps my hand in hers and leads us out of the cell. She pauses and faces the others. "All I ask is that you treat him the same way he treated Lucian and I. Let him writhe in pain every day and die slowly in a cage. I want him to suffer like he made us suffer. I want him to wish for death—no, beg for it—and never be granted that small mercy." I'm startled at the venom and strength lacing each and every one of Soph's words. Not gonna lie, my dick is hard as fuck at her display of courage.

"So-So, are you sure you're okay with him being alive and locked in here?" Kai asks.

"Yes, there's no way he can get out right?"

"No little dove. Even if he attempts to escape, he'll never make it to the top. You have my word babe, he will never get out of here alive, I swear it."

"I agree, he deserves to suffer after everything he has done to us and for everything, he has taken from us!" Ryan grounds out through clenched teeth. With that, Nico slides the cell door shut and turns the key to lock it.

"No, stop! You can't do this; I demand to speak to the vampire council now!" Randall wheezes. Kai turns to him and smiles wickedly.

"I'm right here, what's your complaint?"

"Not you, I want someone else!"

"Too bad Randall, I'm all you got." Randall's eyes widen in fear; it's finally starting to sink in that we're not bluffing. He really will die down here.

"No, I have rights!" he shouts, then he breaks out in a coughing fit.

"You lost those fucking rights when you took my mate and locked my son up! You will never see the light of fucking day again. You will be beaten daily and given a blood bag once a week just to stretch out your lifespan enough for you to hate yourself. You had it all—the power, the army, and the means, but because you are so fucking gutless, you lost it all!" We all turn and make our way toward the elevator, Randall's screams and pleas echoing around us. After a moment, the wolves join in, but their pleas fall on deaf ears.

The next morning, the wolves are executed. Dad dealt with them. He said he needed to do it so his wolf would finally rest and not be so angry all the time. I didn't argue. She was my mom, but at the end of the day she was my dad's *world*. I would want to do the same if it was Soph. I was still shocked that Soph wanted Randall alive and not killed. Yet again this woman was always full of surprises; she never ceases to amaze me. Soph got Mary and the other three ladies set up in the room next to ours. She was with them right now, trying to work out the best way to help them and the other females. I was shocked to learn that this sort of abuse is a common occurrence among the packs. Jax is disgusted and declared he would be traveling to all the pack lands and checking in on all his wolves, making sure that an end would be put to this barbaric way of men thinking they are *entitled* to treat woman this way!

Epilogue

Three months later...

I never, I mean *never*, thought I would be sitting on the back porch of my dad's house with my legs kicked up on the railing while I rock back and forth in my rocking chair. It still feels so surreal to be here on pack lands and not hate every single person.

Oh, by the way, shock of the year is when we returned to the pack lands three months ago and we found Louis hiding out with the women. I, being the calm collected man that I am, dragged him out the house by his throat and was about to end him when more than half of the women begged and pleaded that he wasn't part of the cruelty. I didn't believe them. When Louis told me his story, I kind of felt bad for him, him *kind of* being the keyword. I still think he is a fucking dipshit and want to cave his head in. After what he did to my mate, I still want him dead.

Soph is doing fucking amazing. She and Nina Knox have opened a shelter here on pack lands for women. They offer food, shelter, and security for these women. Jackson put in an offer to all the packs that any man willing could transfer to the

New York pack to "fill in the numbers." The men that did volunteer were under the impression that they were coming to fill in the numbers, since our pack had dwindled in members, but that wasn't the case. The men were brought here to help with security and extra protection for these women.

To say I am proud of Sophia is a fucking understatement. Aurora and Ryan help out at the shelter as well. Nina Knox has been fucking amazing. Soph meets with her twice a week and they discuss their trauma and ways that help them cope. It may not be the healthiest way to heal for some people, but this way seems to be working for my girl, and I couldn't be fucking happier. Lucian helps his mom out as well, and a few of the younger girls in the pack seem quite taken with my boy. I'm stoked for him, but Soph isn't—she is forever preaching about safe sex and taking your time, yada yada yada. My advice—live in the moment. That is the advice my dad gave me many years ago, and I think I turned out just fine!

I hear the back door creak open and look over my shoulder to see my dad, Nico, and Kai walk out.

"What are you guys doing here?" I ask, and Nico narrows his eyes at me. What the fuck is his problem now? I look to Kai and my dad and see that they both have sour looks on their faces as well. What the fuck have I done now?

"Got something to tell us Dominic?" Nico grits out. I cock my head to the side confused.

"Ahhhh, I don't think so?" It sounds more like a question than I want it to.

"Want to know a funny story?" Sarcasm is thick as fuck in Nico's tone, Dad and Kai stand beside Nico like statues. I climb to my feet and look my best friend in the eyes.

"Why don't you just spit out whatever it is that you came here to say?" A wicked smile spreads across Nico's face. *Uh-oh, I don't like that look.*

"Well, your son–my nephew—happens to be best friends with his aunt–my wife–."

"Skip the bullshit, I know how everyone is related. Now get to the point!" I'm starting to get annoyed as fuck at not knowing what the hell is going on here.

"Well turns out being a gossip runs in the family." Now I'm pissed, I know him and Luce have been getting on really well lately, but he that doesn't give him the right to talk shit about my son.

"It was an accident! It just slipped out Dad, I swear." I spin around to see Lucian, Ryan, Nina, and Sophia making their way up to us. I look at Sophia with a raised brow, and she lifts hers in return and shrugs. The four of them come to a stop when they reach us. Ryan heads to stand by Nico, who wraps his arm around her waist and places a kiss on top of her head. Soph stands next to me, and I do the same, except I kiss her full lips and slip her the tongue.

"Dude! Stop doing that shit in front of me!" I turn and grin at Nico, loving the discomfort me kissing Soph causes him.

"You spend just as much time with my sperm as I do, so why are you complaining?" Lucian glares at me; he hates it when I refer to him as *my sperm*. Nico shudders and runs his free hand down his face. Ryan turns and pins me with a look that has the smile dropping off my face. I see Nina Knox move to stand beside my dad. He leans down and whispers something in her ear that has her eyes doubling in size and then her gaze snapping to me and Sophia.

"What the fuck is going on here? You are all acting weird, and Lucian looks like he's about to get a beat down."

Luce growls low in his throat. "I would like to see you try, *old man*." I reel back, in shock that the little shit has the nerve to call me old...again.

"I may be old, but my old dick still made you, asswipe!"

"Dominic, language!" my dad hollers as I continue to stare down my *sperm* while he smiles widely, loving that I just got told off by his grandfather.

"Oh for the love of God, Lucian told us that you proposed to Soph, and Nico is shitty because you didn't ask his permission." Ryan blurts out, and both Soph and I stare at Nico and Ryan for a moment then, in unison, we swing our gaze to our big mouth kid. We haven't found the right time to tell everyone yet, and we're just keeping it to ourselves. The only one that we have told is Lucian; we wanted to make sure he was okay with it before anyone else. The kid lit up like a Christmas tree at the news. Lucian starts to rub the back of his neck and keeps looking everywhere except at his mother and I. At least he has the decency to look sheepish.

"So, this weather is pretty nice, and I think we should go—" Soph cut off his mindless rambling.

"You were supposed to keep it a secret until we said something." Lucian finally meets his mother's gaze, remorse shinning in the depths of his strange eyes.

"Mom, it was an accident, I swear. When I went to see Smurf last week, Unks asked me if there was any news, and I couldn't help myself. It was like my mouth took on a mind of its own, and then it all spewed out." I was trying so hard not to laugh; I had said the exact same thing once.

"Huh!" All eyes turn to my father, who is sporting the biggest shit-eating grin. "That, my boy, is called *Karma.*" Everyone erupts into laughter at my dad's silly outburst.

Fuck. My. Life!

Click the link below to read Kai's story —
Anarchy

Also by Samantha Barrett

Mafia Romance

Murdoch Mafia Series

Played By The Bishop

Tormented By The King

Tortured By The Knight

Tempted By The Queen

Turned By The Pawn

Ruined By The Rook

Murdoch Mafia Novella

Stalemate

Memento Mori Series

Reign Of Royal

Broken By Sin

In Havoc Lays Chaos

Godfathers of the night

London has Fallen

Damned By His Angel

Re Della Strada

Shattered Soul

Fractured Heart

Tainted Essence

Fairytales With A Twist

Condemned Beast

Secret Society/ Bully

Filthy Few

Forever Filthy

Filthiest Of Them All

Masked Men Novella (Pure Smut)

Dirty Priest

Dirty Daddy

Sports Romance

<u>Playing For Keeps</u>

Offside

Touchdown

End Game

Hail Mary

Blindside

RH Sports

Hate Us Like You Mean It

MM

Love Me Like You Mean It

Paranormal Romance

<u>The Veil Of Obsidian</u>

Of Time And Carnage

<u>Curse Of Fate</u>

Dream

Fate

Nightmare

Redemption

Anarchy

<u>Brutal Savages</u>

Savage Lies

Brutal Truth

Savage Beast

Brutal Beauty

Acknowledgments

That's a wrap!
Dom and Soph are done and dusted.
After all the shit they went through they bloody well deserve
their HEA.

Writing this book was something else. All the different emotions
that I went through with Dom and Soph were amazing and so
humbling. This book as opposed to *The Dream Trilogy* is so
different. I loved every minute of it, and I really hope you did as
well. I cannot wait for you to read *Kai's* book!

To the best thing that ever happened to me, my husband. You,
my love, are my inspiration for all of this. Your love stirs
something inside me each day and that pushes me to write these
stories so others can have a small glimpse into what I live each
and every day. Plain and simple, I am so fucking in love with
you and appreciate you so much!

Last but certainly not least, my amazing readers!
Without you, all of this wouldn't have been possible. There are
no words to describe how important you are to me. You make
this dream of mine possible and allow me to live the life I have
always dreamed of. I love you all dearly.

If you enjoyed *Redemption*, leaving a review would be much

appreciated on, **Amazon, Bookbub,** or **Goodreads**, it will
mean a lot to hear your feedback.

Xxxx
Sam

About the Author

Samantha Barrett is originally from Auckland, New Zealand but living in Brisbane, Australia.

Sam writes all things dirty dark and delicious with a side of twisted mind fuck.

She is a lover of all things red flags and an anti-hero is a must.

www.ingramcontent.com/pod-product-compliance
Lightning Source LLC
Chambersburg PA
CBHW050134120726
47903CB00002B/355